P9-CCH-476

MEN
in
UNIFORM

Courteous, courageous and commanding—
these heroes lay it all on the line for the
people they love in more than fifty stories about
loyalty, bravery and romance.
Don't miss a single one!

MEN
in
UNIFORM

New York Times and
USA TODAY Bestselling Author

ELIZABETH BEVARLY

MORIAH'S MUTINY

Silhouette Books

Published by Silhouette Books
America's Publisher of Contemporary Romance

If you purchased this book without a cover you should be aware that this book is stolen property. It was reported as "unsold and destroyed" to the publisher, and neither the author nor the publisher has received any payment for this "stripped book."

SILHOUETTE BOOKS

ISBN-13: 978-0-373-36257-8

MORIAH'S MUTINY

Recycling programs for this product may not exist in your area.

Copyright © 1991 by Elizabeth Bevarly

All rights reserved. Except for use in any review, the reproduction or utilization of this work in whole or in part in any form by any electronic, mechanical or other means, now known or hereafter invented, including xerography, photocopying and recording, or in any information storage or retrieval system, is forbidden without the written permission of the editorial office, Silhouette Books, 233 Broadway, New York, NY 10279 U.S.A.

This is a work of fiction. Names, characters, places and incidents are either the product of the author's imagination or are used fictitiously, and any resemblance to actual persons, living or dead, business establishments, events or locales is entirely coincidental.

This edition published by arrangement with Harlequin Books S.A.

For questions and comments about the quality of this book please contact us at Customer_eCare@Harlequin.ca.

® and TM are trademarks of Harlequin Books S.A., used under license. Trademarks indicated with ® are registered in the United States Patent and Trademark Office, the Canadian Trade Marks Office and in other countries.

Visit Silhouette Books at www.eHarlequin.com

Printed in U.S.A.

ELIZABETH BEVARLY

is a RITA® Award-nominated author of more than sixty works of contemporary romance. Her books regularly appear on the *USA TODAY* and the Waldenbooks bestseller lists for romance and mass-market paperbacks. Her novel *The Thing About Men* hit the *New York Times* extended bestseller list, as well. Her novels have been published in more than two dozen languages and three dozen countries, and there are more than ten million copies in print worldwide. She currently lives in a small town in her native Kentucky with her husband and son.

For my two big brothers, Danny and Jim(my),
who've made my life an adventure
since the very beginning.

Chapter One

The weather on St. Thomas was hot and muggy, but the throngs of people drinking and dancing inside The Green House Restaurant and Bar didn't seem to be affected by it. The band onstage was playing what Moriah Mallory guessed was supposed to be their rendition of a popular reggae tune, but in her opinion they were nowhere near as harmonic or hypnotic as the group who had originally recorded it. Yet the scantily clad bodies that crowded onto the tiny dance floor and spilled into the dining area didn't seem to notice or care. They swayed and sweated in time to the irregular drumbeat, tipping back green and brown bottles of beer, or pink and yellow rum drinks to alleviate the steamy tropical heat.

If Moriah rose up enough from her bar stool and craned her head around the group of inebriated divers beside her, she could just glimpse the harbor of Charlotte Amalie, now hidden in the night, spattered by patches of glittering light that scattered across the darkness, the result of a small fleet of sail-boats and cruise ships anchored offshore. Moriah sighed deeply, inhaling the warm night, and ordered another beer.

Tomorrow morning she would be boarding one of those vessels, or another very similar, and would embark on a two-week cruise through the Caribbean Islands, viewing the lush green jungles, the sparkling, pearly beaches and clear, turquoise-and-emerald waters from the deck of a quiet, softly rocking, tranquility-ridden sailboat. So why this feeling of utter dread that had settled like a cool clump of sand in her stomach? Why the worry that she was about to set sail on a ship of woe? Why did she want so desperately to hightail it back to Philadelphia and forget the entire episode?

Because this whole experience was going to be anything but quiet, and certainly none too tranquil, she amended, re-membering that her three sisters would be accompanying her as usual on her summer vacation. As if she could forget them, she thought morosely, slugging back a deep swallow of cold beer. God, why did she continue to put herself through the misery of these annual vacation excursions? Why didn't she do more than leave a day early to have just a little bit of time to herself? Why couldn't she stick by the plans she made every summer after the ordeal ended, always swearing to God and heaven above that next year she was going to get away alone?

You can't, because they're your sisters, her inconvenient conscience nagged. They're your family. It's tradition.

The four Mallory sisters had been vacationing separately from their parents ever since they were children. Ever since the elder Mallorys, Theodore and Diana, understandably wanting to remove themselves from the shrieks and demands of their somewhat spoiled offspring, had begun a tradition of sending their daughters on a variety of exotic adventures be-fitting the children of a wealthy industrialist and an affluent bank president. Their trips had ranged from island-hopping in the South Pacific to llama trekking in the Andes, from cruises in the Mediterranean to a dude ranch in Wyoming.

And when the sisters had grown into womanhood and undertaken demanding careers, they had still upheld the tradition with vigor, religiously penning the word *vacation* in big red letters over the first two weeks in August in their engagement books. Last year they had gone hiking in the Alps. This year Morgana had thought it would be fun to charter a sailboat in the Caribbean.

Morgana always got to choose, Moriah thought with annoyance. Then her oldest sister would locate her next romance novel in the place and count most of the trip as a tax write-off. Of course Marissa and Mathilda were no better, always agreeing wholeheartedly with whatever Morgana wanted. Moriah couldn't remember the last time they'd accepted one of *her* suggestions. Granted, she had enjoyed the llama trek when she was fifteen. It had surprised her that Marissa had come up with that idea. Her obsession with her physical appearance had been legendary long before she'd become a fashion model. Mathilda had always been the adventurous one, Moriah remembered, recalling the way in which her second-oldest sister had just up and left the sanctuary of her parents' sprawling Rhode Island estate one day to stake her claim on the New York stage. It had been a well-calculated risk. In October Mathilda would be opening in her first starring role on Broadway.

In fact all of her sisters had become very successful, Moriah realized with a mixture of heartburn and pride. Of course, she hadn't done too badly herself. But becoming a full professor of cultural anthropology wasn't exactly the glamour position of the century. And certainly her recently published textbook about the primitive tribes of Peru and Venezuela wouldn't reach the top of the bestseller list the way Morgana's latest, *Lust's Crashing Waves,* had done. Still, Moriah was very proud of her accomplishments, even if no one else in the family was.

Ever since they were children the Mallory sisters had taken their world by storm. At least the three eldest Mallory sisters had. All slender and tall with wide blue eyes and silver-blond hair, Morgana, Mathilda and Marissa had enjoyed one success after another. Spaced only a year apart, they'd each achieved fame, fortune and a faithful following of fans, things they'd even managed to garner on a smaller scale in Newport, where they'd all grown up.

Unlike her sisters, Moriah had arrived nearly four years after Marissa, and where the others were tall and slender, she barely topped five foot two and was much more rounded in the hips and breasts. She, too, was blond, but not with the straight, silky shafts of blinding white and silver that her sisters claimed. Instead her hair was thick and curly, falling past her shoulders in a tumbling mass, what a casual observer might call a rich, dark, honey blond. Moriah had always regarded it as mousy. And in place of the pale, sky-blue eyes that were so striking on her sisters, Moriah's eyes were slate gray, deep and expressive almost to a fault. Friends told her she had compelling eyes. Moriah had always considered them cloudy.

All her life Moriah had traveled in the wake and the shadow of her sisters' accomplishments, both social and academic. She couldn't count how many times she had heard the grumbled comment, "You're not much like your sisters, are you?" Countless, too, were the occasions when her teachers and her dates alike had begrudged her any effort to promote her individuality. And all too vivid still were the nights she had spent home alone because too many times she'd disappointed people for not being a *real* Mallory sister. By the time

Moriah had entered the illustrious Prescott Academy, the other Mallorys had all graduated and become a past glory, each having left Newport to seek education and careers elsewhere. Moriah had been left alone to face the massive burden of carrying on the name and the Mallory mystique. With the name, she had little problem as it was hers by birth. The mystique, however, was something she'd never quite been able to master. Consequently it left town along with her sisters.

So Moriah tried to get by as best as she could. And academically, anyway, she did quite well; her grades were excellent. But then that was to be expected of a Mallory, so her parents had never bothered to congratulate her for her accomplishments. They did, however, continuously bemoan her lack of social achievements, her absence of chatty friends and moon-eyed suitors. They wondered avidly why she didn't have the interest in clothes, cosmetics and the opposite sex that had kept her sisters giggling and shopping all the time. And they were constantly curious about her quiet and solitary habits. Moriah's sisters had certainly never been that way.

Moriah gulped back the last of her second beer and quickly ordered a third. The divers beside her were staking drunken claims on a bevy of sunburned beauties that beckoned to them from the other side of the bandstand. They nudged one another clumsily in the ribs and slurred out their none too chivalrous intentions toward the women.

"Oh, for God's sake, just go over there, toss them over your Neanderthal shoulders and carry them back to your caves," Moriah muttered with sarcastic impatience at the largest of the men.

He turned at the sound of the deep, feminine voice beside him, his movements slow, though as a result of his drunkenness or his anger, Moriah wasn't sure. Like his friends, he was blond and tanned from days spent under the scorching sun, and his numerous overdeveloped muscles let her know that diving wasn't the only sport in which he excelled.

She wondered what had possessed her to speak to the giant amphibian in the first place. It was bad enough that she was sitting alone in a bar. Now she had gone and drawn unwanted attention to herself.

"Are you talkin' to me?" the diver asked her thickly, as if his tongue was having trouble navigating.

"Uh, no. No," Moriah said quickly, her eyes darting from one man to another as her brain scrambled for polite and credible excuses that would cover her colossal blunder. "I, uh, I was talking to myself. Yes, that's it. I'm, uh, I'm schizophrenic, you see. And you know what they say. You're never alone with a schizophrenic."

The diver gazed at her with a foggy expression, trying to comprehend the information she offered him. "I've never heard that," he finally told her, gazing at her with a newfound interest. A predatory light began to flicker in his eyes as another thought struck him. "So if we went to bed together, would that be like getting it on with twins?"

Moriah's jaw dropped fast at the man's blatant suggestion, and she tried to ignore the jeers and leers of his friends. Her slight sunburn from the afternoon spent at Magen's Bay became a deep crimson. "Uh, no, actually," she stammered. "I'm, uh, I'm sure you'd be very disappointed."

But the big, blond diver was not about to be put off by what had become an intriguing idea. His eyes wandered lazily across Moriah's face, down her loose-fitting black T-shirt and short denim skirt, along the length of her shapely legs. On the trip back, his eyes lingered at her chest, where the scooped neckline of her shirt revealed just a tantalizing hint of the swell of her breasts, and he lifted his beer thirstily to

his finely chiseled lips. When he finally lo   ed hi
face, Moriah began to feel more than a little
guy was huge. And he was drunk. There was
what he was going to do next. She took a dee
to steady the accelerated thumping of her heart and gripped
her bottle of beer tightly, as if it were a weapon.

"You know," the diver began slowly, allowing his hand to
travel the short distance of the bar that separated them until
his fingers settled gently over her wrist, "we could have a
really good time together."

"Not tonight, fella, I'm waiting for someone," she lied
with determination, hoping her voice didn't illustrate any of
the unsteadiness she felt.

His hand tightened on her wrist, and his smile became a
disturbing grimace. "Yeah, tonight," he whispered viciously.
"All night. Any guy who'd leave you waiting here alone isn't
worth the effort. I don't live too far from here, and we
could—"

"You've got the wrong woman, pal," Moriah insisted,
trying to free herself from his iron grip. When had everything
gone crazy? she wondered wildly. A moment ago she'd been
sitting quietly, enjoying a beer while she contemplated with
dread what awaited her with the arrival of her sisters the next
day, and now she was suddenly fearing for her safety. How
had this happened?

The muscle-bound giant's grip grew tighter with her struggles. "Oh, you like to wrestle, huh?" he murmured angrily.
"That's fine, baby. I like it rough, too. Let's go." He stood then,
his intentions stated, pulling Moriah to her feet along with him.

"No," she said with as much conviction as she could
muster in her growing panic. She glanced about furiously, but
everyone else seemed oblivious to her situation. The bartender was pouring drinks with his back to her, and the diver's

...s were eagerly egging him on. "Let go of me, you big
...k," she hissed anxiously.

"Ah, ah, ah," the diver admonished her as he grasped her
upper arm painfully with his other hand. "No name-calling.
I don't like that. It's not polite."

His voice had become malicious and low, and Moriah decided then and there that serious times called for serious
crimes. She was just beginning to bend her knee, quickly as-
sessing the exact amount of force necessary to drive it into
the man's private parts and completely incapacitate him with
pain, when another man came suddenly out of nowhere,
dropped his arm casually across her shoulder and cried out,
"Darling! I've been looking all over for you! Hiya, Bart.
What's new?"

Simultaneously Moriah and the diver turned to stare at the
newcomer, one face etched with surprise, the other with wariness. Moriah took in the man's handsome features, ruggedly
bronzed from the sun, his laughing amber eyes and the slightly
curling hair that had probably once been a dark rich mahogany
but was now also streaked with a dozen shades of copper and
bronze. He was taller than the diver who still held on to her,
but not nearly as physically overblown. This man was firm and
muscular, yes, but as a result of physical labor and lean times,
not from afternoons spent at a gym. Moriah could only stare
at him speechless, but her tormentor obviously knew the man
and was disappointed by his interruption.

"Austen," the diver greeted the other man with a reluctant
nod. "You know this babe?"

Austen cringed a little at Bart's statement, but his smile
didn't falter. "Know her?" he asked, seemingly aghast.
"*Know* her? Why, Muffy and I are practically engaged!"

"*Muffy?*" Moriah and Bart spoke as one.

Austen's smile dropped somewhat. "It's a pet name," he

explained to the diver. When he looked over at Moriah, the crooked grin reappeared. She looked as if she wanted to slug him instead of Bart, and he was the one trying to rescue her. When he'd entered The Green House, he'd almost turned right around to leave again. The popular night spot was even more packed than usual, and for some reason he didn't feel like being part of a crowd tonight. Normally he enjoyed a party as much as the next guy, and the more people, the better. But tonight he felt differently. Tonight he felt restless and edgy, anxious even. As if there was something big coming, but for the life of him he didn't know what.

As he'd turned to leave, he'd caught sight of Bart and the boys at the bar, then almost involuntarily his eyes had been drawn to the woman they seemed to be tormenting. It wasn't just the fact that she was beautiful that made him catch his breath; there was something else, too…some raw energy, some unassuaged yearning caged within her, threatening to burst out any minute. The look in her eyes spoke of wild desires that wanted to burn free but that she kept buried with careful control.

He could tell by her expression that Bart was threatening her and she was about to strike back. He'd even noticed her preparation to nail the diver in a place that most men considered exceedingly important. He had to admire her insistence that she was not about to be manhandled by the big gorilla, but knowing Bart the way he did, there was unfortunately no way she would have been allowed to leave St. Thomas intact had she succeeded with such an act. Therefore, Austen had jumped in with both feet in an effort to defuse a potentially explosive situation, hoping unconsciously, too, that like the good guy in all his favorite Westerns, he might also wind up with the girl.

"Thanks for keeping an eye on her, Bart," he told the other man with a wink. "I was afraid she'd gotten tired of waiting for me and taken off." He playfully but meaningfully tugged Bart's hands from the woman's tender flesh, then put his own arm around her waist and pulled her close.

Moriah had no choice but to allow him the liberty, reasoning that at least this man seemed sober and more normally proportioned, and would prove a much less formidable adversary than Bart.

"Yes, uh, Austen," she began slowly, thankful that she remembered Bart's use of the stranger's name. She, too, wound an arm around his lean waist, explaining away the pounding of her heart as the aftershocks of having been placed in a dangerous situation. "It's about time you showed up. I was getting worried."

"Isn't that just like a woman?" Austen said to the group of divers who still gazed at him with no small amount of suspicion. Impulsively he swung the woman around to face him and buried his hands in the hair that had tantalized him ever since he'd entered the bar. Her gray eyes widened in startled surprise, but Austen couldn't help himself. Telling himself he was only doing it to convince Bart he actually knew this woman, he lowered his lips to hers in what he'd intended to be a quick, light kiss. But once he knew the warmth and softness of her mouth, once he tasted her sweetness and passion, Austen couldn't retreat.

At first Moriah was shocked by the man's actions, even if she had thought the arm draped around her waist had brought on some very pleasant sensations. She was being kissed by an absolute stranger! In a public place! While other strangers looked on! But what was worse, she realized, as the handsome, wonderfully muscular man intensified the kiss, she was really beginning to enjoy it.

Maybe it was a result of consuming too much beer or having been far too long without any male companionship, or maybe it was a leftover reaction to the highly tense situation in which she'd been embroiled only moments before. Maybe it was for some other reason she didn't want to think about right now, but almost of their own volition, Moriah's arms crept slowly and reluctantly up Austen's abdomen until her fingers spread possessively across his chest. And that was all the invitation he needed to pull her closer and deepen the kiss. As his hands wandered freely over her back and shoulders, her fingers became tangled in his thick hair. When Moriah felt his tongue graze along the line of her teeth, she opened her mouth to him willingly and nearly collapsed in his arms at the reckless, hot sensations that washed over her at being so filled by him. She allowed herself to become lost in the passionate embrace for a moment, clinging to him as he clung to her, locking her tongue with his in an intimate celebration. But when she realized with a start that she was clinging so desperately and passionately to a total stranger, Moriah gasped out loud and pulled her lips savagely away.

"Stop," she whispered breathlessly, her fingers betraying her as they continued to clutch great handfuls of Austen's pale yellow T-shirt. She was so close to him that she could feel through his faded, tight blue jeans how aroused he had become, and her shame and horror at having provoked him into this state was almost too much to bear. "Please, just stop," she repeated, ducking her head in embarrassment, unable to meet his eyes.

Austen's gasps for breath were ragged and shallow, and he, too, was appalled by what had just transpired between them. He didn't even know this woman's name!

Moriah took a deep, calming breath and expelled it slowly. "The others…" she muttered lamely, looking around the bar fearfully. "Bart…"

Austen glanced quickly over her head to discover that

Bart and his cronies had disappeared from their seats at the bar. With a brief survey of the room, he saw that they had joined a group of giggling beach bunnies, their smiles broad, their chests swelled, enjoying their new celebrity.

"The others are gone," Austen murmured into Moriah's ear. "So's Bart. See for yourself."

She turned uncertainly, her eyes darting between Austen and the recently vacated bar stools behind her, then returned her attention to him. "If that's the case, then why don't you let go of me?" she asked him pointedly, indicating the strong hands still settled possessively on her hips.

"'Cause I don't want to," he told her with a crooked smile, his curiously colored eyes sparkling with humor. "Why don't *you* let go of *me?*" he returned, and Moriah realized with chagrin that she still clung with some insistence to the front of his shirt.

Immediately she released it, nervously running her damp palms over his chest in an effort to smooth the softly worn fabric. "Um, sorry about that," she mumbled sheepishly.

"Hey, no problem," he drawled, loving the feel of her hands caressing his chest.

Moriah, too, was somewhat preoccupied with the motions of her hands, marveling at the strength and hardness she felt below her fingertips. He probably had a really magnificent chest, she thought fondly. Well, of course it was magnificent *now*, with his tight T-shirt straining across the finely tuned muscles. But when he was naked, it was probably incred—

She dropped her hands as if she'd been burned, and pulled away from his now-loosened grip to reseat herself at her original position at the bar. After a long, cooling swallow of beer, she managed to look over at him without feeling her stomach turn inside out, though she did squirm a little when she realized his chest was still at eye level. After clearing her throat nervously, she finally said, "Well, thank you for coming to my rescue, Mister…"

"Uh-uh. No 'Mister,'" he told her. "Just Austen."

"Well, then, thank you, Austen. It was, um, enlightening meeting you, but now I'm more than certain that you have to be going somewhere. Goodbye."

Austen's already handsome face was made radiant by the mischievous glimmer that lighted up his eyes as he seated himself on the bar stool Bart had vacated. "You're damned right it was enlightening," he agreed. "But I don't have to be anywhere until tomorrow morning. And frankly, I'm not sure it's such a good idea to leave you here alone with Bart lurking around. I'm afraid I know the guy. And the way he was looking at you tonight…well, let's just say the old boy's tenacious where women are concerned."

Unconsciously Moriah's hand encircled the wrist that the diver had gripped so painfully, and she gazed at him uncomfortably across the room.

Austen noted the gesture with a frown. "Did he hurt you?" he asked softly, taking her wrist gently in his own hand. Her soft flesh was red from Bart's manhandling, and he traced over her delicate bones with a roughly padded thumb.

Moriah grew warm at the exquisiteness of his caresses, so different from the savage pawing she'd suffered from the other man. "Not much," she replied quietly. "Thanks again for helping me out."

With a casual shrug, Austen brushed off her unnecessary thanks, then caught the bartender's eye. "Stu, bring us a couple of planter's punches."

"Oh, no," Moriah objected. "I've still got a beer here, and I don't want to mix."

"Come on," Austen insisted. "You're in the Caribbean.

Drink something festive. You can have beer any day. Besides, you'll love this. Trust me."

On cue the bartender placed two tall, pinkish-orange drinks on the bar before them.

"Stir it up first," Austen instructed.

"Why?"

"They float one-fifty-one on top."

"One-fifty-one?"

"Just do as I say, Muffy, or I'll have to get ugly."

"My name isn't Muffy," Moriah said with a laugh as she rattled her straw around in her drink. "It's Moriah."

"Wow, what a great name," he remarked with genuine appreciation.

"Really?" she asked, irrationally pleased that he thought so.

"Yeah. Isn't there an old song or something about that?" He thought for a moment and then recited with mock seriousness, "Way out west they have a name for wind and rain and fire.' Or something like that."

"Yeah, the wind is 'wind,' the rain is 'rain,' and they call the fire 'fire,'" she rejoined with a chuckle.

"No, no, that's not it. They call the wind Moriah," Austen corrected.

"Whatever."

"After what happened tonight, though, I'd say the fire should be called Moriah," he murmured in a silky voice.

Moriah tried to pretend she hadn't heard, but she sloshed a good bit of her drink onto the bar as her stirring became more furious. Dropping her straw onto the napkin, she lifted the wet glass to her lips and took a deep sip of her drink. "Hey, this is really good. I could drink a lot of these."

"You'll be sorry if you do," he cautioned. "If not tonight, then tomorrow."

"I never get hangovers," she told him. She neglected to add that it was because she so seldom drank alcohol.

"A lot of people have lived to regret those words. Especially down in the Caribbean."

"Do you live here?" Moriah asked with great interest. She already pretty much knew the answer to the question just from looking at him. Tourists were far too easy to spot in their newly purchased vacation clothes, sunburned from head to toe and dead drunk most of the time. Austen was much too comfortable in his surroundings, and his sun-bleached, rebelliously long hair and basic choice of clothes indicated to her that he wouldn't be flying back to the States for the opening bids at the stock exchange Monday morning.

"Yeah," Austen responded as predicted. "I've been down here about five years. How about you? Do you live here?"

Moriah nearly choked on her drink. Did she *live* here? In the *Caribbean?* Really, it was all too funny. What would the other professors in the anthropology department think? "Do I look like I live down here?" she asked in lieu of an answer.

Austen turned her question into an opportunity to give her the once-over again, and he smiled. Moriah kept any comments to herself, as she realized belatedly that she'd set herself up for his ogling.

"No," Austen answered. "Your sunburn is a dead giveaway."

"Swell," Moriah mumbled as she lifted her drink to her lips.

"But," he hastened to add, "you look like you belong here."

Moriah gazed at him openly, honestly amazed at his statement. "I do?" she asked softly. A small smile playing about her lips and eyes reflected her genuine pleasure at his compliment.

Austen caught his breath at her expression. She looked even more beautiful than before, her face almost childlike in its innocent delight, as if he had offered her the highest of praise. "Yeah," he breathed out quietly. "You do."

Moriah continued to beam. "Thanks, Austen."

"You're welcome," he replied automatically, still entranced by the warmth that emanated from her gray eyes.

For several moments they only gazed at each other as if verbal communication was unnecessary. Then with a start, Austen realized he knew nothing of this woman except that her name was Moriah and she was a damned-nice kisser, and he'd better get his mind in gear if he was going to score any points with her.

"So I guess you're here on vacation?" he asked lamely, realizing they both already knew the answer to the question. When Moriah nodded as she sipped more of her drink, he continued, trying not to sound like the idiot he must surely appear. "Where are you from?"

"Originally from Newport, Rhode Island," Moriah informed him. "I grew up there. Now I live and work in Philadelphia."

"Newport's a big sailing mecca, isn't it?" Austen asked, always interested in things nautical.

"There are a lot of big yachts and sailboats up there," Moriah agreed distastefully. "But boating is something I was never much into, personally," she added with an edge to her voice, remembering all the nightmarish occasions as a child when the family had gone out on their seventy-two-foot yacht, *Teddy's Toy.* Her father had always been determined that his four daughters would be perfect sailors and flawless nautical hostesses, and he'd spent each excursion impressing them with the severity of a drill instructor. Naturally Morgana, Mathilda and Marissa had all passed the tests with flying colors and enjoyed the trips immensely. Moriah, on the other hand, had struggled for years with motion sickness and vertigo, for the most part losing her lunch over the leeward side while her father looked on, shaking his head in disappointment.

Austen detected the bitter note in Moriah's voice and incorrectly surmised that it was there because she harbored a distaste for people who could afford big yachts and sailboats. Therefore he didn't pursue the topic, wanting instead to reestablish their earlier humor and ease of communication. "So what do you do in Philadelphia?" he asked in an effort to change the subject.

"I'm a teacher," Moriah responded proudly, sitting up a little straighter in her chair.

Austen couldn't help but grin at her, so obvious was her love for her job. It seemed like an appropriate profession for her. He got the impression Moriah was the type of person who would take pleasure in giving something of herself to others. She was probably great with kids, too, he suspected, and with her abundant good humor and self-confidence, she must be a great inspiration to her students. They probably loved her. If he'd had a teacher like her when he was in school, he definitely would have been inspired. Not to mention in love.

"What grade do you teach? What subject?" he asked her. Then impulsively he rushed on. "No, wait. Don't tell me. Let me guess."

Moriah sipped her drink slowly and told him, "I'm the most obvious candidate for my position in the world. You'll guess in a second."

Austen looked at her once more, taking in not just her gorgeous body this time, but the carefree clothes that encased it, the tumbling wildness of her dark gold hair, the laughing fire in her huge, beautiful eyes. "You have to teach either art or music," he decided, not sure if the widening of her eyes meant he was right or wrong. "And probably the seventh or eighth grade. Am I right?"

Moriah's laughter erupted uncontrolled from deep inside her, full and rich and uninhibited. Austen thought it the most wonderful laugh he'd ever heard.

"What?" he demanded with a chuckle. Her mirth was highly contagious. "Am I right?"

His question made Moriah laugh even more, the image of her doing something creative and beautiful just too, too funny to imagine. It was true that there was an abundance of artistic genes in the Mallory DNA, but they'd all been used up by the time she'd come along. She had to be thankful that she'd gotten more than her share of the intellectual ones, though, she ceded, Marissa having been shorted a bit there.

"Oh, Austen," she finally managed to say through her giggles. "That's pretty humorous."

"I guess you're trying to tell me that my assumption was a little off target."

"Actually, the only way you could have been further off would be to have placed me at the head of an elementary schoolroom."

"Look, are you going to tell me what you do for a living, or am I just going to sit here looking like a fool?"

Moriah smiled sweetly at him as she announced, "I'm a professor of cultural anthropology at a Philadelphia university. I teach upper-level and graduate classes in primitive South American cultures, and right now I'm studying different tribes of the Carib Indians, trying to discern their original migration routes from one island to another."

"Oh," Austen muttered. Then after a thoughtful swallow of his planter's punch, he added, "You don't look much like an anthropologist."

Moriah's genuine look of bewilderment told him she thought he was out of his mind. "Of course I do," she said simply.

"No, you don't," he insisted. "I always pictured anthropologists as dry and humorless."

"I *am* dry and humorless," Moriah told him simply.

The realization that she actually believed that struck Austen like a freight train, but his consequent shock prohibited him from coming up with the proper denial. Instead he demanded, "How come you don't have your hair pulled back and wear glasses like anthropologists are supposed to? Where's your gray flannel suit and starched white blouse and sensible shoes, hmm?"

Moriah shrugged, and her reply was matter-of-fact. "Actually, I *do* usually pull my hair back, but after all the saltwater and wind and humidity at the beach today, it just refused to be contained. And I only wear my glasses for close-up work. As for the suit and sensible shoes, well, that's kind of an outdated fashion statement even for anthropologists. Besides, they're terribly inappropriate for field study."

She didn't *seem* angry or resentful when she made her statement, Austen thought after she concluded. But there was something, some almost undetectable glimmer in her eyes that indicated she *was* somewhat resentful about the life she led. She'd delivered her words without malice or defensiveness, just plainspoken, unadulterated fact. But somehow he felt that hers was a hollow, inappropriate description, that the way she *did* live wasn't the way she wanted to live. That the person she described herself to be was in fact just a facade to disguise who she really was. What he didn't understand was why she would want to deny herself that way.

Before he could verbally pursue his suspicions, a shutter suddenly fell over her eyes, and he wasn't altogether sure that the look he thought he'd seen was ever there. Instead he only said, "I'm sorry, I didn't mean to—"

"No apology is necessary," Moriah told him honestly, wondering why he should think one was. Everything he'd asserted about anthropologists, save the flannel suit, had been right on the mark as far as she was concerned. And she was every bit as guilty of following the stereotype as her colleagues at the university. She did dress modestly, and she did lack a sense of humor. She knew that because her sisters always complained about her colossal lack of fashion sense and because every time she tried to make jokes among her family or her peers, she was met with either blank stares or condescension. As a result she'd given up just about any attempt to describe the humor she still found in situations, because evidently what she considered funny simply was not.

Austen was silent for a moment, contemplating the puzzle of this beautiful woman, more curious about what made her tick than any person he'd ever met. And in the five years that had passed since he'd moved to the Caribbean, he'd met dozens of strange and wonderful characters. He watched Moriah drain her glass of the sweet pink liquid it held, entranced by the slender length of her throat, inevitably letting his eyes fall to the neckline of her shirt and the subtle swell of her full breasts. A cultural anthropologist. My, my, my. Perhaps if he'd majored in that instead of business he would have wound up a more satisfied man.

But thoughts of the past were behind him now, and as he gazed lustily at the woman beside him, his future was looking brighter. Particularly his immediate future. When two sunburned dancers wearing matching striped rugby shirts fell drunkenly against him with a giggle and a gasp, he turned to Moriah with an idea.

"It's getting awfully crowded in here. What say we go someplace else? Someplace where there aren't so many fods."

Moriah eagerly licked the last of the planter's punch from her lips and offered him a mild grin, beginning to feel the effects of the mysterious concoction. "Fods?" she asked, drawing her brows down in confusion. "What are fods?"

"Fods are all those tourists you see dressed identically alike so they won't lose each other in a crowd," he informed her, trying to ignore what the motion of her tongue did to his body. "It's a widespread, imported phenomenon down here."

"I see." Looking around, Moriah did detect the presence of a number of couples wearing identical sportswear. "It would appear that these fods breed like rabbits," she noted.

Austen smiled at her culturally anthropological observation. "Virtually overnight," he concurred. "Come on, I know a better place. There are still a lot of tourists, but they're cool tourists. They like to hang with us locals. You'll like it."

"Gee, I don't think so, Austen," Moriah hedged. "The rest of my family is coming down tomorrow morning and I should meet them at the airport."

"Where's your hotel?" he asked.

"Bolongo Bay Beach," she told him.

"Hey, that's not bad," he commented, thinking college professors must get paid pretty well these days. "But I wouldn't sign up for any diving lessons if I were you."

"Why not?"

"Bart's one of the instructors."

"You mean that big Neanderthal works in the same hotel where I'm staying?" Moriah's concern was obvious.

"Don't worry," Austen assured her with a smile. "He usually has his head underwater. Explains the waterlogged brain, you know?"

Moriah smiled back at him. Austen had come at her virtually out of nowhere, looking like a bronzed Adonis, rescuing her from the menace of a pack of tiger sharks. He'd made her laugh a lot and enjoy herself immensely this evening, despite the dread she still harbored at her sisters' impending arrival. Not to mention the fact that he was a remarkably talented kisser, too. Austen might have come as a surprise, but it had taken Moriah no time at all to decide that she liked him. A lot.

"Anyway," he went on, interrupting her thoughts, "what I was going to say was that your hotel isn't *that* far from the airport. You won't have to get up too early. You could stay up just a *little* bit longer, couldn't you?"

He's so cute, Moriah thought with no small amount of surprise. She'd never fallen for a cute man in her life. She'd always gotten involved with men who were as dry and humorless and as ignorant of the concept of fun as she. And, of course, that's why she'd always wound up dumping them.

"I don't know," she began reluctantly, obviously weakening in her conviction. "If you knew my family the way I do, you'd understand."

"Hey, if they're anything at all like you, I don't think you'll have any problem," he told her.

But that *was* the problem, she wanted to tell him. The rest of the Mallory clan were nothing at all like her. Or rather, *she* was nothing at all like the rest of the Mallory clan. That's what had always been the problem.

"Come on, Moriah," Austen coaxed as he nudged her shoulder playfully with his. "You're on vacation. Enjoy yourself."

"Actually, it's going to be something of a working vacation," she told him, stalling for time. "I'll be visiting several islands that have university and library facilities, and I've made some appointments with other anthropologists and professors. I'm doing some research for a new textbook that I hope will be a useful tool in classes focusing on primitive Caribbean cultures."

Austen looked at her for a moment without speaking, then

slowly, gradually, a wonderfully wicked, marvelously mischievous grin spread across his face. His amber eyes twinkled
merrily when he finally spoke. "You know, you're right. You
are dry and humorless. But I have the perfect remedy for that."

Moriah blinked. "You do?"

"Yeah." Austen's smile broadened, and Moriah felt her
insides turning into mashed bananas. "Come on, Moriah.
We're going to Sparky's."

Chapter Two

"So what you're saying, Austen, is that these naughty, um, I mean, these nautical nods—"

"Nautical nogs."

"Whatever. What you're saying is that these teeny little drinks are the ultimate cure-all for the world's ills. That if every world leader past and present sat down at a big table at Sparky's and sipped these little drinks, then the world would be a beautiful place. Is that about the gist of it?"

"That's about the gist of it," Austen agreed, smiling down at a flushed, soft, slightly inebriated Moriah.

"What I don't understand, though," she went on, then paused suddenly when she became fascinated by the gold-tipped errant curl that had tumbled over one eye as she spoke. She brushed at it weakly in an attempt to make it join the rest of the unruly mass, but it fell forward again almost immediately. "What I don't understand is what I'm supposed to do with a collection of these little blue-and-white china mugs if they don't make a pitcher to match them."

Austen laughed and glanced at the man seated next to him. Upon entering Sparky's, he had recognized Dorian Maxwell from across the room, no easy feat amid a crowd large enough to rival The Green House. Austen had shouted to his friend and partner, and the other man had waved an invitation to join him and the large group crammed around a small, scarred cocktail table. At Moriah's enthusiastic consent, they had. Dorian was originally from Tortola, but the two men had both lived on St. Thomas for the past five years, having based their business there. So Dorian knew as well as Austen the effect that several of Sparky's nautical nogs could have on a person, and the wide white grin that split the other man's sable-skinned face mirrored the one Austen knew must be fast spreading across his own.

"Well, to be honest, Moriah," Austen said, "very few people walk away from the table with a *collection* of the mugs, and I have to shudder at the concept of what an entire pitcher of nautical nogs might do to someone."

Moriah's eyes narrowed as the information Austen offered her seeped slowly into her brain. She blew an upward gust of breath from her lips and finally sent the unruly curl that had been plaguing her back from her forehead. "Oh," she replied. "Okay. Can we have another one?"

Dorian laughed out loud, a rich, deep rumbling that seemed to erupt from his very soul. He slapped Austen soundly on the knee and said through his chuckles, "Looks like you got her right where you want her, mon. I guess you'll be wantin' the key now to Lionel's apartment."

Austen grinned sheepishly at the other man's reference to a friend's apartment near the bar that they both borrowed from time to time whenever it seemed one of them was going

to get lucky. He mumbled vaguely, "Ah, not just yet." Then
to Moriah he responded, "I think you've had enough nautical
nogs for one evening. They have a tendency to hit you when
you're not looking."

Moriah gazed at him with a puzzled frown until the mean-
ing of his statement hit her squarely in the brain. "Are you
insinuating that I'm *drunk?*" she gasped in horror. "Why, I'll
have you know that I have never, never, never, never, never
in my entire life been under the influence of *anything.*"

"Moriah…" Austen began to apologize.

But Moriah pushed on as if she hadn't heard him. "Except
for that Valentine's Day dance at Barry Masterson's house
when I was sixteen. But that was Marissa's fault. Hers and
that geeky boyfriend's of hers, Bra-ad." She said the name in
a singsong voice, rolling her eyes as she did so.

Austen's smile broadened. He was having more fun tonight
than he'd had in a long, long time, and he owed it all to the
honey-haired, lushly curved, slightly sunburned woman at his
side. Moriah was such a far cry from the numerous and redun-
dant bleach-blonde, salon-tanned, surgically perfected, empty-
headed women with whom he normally took up on St. Thomas.
The ones who came down from the States with the dual intentions of toning up their tans and getting lucky with the locals.
Even under the influence, Moriah was bright and fascinating,
and the more time Austen spent with her, the deeper he felt
himself falling into the inviting depths of her dark gray eyes.

"So what did Marissa and geeky Brad do?" he encouraged
her to finish the story she'd left hanging.

"Hmm?" Moriah responded, gazing at him with warm,
liquid eyes, thinking that this man was just about the most
gorgeous one she'd ever seen.

"The Valentine's Day dance when you were sixteen?" he
prodded. "You got drunk that night?"

Moriah's eyes narrowed suspiciously. "How did you know about that?" she demanded.

"You just brought it up," he told her.

"I did?"

"Yes, you did."

"Oh."

When she didn't continue, Austen tried again. "So what did Marissa and Brad do?"

Moriah frowned, drawing her brows downward comically. "They slipped me a Mickey," she said with melodramatic bitterness. Almost immediately her face cleared of its feigned dark expression and she smiled broadly. "But I got even," she announced.

"What did you do?" Austen tried not to laugh but found it nearly impossible.

"I countered with a Donald," she told him, slapping a hand over her mouth to hold in the giggles she felt erupting. "Then we all went out and got Goofy," she added through her chuckles. "Get it? Mickey? Donald? Goofy? Isn't that hilarious?"

"Hilarious," Austen agreed, though his own mirth wasn't so much a result of the joke as it was from watching Moriah.

"I read that on a greeting card," she said when she'd regained control of herself. "I love telling that story now. It used to be no fun at all."

Austen shook his head as if to clear it. "I'm not sure I want to know where you shop for greeting cards."

"What? Why not?"

He sighed. "Never mind, Moriah. You want to dance?"

Immediately her eyes cleared of their wariness and she answered enthusiastically, "Oh, yes. I love to dance."

"Earlier this evening you told me you didn't know how to dance," he reminded her, referring to the talk they'd had as they were walking to Sparky's, a talk in which Moriah had tried once again to convince him that she was every bit as humorless as she claimed. He eased out of his chair now, pulling Moriah gently behind him.

"I did?" she asked as she stood up and straightened the neckline of her shirt. "Why would I have said that? I don't understand."

"There's a lot about you I don't understand," Austen mumbled under his breath, then added silently, But it's going to be a pleasure figuring you out.

As they neared the dance floor, the duo performing onstage began a slow acoustic rendition of a relatively unknown Jimmy Buffett song. It was one of Austen's favorites, and he pulled Moriah close, wanting to savor the tune and the woman who made the moment ideal. Swaying rhythmically to the gentle strains of the guitar and softly uttered words of the very romantic song, Austen tucked Moriah's head under his chin, closed his eyes and sighed with complete contentment.

Moriah felt utterly at peace in Austen's arms, marveling at how easily and naturally the two of them were getting along. She usually wasn't very open to strangers, especially those of the masculine persuasion. And Austen was extremely masculine in his persuasion. Almost as if to illustrate that thought, her fingers pressed into the strong flesh on his back and waist, loving the firm muscles she encountered. In response to her exploration, Austen pulled her closer, and she gasped as her body was thrust once again into intimate contact with his. Instead of pushing away, though, Moriah found herself snuggling even closer to him, drawn by his warmth and strength, attracted by whatever it is that draws a woman so irrevocably to a man. She inhaled deeply the fragrance that surrounded him, something wonderfully elusive and utterly reminiscent of the sea.

Austen was so unlike other men she knew, so far removed

from the dry, overly academic professors and the insecure, pseudo-intellectual students with whom she came into daily contact. Moriah only dated occasionally, and then never anyone outside her social or academic circles, which basically were one and the same. She shared common interests with men of her acquaintance, and she generally had a good time when she went out, but never had a man excited her the way Austen had within moments of meeting him. He was handsome in a rebellious, carefree sort of way, completely confident and self-assured. He was clever and interesting, and along with Dorian had told her some of the most wonderful stories about the Caribbean she'd ever heard. He made her laugh, and feel oh so good. Was it any wonder then that she found herself liking Austen, liking him a lot?

As one slow song faded into another, Austen continued to hug Moriah's warm, softly curving body more expressively against his, unwilling to put an end to their intimacy just yet. Dancing with Moriah was the only socially acceptable way he could think of to be this close to her, but he realized unequivocally that even this closeness wasn't enough. It shocked him how good she made him feel so soon after meeting her, but it was more than the sexual yearning she aroused in him. Hell, just about every night he met a woman he wanted to take to bed. With Moriah, though, the attraction was more complex, more puzzling. He figured that if he plied her with a few more drinks, he could probably talk her into anything. She seemed more than willing right now. But for some reason, sleeping with her tonight was the last thing he wanted to do. She wasn't meant for one-night stands, and he knew a one-night stand wouldn't even come close to satisfying what he wanted with her.

For the first time that he could ever remember, Austen wanted to get to know a woman, wanted to delve into her soul and discover everything he could. He wished fervently that he didn't have so much work looming before him. Tomorrow afternoon he would have to leave St. Thomas, and he wouldn't be back for almost a month. By that time Moriah would be long gone, back to Philadelphia and the stuffy, stifling world of anthropology, and he'd never have the chance to further explore these curiously tumultuous sensations that had been speeding through his body ever since he'd laid eyes on her.

He suddenly ceased the slow movement of their bodies that had passed for dancing and pushed her at arm's length. Searching her face earnestly, focusing his amber eyes on her dark gray ones, he asked quickly, "Moriah, how long will you be staying on St. Thomas?"

The quickness of his movements and the intensity in his voice surprised her, and her eyes widened with confusion and concern. "Until tomorrow," she told him.

He shook his head slowly as if he didn't understand. "But you said your family is coming down tomorrow. How can you be leaving?"

"They are coming," she assured him. "But we're not staying here. We're going island-hopping for the next two weeks, all over the place. It was my sisters' idea." And now I have another reason to resent them, she thought. Their decision to charter a boat and leave St. Thomas meant she wasn't going to be able to meander down this new avenue her life had stumbled upon.

Austen's thoughts suddenly became urgent. He didn't know why, but somehow he had to see her again. "What islands?" he pressed. "Maybe we could meet up on one of them. I'll be traveling, too, for the next four weeks."

Moriah thought for a moment. It would be fabulous to meet up with Austen at some point during the cruise, especially since she knew her sisters would have more than their share of invitations from men. It was always the same. Morgana, Mathilda and Marissa would dazzle everyone who happened to meet the group of sisters, and Moriah would be unwittingly pushed into the background. It wasn't that she was particularly unattractive, uninteresting or inept. It was just that the three elder Mallorys were, in a word, spectacular. Moriah, by comparison, was pretty, nice and well-bred. And most men, given the choice, would choose dazzling over decent any day.

Yet somehow Moriah sensed that Austen would be different. He wasn't shallow and superficial like the men her sisters generally dated, and she felt he wouldn't be impressed by the fame and fortune and flutter that surrounded them. Austen liked *her;* she could feel it. And even the looming specters of her sisters would fail to turn his head. She hoped.

"I…I'm not sure," she replied honestly. "My sister has our itinerary, and to tell you the truth, I had very little to do with the planning." That was a laugh, she thought. She'd never had any amount of input into the preparation of their vacations. Her sisters always chose the destinations and activities, always organized every detail, even decided what they'd order for dinner at the restaurants they selected. They never bothered to consult Moriah. Why should they? Every Mallory knew that little Mo was far too inexperienced to make suggestions of such magnitude. Every spring Moriah received a letter from Morgana telling her where they were going, when they would meet and how much she could expect to spend. And like the unobtrusive little sister that she was and had always been, Moriah went along obediently and silently.

"You came to the Caribbean for a vacation and you don't even know where you're going?" Austen asked incredulously.

Moriah became defensive at his tone of voice. "I'm not

very good at organizing things," she explained lamely. Then she quickly remembered that her flight home was from St. Vincent. "I know we'll be in St. Vincent at the end of the trip," she offered hopefully.

"Great." Austen breathed with a sigh of relief. He was going to wind up there, too. "When?"

"We should be arriving on the fourteenth sometime, because our plane back to the States leaves the afternoon of the fifteenth."

Austen couldn't believe his good luck. "That's terrific!" he exclaimed happily. "I'll be there the fourteenth through the sixteenth!"

Moriah's shy smile told him she was as happy about that as he.

He let his hands roam up to her shoulders and give them an affectionate squeeze. "We could meet there somewhere," he told her uncertainly. "If you want to, I mean."

She nodded slowly, confused by the sudden case of nerves that was invading her body. Her stomach tightened into a fist, while her heart pounded erratically in her throat. She felt as if she was a teenager again, back at The Prescott Academy, hanging out by the boys' gym in hopes of catching a glimpse of the school quarterback. "Yes," she answered breathlessly. "I'd like that a lot."

"Great," he repeated, then felt like an idiot for suddenly losing track of his normally extensive vocabulary.

"But I don't know anything about St. Vincent," she told him. "I don't know where anything is."

"No problem," he assured her. "It's not that big an island." He wracked his brain to come up with a place where he could meet her that would be appropriate. Normally he saw very little of the islands he visited, usually restricting himself to the bar life—waterfront bars at that. But Moriah wasn't exactly the type of woman to frequent such haunts. The Green House and Sparky's were great places to go when he was home on St. Thomas, crawling with tourists and locals alike who might want to hire him and Dorian, or else put him in touch with someone else who would. But when he worked, he generally needed the distraction and escape that came with little hole-in-the-wall dives, wanting to get away from the demands of his employers, usually self-centered, whiny, red-faced little people who wanted to spend their vacations throwing their weight around because they'd been pushed too far by their own bosses at home.

After a moment's thought, he came up with a brilliant idea, the perfect spot for trysting lovers. Somehow that's the way he viewed their next meeting. "The airport is in Kingstown," he told her. "Just north of town is the botanical gardens. They're gorgeous. Any cabdriver can take you there. Meet me the evening of the fourteenth at, say, five o'clock?"

"Okay," Moriah agreed. "Five o'clock it is."

"I'll be at the front entrance with a red hibiscus behind my left ear," he said with a smile.

"I'll find you," she promised.

They gazed at each other for a long time, having forgotten that they were still standing in the middle of the dance floor until another couple bumped into them during the duo's lively rendition of a popular Jimmy Cliff tune.

"Oops," Moriah mumbled sheepishly as she was thrown once again into intimate contact with Austen's tall, muscular form.

He caught her in his arms, steadying her even though there was very little need to do so; she had righted herself by gripping his big biceps possessively. He smiled when she looked up at him shyly with wide, questioning eyes. Almost involuntarily he lowered his mouth to hers, nibbling provocatively at her lips, tasting the corners of her mouth with the tip of his tongue, pulling her closer still until she wasn't sure where she ended and he began. Moriah closed her eyes then and kissed him back, softly at first, in response to the gentle request in his actions, then more intensely as the passion built. Amid the sweating, gyrating, laughing dancers on the floor, Austen and Moriah became oblivious to everything except each other— exploring, touching, tasting as if they'd never experienced the glory that could be found with another human being. Only when a couple of islanders danced by and muttered, "Eh, go for it, mon," did they put an end to their extensive research, standing still at the center of a crowd, feeling muddled and uncertain, gasping for breath and confused as hell.

"I'm sorry," Austen whispered.

"For what?" she rasped through ragged breaths.

"I shouldn't have kissed you like that. Not out here in front of all these people."

"I thought I was the one who kissed you," Moriah told him.

"Did you?"

"I don't know," she confessed with a laugh, honestly confused. "I don't know what's happening between us. It's like…"

"Like nothing you've ever experienced," he finished for her.

"Yes," she agreed with a slow nod.

He nodded, as well. "Me, too," he said softly. After a brief instant he added, "Come on. Let's go back to the table."

When they returned to their seats, most of the original group had dispersed, leaving only Dorian and his date, Maggie, a very beautiful and exotic-looking woman from St. Lucia who was wearing the most form-fitting red dress Moriah had ever seen, and another couple from St. Thomas that Austen had called old friends, a sixty-three-year-old Norwegian named Gustav and his twenty-two-year-old Swedish wife of four years, Anna. They were passing around photographs of their eight-month-old twins when Moriah and Austen returned, and it occurred to Moriah then, that since she had arrived in the Caribbean, she hadn't met a single person who wasn't interesting in some way.

Despite Austen's warnings, Moriah ordered another nautical nog, arguing that since the drink had coffee in it, she couldn't possibly get that drunk from one or two more, and the group lapsed into lively conversation. Seated beside Austen, feeling more and more mellow as the night wore on, Moriah began to experience a most remarkable sense of well-being, as if the entire earth were beginning to rotate specifically as she dictated. All of a sudden her life seemed more appealing, her future more promising. And then, with surprising clarity, something very odd and very significant occurred to her.

For the first time that she could ever recall in her life, Moriah Mallory felt as if she was in the center of things instead of in the background, like she was a part of what was going on instead of a witness to it. Her insights into the dialogue surrounding her were well-heard and appreciated by the others, and their responses in return were pertinent and respectful. She simply wasn't used to such reactions after years of being ignored or pooh-poohed by her family as too young, too inexperienced or too naive to know what she was talking about. Moriah liked Austen's friends almost as much as she liked Austen, and she was startled to discover that she felt more at home in the dimly lighted, character-infested bar than she had ever felt among her family at home or her colleagues at the university. On top of everything else Austen had made her feel that evening, he'd given her the opportunity to be a part of something, had made her feel as if she belonged.

And for that more than anything else, she felt she owed him the greatest thanks.

When the hour grew late and the conversation lagged, the group reluctantly but unanimously agreed that it was time to part ways. Gustav and Anna were going to head home, while Dorian and Maggie invited Austen and Moriah to an all-night party at the home of a mutual friend near Red Hook. With an expressive glance toward each other, both simultaneously declined. Instead Austen drove Moriah back to her hotel, taking a roundabout route to give her a casual tour of the island along the way. Even in the dark, the moonlit views were spectacular, and Moriah breathed deeply the balmy Caribbean night, so different from the stifling, stale heat that had pervaded Philadelphia all summer. What was it about the tropics that made the heat not only bearable but enjoyable? she wondered. Then gazing along the way at the silver moon and crystal stars that hung above the lush whispering palm trees and the long ribbon of surf that stretched around the U-shaped beach at Magen's Bay, she realized the answer to her question. Who wouldn't prefer this to the city?

Probably anyone who couldn't find a job down here, she told herself drily. Too bad the number-one business was tourism, she added silently. She hadn't gone to school for seven years and suffered through her thesis and dissertation to become a hotel manager or bartender or diving instructor. And even if her studies focused on primitive Caribbean cultures right now, there weren't too many universities down here that could offer her the funds, the staff or the resources she needed to facilitate her research.

Moriah sighed heavily at the realization, and Austen glanced at her from the driver's side of his Jeep. Every time he looked at her, she was more beautiful, he thought. And now, with the moon glinting off her curls like honeyed silver, her hair tossed about furiously by the wind, she nearly took his breath away. When they finally arrived at her hotel, he pulled into the parking lot and got out along with her, suggesting that they end the evening with a stroll along the beach.

"But it's after one o'clock in the morning," she protested reluctantly, beginning to feel a significant buzz from her drinks at Sparky's but still unwilling to end what had been an exceptionally pleasurable evening.

"Just a short one, Moriah," he entreated. "Please?"

She smiled at him and capitulated easily. "Okay."

They found their way down to the beach through the nearly deserted hotel lobby and kicked off their shoes when they touched the warm, powdery white sand. They both reached automatically for the other's hand as if it were the most natural thing in the world to do, and Moriah found herself gazing up toward Austen's face expectantly, as if he might be able to reveal to her all the secrets of the universe. Instead she saw a man whose burnished skin made him ruggedly handsome, whose charmingly crooked smile displayed a row of even, white teeth and gave rise to deep slashes on his square jaws that she supposed were meant to be dimples. A funny little heat seeped into Moriah's stomach, as if she'd consumed a flaming dessert before the fire was extinguished. It spread into her heart and her breasts, creeping up her neck to her face, and she knew her temperature must have risen ten degrees just looking at him. Somewhere in the distance, perhaps at one of the bars or other hotels or maybe just somewhere in the hidden darkness of her feverish imagination, Moriah heard steel drums picking up a lively, joyful tune, something that reminded her of endless oceans and long sea voyages, of hot passion-filled nights and tranquil summer days.

Austen seemed to hear the magic, mystic music, too, because he stopped suddenly and turned to her, searching her face for something he didn't voice. As the warm surf lapped playfully about their ankles and the cool breeze lifted their hair, Austen brought his hands up to gently cup Moriah's face. For long moments he only looked at her, and gingerly, she covered his hands with her own and waited. Finally he dipped his head quickly and brushed her lips with his, so softly that Moriah thought at first she must have imagined it. But then he kissed her again, and again, this time gently urging her shy mouth with his, asking permission, petitioning, pleading.

Eagerly she answered him with a need and desire to rival his own, running her fingers down the length of his bent arms to rest on his shoulders, coming up on tiptoe to press her mouth anxiously against his. With a groan, Austen wrapped his arms tightly around her waist, lifting her easily from the sand to bury his face in the thick, sea-scented tresses that fell over her shoulder. Hungrily he kissed her neck and collarbone, her jaw, her cheek, her forehead. Then once again his lips traveled down to capture hers, hot and insistent. He traced her mouth with the tip of his tongue, then nipped and tasted her lower lip as if he couldn't get enough.

"Moriah," he rasped out softly, pulling her tightly into his arms, tucking her head snugly beneath his chin, "we have to stop this right now."

Moriah's heart banged against her rib cage with the speed and force of a battering ram. What am I doing? she asked herself frantically, realizing with utter shock that her behavior tonight was so unlike her usual stern reserve and propriety. It was as if she had become another person since she had met Austen. As if her personality had just split down the middle and now she was acting like some wanton, hedonistic, mindless being. Good heavens! She was acting like one of her sisters! It simply was not like Professor Mallory to pick up a man in a bar and follow him all over town. Never in her life had she reacted so wildly and impulsively to a man the way she had to Austen. Not with professional and academic men she had known for months and years, and certainly not with some beach bum she had just picked up in a bar.

Virtually all of her life she'd been building up sturdy walls and barriers to keep away the pain that came with continuous rejection, to protect herself from ever being thoughtlessly hurt again. But somehow, and in a very short span of time, Austen had managed to tear down those walls, break through those barriers and had experienced very little difficulty in doing so. Moriah had to admit with a good deal of surprise that she had been perfectly happy to let him do it. And standing here now on the beach of a tropical island, digging her toes into the sand, breathing in the fragrance of the summer night and the handsome, exciting man beside her, savoring the kiss of the breeze on her skin and watching the shimmery light of the wide silver moon dance across the tranquil water…it suddenly occurred to Moriah that this was exactly where she belonged. The scent of her stale, stark campus office was exactly where it belonged right now, too—a million miles away.

Moriah told herself that it was precisely because she *did* feel like another woman that she made her next suggestion. Because she was free of the restrictive leashes that her job and her relatives choked around her, free of the academic and familial mores that dictated she be stark and stale, too. With Austen, she was no longer Mo Mallory, underachieving younger sibling of the spectacular Mallory sisters, nor did she have to perform to the high standards and intellectual level of Professor Moriah Mallory, Ph.D., cultural anthropologist. Here, with him, she could be anyone she wanted to be, and for tonight, she just wanted to be Moriah, a woman with wants and needs like any other, a woman whose feelings were fierce and whose desires ran deep. A woman who wanted and needed the man who held her close in his strong arms.

"Austen," she whispered quickly, breathlessly, fearful that the wind would whisk her words before he heard them, "I want you to spend the night with me. I want to make love with you."

She heard him catch his breath, felt his heart begin to fire rapidly in his chest. For long moments neither of them moved, and she began to worry that Austen wasn't going to answer her. Finally his softly uttered words splintered open the dark, quiet night.

"Moriah, you don't know what you're saying," he told her softly.

"Yes, I do," she insisted.

He pulled his head from above hers and looked affectionately down into her eyes, then shook his head slowly back and forth. "No, you don't," he repeated simply.

"Austen—"

"Moriah, you're here temporarily on vacation," he interrupted her. "And the Caribbean is a far cry from Philadelphia, believe me. It's very, very easy to get things mixed up down here, very, very easy to confuse your priorities and values."

"But—"

"I went a little crazy myself the first time I came down here, and when I went home, I had to do some pretty serious thinking before I decided to change the way I was living. It took me months to make the decision. You've only been here for one day." He bunched a fistful of curls at her temple into his palm and gazed into her eyes with an expression Moriah didn't understand. "You have no idea what you're saying right now. Trust me. It's your heart talking, not your head."

She lifted her chin a little defiantly. "And what's so wrong with that?" she demanded. "Maybe if everyone thought with his heart instead of his head the world would be a better place."

He smiled at her, a smile that was sweet, serene and sad. "That's never going to happen. Everyone would grow up to become a fireman or a ballerina, and we'd all do nothing but lie on the beach and eat out."

"But, Austen," she protested, "I've never met a man like you before. You're…" She paused for a moment, uncertain what it was exactly she wanted to say. Finally she just told him, "I don't want anything to happen. I don't want you to disappear and then never know what it's like to…"

When her voice trailed off, leaving her statement unfinished, he smiled at her again, but this time his smile was gentle, happy and warm. "You're not going to lose me, Moriah," he assured her.

Her eyes searched his frantically. "You promise?"

He nodded slowly and pushed back her hair with his hand. "I promise," he vowed, leaning down to seal the bargain by placing a soft kiss on her forehead.

"Well, could we stay out walking a little longer anyway?" she asked him hopefully.

"What about your family tomorrow? Didn't you want to get up early to meet them?"

Moriah pushed the annoying thought of her sisters to the back of her brain. "Oh, who cares?" she muttered irritably. "Let them get a taxi to the hotel, they're not helpless." She circled her arms around Austen's neck and arched her body closely toward him. "I don't want this night ever to end," she said quietly.

Oh, God, he groaned inwardly, loving the way her body felt pressed so intimately against his, neither did he. He began to reconsider the wisdom of his previous statements to Moriah. Maybe he'd been a little rash in suggesting that she didn't know what she was saying when she told him she wanted to make love. Hell, she was a grown woman; she knew what she was doing. What would be so wrong about the two of them spending the night together? When had he become so damned noble, for God's sake? And *when* had he developed a conscience?

"All right," he ceded to her request. "Just a little farther up the beach. But then I have to leave. I've got to work in the morning."

Moriah was about to ask him what exactly it was that he did for a living, surprised that the question hadn't come up before now, but at that moment, the steel-drum music started up again, a catchy mambo number that made her want to dance. "Let's go find out where the music is coming from," she said with an excited smile.

"Moriah, I just told you, I have to work in the morning."

"But tonight you introduced Dorian as your business partner, so I assumed you have your own business. Don't you?"

"Yes, but—"

"So if you're the boss, can't you go in late for once?"

"No, it's not like that. I can't—"

"Please, Austen?"

She looked at him with such pure and childlike hopefulness that Austen had to smile at her and give in. What was wrong with him, thinking about work when he only had a few more short hours to spend with Moriah? "All right," he surrendered, laughing at the look of naked relief and joy that spread across her beautiful features. "We'll go and find out where the music is coming from."

Moriah had never stayed out all night long before, but tonight had been full of firsts, she decided, so why not add one more? They wandered up the beach until they came to an open-air pavilion surrounded by dancing, laughing people. As they pushed their way through the crowd, they too became infected with the high spirits of the others. When they finally broke into the front of the group, they saw a tiny stage encircled by blue-tipped flaming torches, where four islanders wearing bright red shirts and white pants danced and shouted as they pounded out on their green-and-yellow steel drums the most wonderful music Moriah had ever heard. She laughed out loud at the feeling of fun and life that went rippling through her body while she watched them, and she scarcely paid attention when her feet and hands took up the rhythm of the drums. Someone pressed a tall tropical drink into her hands, and she consumed it thirstily, only to discover it replaced by another, then another when she was through.

For what seemed like hours she and Austen danced and sang and laughed, so caught up in their revels that they barely noted the passing time. When the musician reluctantly announced that their set was over, Moriah and Austen voiced their playful disappointment with the others and then made their way slowly back down the beach. Reaching absently for each other's hand, they strolled in comfortable silence back to Moriah's hotel. But when they arrived at her room and Moriah opened the door to the expansive pale-peach-and-white suite, she discovered to her annoyance that it was spinning and pitching precariously and that all she could do to make it stop was cling to Austen like there was no tomorrow.

"What's wrong?" he asked her when she spun quickly and clumsily around to grab him.

"Room's jumping around," she mumbled into his broad, muscular chest.

"The room's fine, Moriah," he assured her with an affectionate chuckle, tugging at the arms that were circled possessively around his neck. "But I think you might be just a little bit tipsy."

Instead of letting him go, she buried her face against his chest and clung more tightly. "No, no, no," she said as she shook her head fiercely. "I told you I never, never, never, never, never…" Her words trailed off as she lost track of what she was going to say.

"You never get drunk," Austen reminded her.

"Right." This time she nodded her head eagerly up and down. "I never do."

"Well, maybe you're just a little bit tired then," he corrected himself magnanimously.

"Yeah," she said on a sigh. Then realizing somewhat foggily that if she was tired she wouldn't be able to talk Austen into doing what she wanted so desperately to do, Moriah quickly changed her mind. "I mean no!" she exclaimed frantically, lifting her head enough to gaze groggily into his eyes. "I'm not tired! I'm not! I swear!"

Austen couldn't help grinning. God, she was sexy. Her hair, that wonderfully thick mass of spun gold that he had delighted in touching all night, cascaded wildly about her face and shoulders like a crooked halo. Her huge, dark eyes danced dizzily with excitement, and her warm, curvaceous body was soft and pliant as she pressed it against him in an effort to remain standing. The scooped neckline of her black T-shirt had slipped over one shoulder to reveal sun-pinkened skin and the top of one lush, creamy breast. When Moriah rubbed herself against him unknowingly, Austen felt himself growing hard with need, felt all his good intentions about keeping his distance dissolving into a warm mist.

"Austen?" she whispered thickly against the tanned, salty skin of his neck. Her warm breath stirred him even more, and unconsciously he dropped his hands to her hips to steady her, pulling her even more intimately against him, getting little relief from the desire that was fast ripping through him.

"What, Moriah?" he rasped out raggedly. He had to get her into bed this instant. Alone. The longer he had to hold her up, the closer she'd pull herself next to him. And the closer Moriah got to him, the more dangerous their predicament became.

"Don't go home tonight," she murmured softly against his chin, following her words with feathery little kisses to his jaw. "Stay here with me."

The hands that had been wrapped tightly around his neck now loosened, and Austen relaxed somewhat until he felt Moriah's fingernails go scoring down his chest. He sucked in his breath as she spread her palms open across his flat belly and continued to kiss the warm flesh of his neck and collarbone. But when she came up on tiptoe to flick his lower lip with her tongue, reaching for the button of his jeans as she did so, Austen's breath caught in a strangled gasp in his throat. "Moriah, don't," he warned her as he felt the first button slip through its hole.

"Austen," she whispered on a seductive sigh. "I want you."

The next button popped open at the same moment her lips fastened intently over his. Austen made a halfhearted effort to pull his mouth away from hers until he felt her fingers dip gently inside his waistband, then out again to stroke the hard fullness in his jeans.

"Oh, damn," he muttered brokenly. "Moriah—" But his words were cut off as she cupped him fully in her palm and pressed her hand urgently against him.

That was the last straw. If she wanted to make whoopee, Austen thought, then damn it all, they were going to make whoopee. With the swiftness and grace of a pouncing jaguar, he swept Moriah into his arms and tossed her into the center of the flowered coverlet on the king-size bed. While she gazed at him with hungry intent, he reached back over his shoulder to bunch his T-shirt in one hand, then pulled it over his head and let it fall to the floor.

For a long moment he stood towering over her, his bronzed, naked chest sprinkled with coils of gold-tipped hair rising and falling rapidly with the passion she had raised in him, looking to Moriah like a glorious island king. Feeling more excited and reckless by the moment, she opened her arms to him in invitation, and with a deep and ragged groan, Austen threw himself onto the bed beside her.

For a moment he was too overcome with desire to know where to begin. He'd never, ever, wanted a woman the way he craved Moriah now. His arousal strained painfully against the heavy denim of his jeans, begging to be set free and buried deep inside her welcoming warmth. But Austen wanted this to go slowly, wanted to take his time savoring the gifts she had to offer, wanted her in turn to hit new heights with him she'd never known before. As she lay flat on her back feasting her eyes hungrily upon him, he felt as thought they had all the time in the world to satisfy each other, felt as though this night would be one that continued forever.

Wordlessly, his eyes never leaving hers, Austen dropped his fingers to the hem of Moriah's denim skirt, spreading his hand open beneath her warm thigh before rubbing his palm urgently under her skirt to cup her hip tightly. Her pupils widened with wanting when he kneaded her flesh with determination, and she moaned out loud when his fingertips dipped quickly and firmly under the lacy fabric of her panties. He wedged his thigh between hers then, pressing it up feverishly to settle against the heated feminine core of her, pulling her body adamantly toward him to rub even more intimately against her. As Moriah arched her back and cried out loud,

Austen's other hand gripped the neckline of her shirt and urged it farther down her shoulder until he exposed one soft, supple breast. With a muffled growl he lowered his head to the swollen mound and took the rosy peak into his mouth. Moriah tangled her hands insistently in his hair and pulled him closer, crying his name out on a gasp, begging him please to never, ever, stop.

With one quick move, he pulled her T-shirt over her head and tossed it to join his on the floor, then bunched up her skirt around her waist and settled himself once again between her thighs. Grasping both of her slender wrists in one hand, he pulled her arms above her head until she was helpless to do anything but surrender to him. Her eyes grew stormy when she understood his intentions, and a wicked gleam joined the fire in Austen's eyes. Bending his head once again over her breasts, he slowly circled the dusky peaks of one with the tip of his greedy tongue while thumbing the other to life with his rough, callused hand.

He'd never known a woman to be as sweet as Moriah, had never known a woman's skin could be so soft, so warm, so incredibly responsive. As he touched and tasted her with quiet reverence, letting his fingers and his kisses blaze trails across her flat belly, Austen felt his own body coming alive for the first time. It was suddenly as if any other sexual experience he'd enjoyed in his life had only been a preliminary to this one, as if this time with Moriah were his first. All the anxiety and excitement of his first time paled in comparison to the feelings that burned and bothered him now.

When a new thought invaded his muddled mind, Austen raised himself up on his elbows and gazed down anxiously into Moriah's drugged, delirious eyes. "Moriah," he asked her urgently, "are you protected?"

She gazed at him blankly, clearly confused by his statement. "What do you mean?"

Austen dipped his head down with a defeated sigh. "No, for some reason, I didn't think so."

"What are you talking about?" Moriah demanded, feeling her blood start to cool rapidly at his seeming disappointment in her, suddenly feeling very tired.

"I mean, are you using any kind of birth control?" he clarified for her.

Her eyes widened in shock. "Birth control?" she repeated, aghast. "Why on earth would I be using *birth control?*"

He lifted an eyebrow suggestively and looked down meaningfully at their half-naked, intimately entwined bodies.

"Oh," she said in a very small voice.

"It's okay," he reassured her. "I never leave home without one."

Moriah was confused again, and Austen's strange desire to have a conversation right now was really making her sleepy. "Without one what?" she wanted to know, successfully stifling the yawn she felt threatening.

But Austen had already started looking for the essential square, foil-covered packet that he always had tucked away in his wallet. As he pushed aside an assortment of business and credit cards, dumping a collection of bar receipts and hastily scribbled phone numbers onto the bedspread, he began to panic. He knew he had one in there, but where had it gone? Yanking out the contents of one of the wallet's many compartments, he discovered an old photograph that he thought he'd lost, one of his father standing proudly beside the old man's fishing boat. He smiled warmly and briefly at the picture, then remembered the task at hand. Dammit, where had he put it?

"Aha!" he cried triumphantly when he finally uncovered the small packet beside a torn, yellowed clipping from the *Miami Herald* that his mother had sent him some time ago, one about his ex-fiancée. "It's all right, Moriah, I—" he turned quickly to Moriah, brandishing his find like a trophy "—I found it." His shoulders drooped in comical defeat.

The woman who had lain so eagerly and anxiously at his side, the woman who had made him feel giddier and more aroused than he'd ever been in his life, the woman whose dangerous curves had promised the most enervating, exquisite, enlightening road to heaven, was now snuggled up against him like a child, fast asleep.

Chapter Three

When Moriah awoke the following morning, it was because a boisterous wrecking crew was slamming a big concrete ball with aching and annoying regularity against the tender membrane beneath her already-shattered skull. In addition to that, something furry and poisonous and foul had found its way into her mouth and died there, rotting away into some sort of linty gelatinous goo that had oozed all over her teeth and tongue. She opened her eyes slowly and painfully, wincing at the stabbing white light of early dawn that pierced her pupils, recoiling at the lurching, nauseating swells that washed up and down in her stomach. This was not a good sign, Moriah thought glumly, wondering where in the hell she was and how she had managed to sleep through the night while all of these terrible things had been happening to her.

It took her all of five minutes to finally inch onto her back so that she could gaze up curiously at the ceiling. Little by little she took in her surroundings and realized she was in a hotel room, and quite a nice one at that. From the sound of the quiet surf that met her ears through the open French doors to her left, Moriah brilliantly deduced that she must be at the shore. But she hated going to the Jersey shore, she remembered with a puzzled frown. Especially in the summer when it was so crowded. It *was* summer, wasn't it? Yes, she was certain that it was. Hadn't she been planning a vacation a short time ago? she wondered, her muddled brain beginning to function a little more clearly now. She vaguely recalled buying some sunscreen at the cosmetic counter in Wanamaker's. Heavy sunscreen. Because she was going to be vacationing in…the Caribbean! Yes, that's it! The Caribbean, that must be where she was. She was supposed to be meeting her sisters on St. Thomas at her hotel on Bolongo Bay Beach. That's where she was all right. She remembered everything now. Sort of.

The prospect of seeing her sisters again in the very near future filled Moriah with a new kind of nausea and dread, and as her stomach revolted once more, she realized she had better haul herself up and out and get herself pulled together before they arrived and did it for her.

With a muffled groan she wrenched her stiff, aching body out of bed, then covered her burning eyes with both hands and stumbled into the bathroom. She leaned her forehead against the cool white tiles of the wall while waiting for the sink to fill with cold water, begging whatever was sloshing and spinning around in her stomach to stay there. When the water reached almost to the rim of the sink, Moriah took a deep breath and then dunked her head into its icy depths, trying to ignore the overflow that swept onto her bare feet. After that, with the assistance of a big glob of blue toothpaste she squeezed weakly onto her toothbrush, she scrubbed away the last remnants of death from her mouth and swallowed three aspirins with a very large glass of water.

The hot sting of the shower's spray chased away a good deal of what was left of her hangover, and by the time she had towel-dried her hair, knotted the sash of her pale yellow terry bathrobe around her waist and called room service, Moriah felt almost human again. Of course her sisters were going to be highly perturbed when she wasn't at the airport to meet them, but they were perfectly capable of finding their way to her hotel. As any civilized woman knew, when one awoke with a severely debilitating hangover, one simply had to get one's priorities in order. And one's first and foremost priority was to bring oneself back among the living.

A knock at the door alerted Moriah to the arrival of priority number two: a very large carafe of extremely black coffee. As she slowly sipped the dark, pungent brew, hoping to absorb even more caffeine by inhaling the fragrant steam, she finally began to relax, feeling for the first time that morning as if there was probably a chance for her, after all. She strode lightly and cautiously across the room to open wide the French doors so that nothing stood between her and the fresh Caribbean morning. Clutching the white china mug of coffee to her heart, Moriah breathed deeply the warm air and let her eyes rove appreciatively over the pearly beach and clear, sapphire ocean. It was going to be a gorgeous day. The sun hung in the sky like a beacon, children frolicked outside her room in the twinkling surf, her coffee tasted rich and smooth and delicious, and—

And she had picked up a strange man in a bar last night and brought him back to her hotel room so they could have sex.

The sudden, shocking realization hit Moriah squarely and blindly in the brain like a great big bag of wet sand. Oh, my

God, she thought silently, gasping as hot coffee spilled onto her fingers when they trembled on the handle of the mug. Had she really done that? Had she actually been sitting in a bar last night and met a man with whom she'd spent the entire evening and at least part of the night? Moriah shook her head slowly as if trying to clear away the fog that had settled over her memories. She tried to retrace her steps of the previous evening, tried to remember *exactly* what her actions had been.

She recalled feeling restless after returning to her hotel from Magen's Bay yesterday, so she went to The Green House to have a beer, one of her students having told her it was *the* place to go on St. Thomas. She remembered having had some problems with a group of obnoxious divers there, then being rescued by a very gallant and handsome man, leaving to go to another bar with him, dancing, walking along the beach, and then something about a steel band…

Austen. That had been the man's name, and he had been very funny and pleasant to talk to and, she recalled with a warm feeling in her midsection, incredibly sexy. He'd brought her back to her room last night, and then… Moriah felt her flesh grow hot when memories of what followed came rushing over her like a boiling river.

"Oh, dear," she said quietly. She also remembered that she had agreed to meet up with him on St. Vincent in two weeks before she was to fly back to Philadelphia. Well, that was certainly one appointment Moriah had absolutely no intention of keeping—even if Austen *had* been charming and wonderful, and even if she *had* enjoyed herself more with him than any man she'd ever known. There simply wasn't any future in taking up with a beach bum who didn't know the first thing about responsibility and probably couldn't even hold down a decent job.

For a moment Moriah stared wistfully out to sea, thinking

about warm, brandy-colored eyes and laughter that rumbled up freely and easily from a brawny, sun-browned chest. She thought about his reckless, confident masculinity and the urgency of his need to claim her, so much more exciting and tumultuous than the tentative fumblings she'd known from other men. Then reluctantly she forced herself to push thoughts of Austen away. She didn't even know his last name, she realized sadly. And now she would never see him again.

She drained her coffee mug of its quickly cooling contents, then refilled it from the carafe on the table. The clothes she had been wearing the previous evening were folded and stacked neatly on a chair beside the bed, Moriah noted, and she smiled a little regretfully that even in her drunken state she had been her usual tidy self, having awakened in her regular sleepwear. But when she went to retrieve her clothes to pack them, she noticed for the first time a sheet of hotel stationery that was folded in quarters and tented on top of her shirt. In a bold, masculine script, her name was scrawled across the side that faced her, and her heart began to dance when she picked it up gingerly, cradling it in both hands. She opened the white vellum paper slowly and carefully, as if it were some ancient manuscript that might dissolve into time-less dust. Unwittingly she held her breath as she read the words contained within.

Don't forget: St. Vincent on the fourteenth at 5:00 p.m. at the botanical gardens. Don't stand me up, Moriah, please. If you can't make it, CALL ME. My number on St. Thomas is 9653. Don't disappoint me, lady. I have to see you again, and I don't even know your last name. If you leave me without saying goodbye, I'll never speak to you again.

Austen

Moriah was touched that he had taken the trouble to leave her a note, then remembered, of course, that Austen must have been as drunk as she was last night. She realized somewhat sadly that he had probably left it behind thanks to the same state of inebriation that had made her do things that she would normally never do. More than likely he was somewhere right now regretting the evening as much as she, worried that the troublesome woman he'd met at The Green House last night was going to be dialing his number this morning and putting him on the spot about his note.

Well, he needn't worry, she told herself as she wadded up the scrap of paper in her hand. She was about to throw it into the wastebasket near the chair, but something stayed her hand. Carefully she opened the note once more and reread the wrinkled words, then chuckled a little nervously. Here she was at the ripe old age of thirty, and Moriah Mallory had just received her first mash note. Sort of. Refolding Austen's letter carefully along its original creases, she tucked the paper into her weekender bag and smiled a secret little smile. Maybe she'd never see the man again, but he'd definitely given her something to remember.

The three elder Mallory sisters arrived in a flurry later that morning, creating a stir and a ruckus that Moriah sensed even before she heard it. Leaving the sanctuary of her room to view the commotion, she watched her sisters' advent with eyebrows raised and lips curled in speculation. Amid a blur of tailored luggage and the very latest designer vacation wear, with the sun glinting blindly off perfectly coiffed silver-blond hair and excessively applied lip gloss, between demands for assistance and complaints about the service, Morgana, Mathilda and Marissa Mallory floated into the hotel lobby with all the splendor of a thousand doves released into the sun-drenched azure summer sky. At least that's how Morgana would have described it, Moriah thought drily. To her it seemed as if they simply stumbled in from the street.

"Over here!" she called out to them.

As if the three of them shared one brain, they all turned at once with an identical expression of inquiry. Leaving their luggage where it lay—no one would dare have the audacity to steal Mallory luggage—they strolled carelessly to where their youngest sister awaited them. Each appraised Moriah with a critical eye, and none of them liked what she saw.

"Honestly, Mo, what are you trying to prove dressed that way?" Marissa asked in reference to Moriah's attractive, pale blue sleeveless cotton dress. "You *know* you have Grandma Maxine's fat calves! Why do you keep wearing those *awful* short skirts? Haven't you listened to anything I've ever told you about fashion?"

"And my God, Mo, do something with your hair!" Mathilda instructed, her voice filled with horror at the rambling cascade of gold that fell over the shoulders of her youngest sister. "I'll braid it for you before we get to the boat. You'll thank me when we get out in that wind."

"Mo, where are your glasses?" Morgana wanted to know. "I hope you haven't left them somewhere again like that time in Fiji. We lost an entire day looking for them. I think it would be a good idea if you just wore them all the time on this trip. Now, where's your room? We'd like to freshen up before you check out."

Moriah took a deep breath and surrendered to her sisters. It was far easier than arguing with all three of them, she knew. The Mallory family history was long and vivid, filled with the bloody battles she had waged with her relatives and lost mightily. When they returned to her room, her sisters pounced on the mirror while Moriah changed into a pair of baggy khaki trousers and a white safari shirt. She fished her horn-rimmed glasses out of her purse and donned them obediently while Mathilda wove her thick, unruly tresses back into a long French braid. When she looked sufficiently anthropological, her sisters, as one, expelled a long sigh of relief, thankful that Mo was back and that the strange, vivacious-looking woman who had met them was now gone.

While her sisters chatted and rearranged their belongings, Moriah observed them with a casual eye. A lot of people claimed that they had trouble distinguishing one Mallory from the other, except for the youngest one, of course, but Moriah didn't see how that was possible. Each one of her sisters looked exactly like who and what she was.

Morgana Mallory was the oldest and, for now, the most famous of the four, having recently seen her newest novel go skyrocketing up every bestseller list in the county. She wrote her first book, *Up on Rapture Mountain,* over ten years ago, but it wasn't until her third, *They Call Me Hussy,* that she'd made it onto the *New York Times* bestseller list. The one following that, *Passion Rides a Spotted Horse,* was turned into a miniseries, and since then, the name Morgana Mallory had meant gold to booksellers everywhere. Some time ago she'd started wearing tailored suits and conservative separates, and she'd had her long tresses shorn into a chin-length blunt cut. All this was done at her publicist's suggestion, in the hopes that it would make her appear less frivolous and more like a "serious writer." Moriah had recommended that her eldest sister give her books serious titles if she wanted to be taken more seriously. Morgana had responded by demanding what Moriah knew about the publishing industry anyway, quickly cutting her off before she could mention that little piece of anthropological fluff she called a textbook.

Mathilda Mallory was a fast-rising star on the Broadway

stage, quickly catching up with Morgana in the fame department, something which Moriah was certain annoyed her eldest sister to no end. She had never seen her sister act, but her parents had, of course, and were forever gushing about the rampantly flowing ocean of talent in their family. If Moriah gave it much thought, which she seldom did, she would probably admit that Mathilda had more common sense than her other sisters and was probably capable of freethinking if left to her own devices. There were times when Moriah felt that Mathilda was as much a victim of the Mallory mystique as she, and believed that Mathilda might possibly have turned out to be rather interesting if she hadn't so closely resembled the others in looks and been forced to comply with family expectations. Mathilda still broke out of the mold every now and then, Moriah noted, wearing berry shades of lipstick and rouge instead of the traditional peach, styling her shoulder-length hair into complicated creations instead of letting the silvery sheaths flow like a celestial river as the others did.

Marissa Mallory posed the biggest irritation to Moriah. Next to her in age, Marissa had always been closer to what was going on in Moriah's life, had always known exactly how to draw the most blood. Like a perfect stereotype of the glamorous supermodel, Marissa was shallow, vague and superficial, her vocabulary consciously restricted to less than a hundred words. With hair that streamed to her waist and a body that most men would kill to possess, she'd also delighted throughout childhood and adolescence in pointing out what she considered an abundance of physical imperfections all over her little sister's curvy form. And now that Marissa was earning hundreds of thousands of dollars a year to be so beautiful, she could smile in just such a way as to tell Moriah she was thinking, "I told you so."

And to look at the four of them now, Moriah would say she was right. There was something very significant in the fact that her three sisters vied for the mirror on one side of the room while Moriah sat apart watching them on the other. It was today as it had always been. Morgana, Mathilda and Marissa looking sleek, beautiful and perfect in their glamorous new clothes, chatting like magpies as if the world was theirs to plunder. And then there was Mo. Plain, quiet, malleable, unobtrusive Mo. A cultural anthropologist who was anything but spectacular and sexy and romantic like her sisters. Mo, who had never quite made it into the upper echelons of the Mallory household. Mo, who would never garner the recognition and awe that the others inspired. Mo, who...

"Mo, could you carry that makeup case for me?" Marissa asked sweetly from the other side of the room, talking to Moriah's reflection in the mirror if not to Moriah herself. "I just redid my nails and they're still wet. Thanks, love," she added quickly before Moriah could respond, knowing naturally that her sister would unfailingly comply with her request.

"Of course, Marissa," she replied tonelessly. "I'll be glad to."

Here we go, Moriah added glumly to herself. Another wonderful, relaxing vacation with the Mallorys. All right, ladies, let the games begin.

Austen Blye awoke that morning in a much better state than he figured Moriah did. His alarm went off at seven as usual, and despite his late hours, he awoke for the most part feeling refreshed and invigorated. He rolled out of his bunk in the aft cabin of his Shannon 51, *Urizen*, stark naked and completely at home. Without dressing he wandered aimlessly into the galley and started a pot of coffee, then ambled to the head for a quick shower. When he was dressed in a pair of ancient, low-slung cutoffs, Austen poured himself a generous cup of coffee and came up from below to greet the sunny Caribbean morning.

"Hi, guys!" he called out to the crew of the Coast Guard cutter that was slicing through the water near his anchorage when he walked on deck.

"Hey, Austen!" a youthful, sandy-haired boatswain's mate shouted back. "We're headed out to Pilsbury Sound! Gonna do some fishing!" he added with a broad grin.

"I'll see you there!" Austen returned amiably. "I've got a charter full of women getting under way this afternoon!"

"Great!" another crew member in his dark blue uniform called out eagerly. "Can't wait! See you later!"

Austen lifted a hand in farewell to the departing eighty-two-footer, unable to keep his grin from disappearing when they were sufficiently out of sight. From all the correspondence and conversation he'd had with the organizer of this particular charter, he had a feeling none of the guys in the U.S. Coast Guard was going to want anything to do with these women. He'd never been one to make snap judgments about people before he even met them, but in this case it had been impossible to avoid it. Without even seeing the woman who'd made the arrangements for this cruise, Austen had the feeling that the next two weeks were going to be particularly long and grueling ones.

He hadn't started out to be a charter-boat captain, he reminded himself as he sat down in the cockpit with his coffee and yesterday's paper. Yet he couldn't even remember now what he'd wanted to do when he was a boy. Then again he'd never really had the chance to decide. He'd enjoyed growing up in Key West, working on his old man's fishing charter, fascinated by the sea and all things nautical. But for as long as he could remember, his father had sworn that *his* son would never wind up a slave to the fickle ocean the way *he* had been forced to do. *His* son was going to go inland for college, his father had told anyone who would listen, and *his* son was going to study business and finance and important money-making stuff like that. *His* son was going to work for some big bank in Atlanta or Dallas or Detroit. No way would he ever have to rely on the sea for his living. Best just to get the boy away from the ocean altogether.

Austen knew deep down that his father's intentions had been good, that he really had thought what he insisted upon for his son was the right thing. And Austen had to admit that he'd allowed the man to dictate his life all those years, wanting to please his parents and become the financial mogul they envisioned him to be. But he'd grown up on Key West, for God's sake, and had always, *always,* been captivated by the ocean. He couldn't have escaped its hold on him if he'd lived to be a thousand years old.

For a while, though, he had left it all behind. He *had* gone inland to study business, and he *had* worked in a big bank for nearly ten years. *Ten years,* he marveled now. Had he really surrendered that much of his life to The Global Bank in Atlanta? It was hard to believe. With all the hustle and stress that had gone along with being a very young vice president, was it any surprise that everything had blown up in his face five years ago? Had he really been surprised by his decision when the time came to choose between his job—with its posh corner office and big black limo, with the twelve-hundred-dollar suits and twenty-eight-room mansion that came complete with wife and kids—and his desire to just live quietly alone on a boat by the sea? By the time he'd abandoned it, his life in Atlanta had become virtually unlivable. But it was all a distant memory now, and the only reminders he ever received these days were the ones that his mother mentioned, like the clipping of his ex-fiancée in her recent letter. He supposed it was possible that Pamela felt remorse for everything that had happened between them all those years ago, but even that old ache didn't hurt anymore. Even her memory had been replaced in his thoughts.

Immediately Moriah's face appeared before his mind's eye, and Austen couldn't help but smile. He wondered how she felt when she woke up this morning. Probably not too great. He wished he could relive the events of the previous evening so that the night hadn't ended so…unsatisfactorily. But up until that point he'd had a wonderful time. She sure did know how to make a guy laugh. He liked that in a woman. Hell, he liked just about everything in this particular woman. He sent up a mental prayer to whatever gods might be listening that she meet him on St. Vincent in two weeks. Otherwise she had damned well better call. Looking up into the clear blue sky, though, he became perfectly content. Somehow he knew that he would see Moriah again, and somehow he was sure it would be soon.

Glancing at his watch, he realized the immediate future was going to have to take precedence over any long-range goals, though, and Austen prepared to leave his anchorage to return to his slip at the marina. His lips turned down in a frown as he contemplated once again the dreaded and potentially hellish charter on which he and Dorian were about to embark. He thought once again about the contemptuous, self-important letters he'd received regarding information on his charter service, remembered distastefully the condescending, snotty-voiced woman he'd spoken to on the phone when finalizing the itinerary for her and her companions.

He'd already decided that this cruise wasn't going to be a pleasant one, and now, because the four women would be keeping him from the lovely Moriah, he had an even better reason for disliking them. Pulling up anchor and revving the sailboat's engine to life, Austen sighed in discontent. He was not looking forward to meeting the Mallory sisters.

Moriah had a seat to herself in the big open-air awning-covered taxi, albeit the backseat. The three elder sisters' luggage took up the front seat, while behind it a group of sunburned, vacationing surgeons were laughing and falling in love with Morgana, Mathilda and Marissa, who crowded into the seat behind them. Moriah shared her seat with her small canvas weekender bag, the only one she'd brought with her, and instead of playing verbal footsie with their three male companions in the taxi, she decided to take in a little of the local scenery.

St. Thomas was the second largest of the American Virgin Islands, and away from town it was green and lush with some of the most beautiful beaches Moriah had ever seen. The main town of Charlotte Amalie was in many ways just one big open market where shoppers could uncover bargains on everything from limes to Limoges, from rum to Rolex watches. A lot of people complained that the city was crowded and noisy and dirty. But Moriah viewed it as a wonderful collision and clutter of cultures. Having spent only one full day there, she'd met people from seven different countries on four separate continents. She was fascinated, both personally and anthropologically, by the local language, the clipped staccato dialect that mellowed into a slow melodic calypso accent when the locals turned their conversations from one another to the throngs of tourists. And when the sun went down, the island remained alive, the hillsides dotted with lights like tiny inset jewels. Remembering all the fun she'd had the night before with Austen and the colorful cast of characters he called friends, she couldn't help but smile. Yes, she liked St. Thomas a lot.

"And that's our sister, Mo," she heard Marissa say in passing. Moriah knew her sister was still talking to the surgeons, because her voice still held that flighty, fluffy quality it contained whenever Marissa talked to men.

"She's your sister, *too?*" the surgeon with the most ominous receding hairline asked incredulously.

Moriah nodded vaguely at the man, thinking a sunburned scalp that exposed must be plenty painful. "Yes, I am," she assured him with a smile.

"Boy, you sure don't look like your sisters!" he exclaimed, sounding quite pleased that he'd made the observation.

Moriah's smile fell, and she sighed in resignation as she gazed unseeingly out at the harbor. Why did everyone who uttered that statement always make it sound like such an insult? she wondered. And why after all these years did it still hurt so much to hear it?

"Were you adopted?" another of the men inquired bluntly.

Moriah closed her eyes and placed her fingertips lightly against her forehead. "Not to my knowledge, no."

"She wasn't," Morgana told them all readily. "I still remember when our mother was pregnant with her. I even remember when she had Marissa."

"Oh, you do not," Marissa challenged. "You were only two years old when I was born."

Morgana sighed loftily. "Many exceptionally creative people have vivid memories of their early childhood, Marissa. Of course, you'd know nothing about that. You probably don't remember what you ate for breakfast this morning."

Marissa lifted her chin defiantly and pulled an atomizer of mineral water out of her purse. Spraying a fine mist delicately about her face gave her a few minutes to think about it, Moriah supposed. Finally the model answered succinctly, "Fruit cup."

But Morgana had lost interest in baiting her sister and instead pulled a rose-and-pink tapestry-covered notebook from her purse. "Now, girls," she began, sounding like a Sunday schoolteacher leading her flock to worship, "when we get to the marina, we want to look for a nice, big sailboat called the *Urizen*."

"How big?" Moriah wanted to know.

Morgana consulted her notes, then glanced back at her youngest sister with a frown. "Very big."

"That certainly narrows it down, Morgana," Mathilda said drily.

Morgana's lips thinned irritably. "Slip number seventy-two," she announced through gritted teeth.

"What's the captain's name?" Marissa wanted to know.

"Blye," Morgana told her. "Captain Blye."

Moriah chuckled with delight. "You actually chartered a boat from someone named Captain Blye?" She never knew Morgana to have a whimsical streak. Maybe this wouldn't be such a bad trip, after all.

"So what's the big deal with being named Captain Blye?" Marissa asked.

The other three looked at her hopelessly, none of them bothering to explain.

"It's spelled differently," Morgana stated in lieu of an answer. "There's no need to get mutinous."

"I didn't mean—" Moriah began, but Mathilda cut her off. "Never mind, Mo, we're here. Help me with my bags, will you?"

Of course she would, Moriah replied dutifully to herself. And she'd naturally help Morgana and Marissa with theirs, too. Service with a smile, you know. Little Mo, always happy to oblige.

When their bags were piled high on the sidewalk beside the taxi, Morgana instructed, "Pay the driver, will you, Mo? All I have are traveler's checks."

Moriah dug in her pocket for some loose bills, paying and tipping the driver only to turn around to find her sisters gone. She finally spotted them, each clutching their small makeup cases, walking down the pier alongside the group of surgeons. They had each left behind their larger bags, knowing from experience that Mo would bring them along with her. Straightening her glasses bravely and squaring her shoulders in resignation, Moriah arranged the four pieces of luggage as best she could under her arms and in her hands, gritting her teeth tightly as she followed behind the three silvery-blond heads glinting starkly in the noonday sun.

By the time she caught up with them, they were exchanging vital statistics with the surgeons beside a long, sleek ketch the color of a beautifully preened swan. Moriah dumped the suitcases unceremoniously on the dock, eyeing the big yacht enviously and thinking that somehow Morgana had managed to do this thing right.

As her sisters said their final farewells to the Cedars-Sinai trio, Moriah's eyes settled on the bow of the boat, widening with surprise at the sudden appearance of a young boy. He grinned at her mischievously, his bright white smile rivaling the sparkle of the sun on the water, his black eyes dancing with the excitement of a new adventure.

"Hello, lady," he called out to her.

Moriah giggled and grinned back at him. "Hello, yourself. Are you Captain Blye?"

The little boy's laughter rang out like the music of wind

chimes on a blustery day. "No way," he assured her. "Captain Blye, he big. Me very, very small. But someday I be just as big. Den I'll have a boat even bigger dan Captain Blye!" He threw his arms wide in an effort to illustrate. "My name is Christian. My brother works with Captain Blye."

"So you're Mr. Christian," Moriah said with a smile. "It's very nice to meet you. My name is—"

"Mo, come on, we need our stuff," Marissa called from where she stood beside the gangway that led to the deck of *Urizen*. Apparently her other sisters had already boarded.

"Coming," Moriah told her sister.

"Mo," Christian said with a childish chuckle. "Dat's a very funny name. But I like it anyway."

"Thanks, Christian," she acknowledged with a crooked smile. "I think."

She turned back to retrieve the stack of luggage from the dock, then bent to fix the ankle strap of her flat sandal. When she looked up again, Christian was gone, and she shrugged at the fickleness of children. She had been hoping he would give her a hand so she wouldn't have to maneuver the skinny gangplank alone. Oh, well, she decided after a moment. Nothing ventured and all that. She'd been living dangerously since she'd arrived in the Caribbean. Why the sudden concern for safety now?

Once more Moriah stooped to retrieve the suitcases, balancing them precariously around her body. When she turned again, Marissa had already accompanied the others onto the boat, and with another resigned sigh, Moriah took steps to join them.

"Dammit," Austen snapped under his breath as he slapped a greasy palm ineffectually against the engine. "Nothing like completely losing power on the day I'm supposed to take a bunch of rich, pampered debutantes out for an excursion," he muttered irritably to no one in particular.

He rubbed his palm furiously over his cheekbone to wipe away the perspiration, probably leaving a jagged streak of black grease in its wake. His chest, too, was wet from the stifling heat of the tiny unventilated engine room, the thick spattering of hair marred by a number of black smears similar to the one that decorated his cheek. He was still dressed in his cutoffs, and he rubbed one bare foot with the other in an unconscious gesture of agitation. His long, sun-streaked hair was thick and unruly from the humid day and fell forward over amber eyes that gleamed with impotent frustration at the silent machine that tormented him.

"Dorian!" he finally bellowed out angrily, letting his animosity toward the engine get the better of him.

"Yeah, Austen?" His partner's worried face appeared upside down through the hatch in the passageway near the engine room. "What's de problem, mon?"

"This damned engine is as temperamental as a sexually repressed librarian," the other man complained.

"Eh, watch it. Maggie is a librarian," Dorian said of his girlfriend. "And she's anything but sexually repressed. If you'd go out with dat friend of hers, you'd see what I mean."

"Dorian! Austen!" a small voice interrupted them. Christian's smiling face appeared beside his brother's in the hatch. "You'd better come quick. Some ladies out here say dey're your charters."

"Great," Austen muttered savagely. "This is just great." He slammed the wrench he'd been holding against the top of the engine and accidentally raked his knuckles across a cooling grate. "Dammit," he rasped out, unconsciously raising his wounded hand to his lips. "Listen, Dorian, you know more about this piece of garbage than I do. You're going to have to fix this thing, man. I've got to greet our guests."

"No offense, Austen," the other man began delicately, "but you look more like a pirate dan a captain right now. Maybe you should let me be de one to meet de ladies."

"What are you talking about?" Austen screwed his face up in anger. "I'm always the greeter," he added crossly. "I'm the one with the charming personality, dammit, and don't you forget it."

"Charming," Dorian repeated drily. "Right. You look like hell."

Austen glanced down at himself. He was sweaty and dirty, and holding up his bruised knuckles for inspection, he noted he was also bleeding.

"Don't worry about it," he told his partner as he pulled himself up through the hatch. "Rich women love this stuff. It's better than the being-seduced-by-the-dirty-gardener fantasy. You just get this baby roaring, okay?"

Dorian laughed. "I'll do my best, Captain. I'll do my best."

Austen's cross mood began to lift quickly when he looked toward the bow of the boat and beheld three silver-blond heads atop three perfectly slender female bodies. Definitely sisters, he thought to himself. Gorgeous sisters at that. Maybe this cruise wouldn't be so hellacious, after all.

"Ladies!" he called out to them, switching on the old Blye charm. When the three turned to him at once, he caught his breath at the picture they made standing there on his deck in the glittering early-afternoon sun. Oh, yes, this trip was definitely becoming more promising by the minute. "I'm Austen Blye, your captain. Welcome aboard!"

Apparently he'd been right about that gardener fantasy, he thought, because as he approached the three women, he felt all three pairs of eyes skim slowly over him from head to toe, as if he were a big prize bull there'd been rumors about at the marketplace. When they all smiled at him provocatively, he knew for certain that he'd been a hit.

"Captain Blye." The one with the shortest hair, who stood in front of the others, extended her hand gracefully and smiled, arching an eyebrow speculatively. "I'm Morgana Mallory. I believe we spoke on the phone. These are my sisters, Mathilda…"

The one with the softly curling hair stepped forward, hand also very gracefully extended. "Nice to meet you, Captain," she murmured.

"Same here," Austen replied, noting the coolness of her slender fingers.

"…and Marissa," Morgana continued, indicating the third woman.

She, too, stepped forward and took Austen's hand, boldly running her middle fingertip over the rough flesh of his palm as she spoke low. "You have a gorgeous boat," she told him throatily with a cryptic smile. "It's so big. Is it that big all over?"

Austen raised his eyebrows at her statement and bit his lip. "Uh, thanks," he responded delicately, then thought, what the hell. "Yeah, it's big…Marissa, is it?"

"Yes," she purred. "Marissa Mallory. The model."

"The model," he repeated blandly, uncertain how the revelation was significant.

"Oh, yes," Marissa enthused. "Morgana's the writer, Mathilda's the actress and I'm the model."

"I see," Austen said with an understanding nod. "But I was under the impression that there was going to be four of you."

"Oh, yeah." Marissa's smile fell somewhat. "Our sister, Mo, came, too."

"Mo?" Austen asked. Morgana, Mathilda, Marissa and *Mo?*

"She's over there," Marissa said absently, waving her hand airily toward the gangway.

Austen turned in time to catch sight of the most wonderfully curvaceous bottom he'd ever seen, bent over a pile of luggage on deck, swaying provocatively as its owner struggled to keep the suitcases from falling overboard. A long dark honey braid fell past the woman's shoulders, swinging along with the unconsciously seductive motion of her rump. He couldn't prevent the lascivious grin that spread across his face. Oh, man, this was gonna be great! Just he and Dorian, alone at sea with four beautiful women. Well, three beautiful women at least, and one with a really great backside. But, hey, if she looked anything at all like her sisters, then...

At that moment the fourth woman glanced up from her burden and quickly straightened. She looked right at Austen and paled, then took three slow steps back toward the gangplank as if trying to escape. With her thick dark blond hair and the wisps of curls surrounding her bespectacled face, with her lush curves and ample breasts, she did not resemble her sisters in any way. However, she did look familiar...

His thoughts ended there, and he took several measured steps toward the woman standing nervously beside the gangway. When he was finally in front of her, with only a few inches separating them, he made a slow circle around her, thoroughly surveying her as he went. He took in the loose-fitting, unflattering clothes, the severely pulled back hair, the huge horn-rimmed glasses. And then he saw her eyes. Big, beautiful dark gray eyes, eyes so full of emotion he wanted to reach out and touch her. But he couldn't do that. Not to a total stranger.

Finally he stopped in front of the fourth Mallory sister and placed his fists on his hips in challenge. In clear, clipped tones he demanded, "All right, who are you, and what in the hell have you done with Moriah?"

Chapter Four

Moriah scrambled frantically for something, anything, to say. She had thought she would never see him again, had believed that what happened last night could be chalked up to poor judgment and intoxication, then filed under *N* for Nostalgia in her brain. Yet here he was, larger than life, sexy as hell, dirty and sweaty and more gorgeous than she could ever have remembered him. Austen. Austen Blye, apparently. *Captain* Austen Blye, who would be the commander in chief of her vacation for the next two weeks. Her heart pounded erratically against her rib cage, and color crept mutinously up her throat and into her cheeks. If she wasn't careful, she thought, she was going to start hyperventilating, and then she'd really be in trouble. Moriah closed her eyes briefly and swallowed hard, groping for words that would not come.

"Well?" he insisted, hands still resting on his hips in the ultimate gesture of challenge.

"I, uh," Moriah began lamely. "That is… I mean…" But explanations and excuses eluded her. As the seconds stretched into minutes, as amber eyes raked over her with animosity, anger and accusation, Moriah felt her grip on reality slowly begin to loosen, felt it dissolving bit by bit into a stark staring panic.

"Do you two know each other?" she heard Morgana utter from a great distance away, feeling suddenly as if she were an insect trapped beneath a jar.

Despite the fact that Moriah was still having trouble forming words that were accepted as part of common English usage, Morgana's question was evidently all it took to bring Austen back into the stream of things. He looked first at her oldest sister, quizzically, as if he'd forgotten the other women were there, then turned his gaze once again on Moriah.

"Know *her?*" Austen asked quietly and not a little breathlessly. "No, I don't believe she and I have ever met before." His voice dropped to a smooth whisper only Moriah could hear, and his eyes never left hers as he spoke further. "But I met a woman once who looked a little like her, a woman full of life and laughter. A woman full of spirit. Apparently I was mistaken. She looks nothing like that woman at all."

It was only then, after he turned his back on her, that Moriah was able to find her voice. She, too, spoke softly, words meant for his ears alone. "That woman wasn't real, Austen," she assured him almost ruefully. "She doesn't exist."

The only indication that he had actually heard what she said was a slight stiffening of his shoulders. When she looked past him at the other Mallorys, her sisters were watching them both with narrowed, curious eyes. Marissa began to open her mouth to speak, but Moriah intercepted any question or speculation that might have escaped the model's lips by saying, "Marissa, I heard something that sounded like it was broken when I put your suitcase down on deck. I hope it wasn't your mirror. You know, the one with the five different light adjustments?"

Marissa forgot anything she had planned to say and raced toward her bags lying heaped on the deck. "Where are our rooms?" she asked Austen urgently as she gripped her bags in her own two hands, clearly not trusting Moriah to go anywhere near her things. "I want to unpack as soon as possible."

"Right this way, ladies," Austen responded automatically, gesturing toward the open hatch.

He sounded to Moriah as if his spirits had lifted once again, but she could still detect a glimmer of something akin to disappointment in his words. She felt herself yearning to reach out to him, wanted to see just once more that look in his eyes that made her nerves dance in anticipation of what his touch would do to her skin, indeed her very soul. Memories of all that had happened between them washed over her like a hot, rushing river, and her heart quivered with the passion that welled up inside her as quickly and vividly as the night before. Just for a minute she let herself relive the feverish, sexually charged moments when his fingers and mouth had claimed her, let herself feel once more the heightened awareness of her surroundings and the scintillating heat that had turned her body into a writhing, pleasure-seeking mass of raw—

Moriah snapped her eyes open in shock. She was seeing herself as a character in one of Morgana's books, she realized with stark horror. She told herself for perhaps the thousandth time that she really did hate her sister's novels and only read them out of a sense of duty to Morgana. She could *not* identify with the women her sister created, Moriah vowed solemnly to herself, and she was *nothing* at all like them. She wasn't. She was Professor Moriah Mallory, Ph.D., expert on primitive South American cultures and all-around intellectual. She was also the awkward little sister of three of the most spectacular women who'd ever walked the earth, she further reminded herself, and she did not entertain any delusions of imitating their successes with the opposite sex. Therefore, why she continued to indulge in these silly little fantasies where she was actually wanted and pursued by men was a mystery.

Last night had happened only because she had indulged entirely too freely. She had been swept away by an unusual set of circumstances, a breathtakingly beautiful island and an uncommonly romantic series of events. She had been thoroughly removed from the crowded, dirty streets of her everyday life in Philadelphia, had left the musty, chalk-scented classroom behind. And she had fallen into a tailspin over an incredibly compelling man who had carried her into a blissful world unlike any she had ever known. And of course the only reason Austen had responded to her was because she had offered him exactly what men like him seek—a free tumble in the sack with no strings attached. Any man would have reacted the same way, she was ashamed to admit. The one thing that had attracted Austen to her was also the one thing that was nowhere to be found in the essential makeup of her character—an ease and independence of spirit that stopped just short of promiscuity.

The word stuck in her throat mentally just as it would have if she had been speaking aloud. Moriah did not consider herself prudish or square and was more than aware of the lenient lifestyles in which some of her students and colleagues alike indulged. Certainly she criticized no one for choosing the number or frequency of their bed partners, nor did she feel it her right or her place to judge. In addition to that, her studies of primitive cultures often revealed populations that practiced polygamy for both men and women. She was neither shocked nor bothered by such behavior. Except where she herself was concerned. Moriah Mallory wasn't precisely an innocent, nor was she widely read in the annals of romantic experience. Since leaving the closely guarded circle of her family, the few relationships she had managed to garner had been in the very advanced stages of development before she would even consider physical intimacy. And when she had finally decided to take the enormous step toward such an activity, she had always been left nonetheless with feelings of regret and unfulfillment.

Then Austen had come along. Austen, with his roguish good looks and irreverent sense of humor, with his solid, muscular body and soft, tentative touches. In virtually no time he had claimed part of her heart that she'd never again call her own. It scared her, the immediacy and insistence of her feelings for him, frightened her that after only hours in his presence she had been not only ready but more than willing to enjoy the activity that in the past she had only allowed after careful and lengthy consideration. What was it about Austen that had made her want to forget every principle and value she had spent her life nurturing, made her want to break every rule that she had ever made?

As Moriah followed her sisters along the deck, her troubled thoughts caused her to shudder, despite the heat of the sun that radiated through her shirt and sent rivulets of warm perspiration streaming down her back. She welcomed the relative coolness that greeted her hot skin when she wandered down the stairs into the passageway, only half listening as Austen pointed out the galley and the head, sheepishly greeting Dorian as they passed the engine room and intensely grateful upon reaching the staterooms they had been assigned. Morgana was to share a double berth with Mathilda on the starboard side of the boat, while Moriah and Marissa would be occupying the forward cabin. Austen and Dorian slept in over-under berths on the port side while Christian, when he was cruising with them, chose to bunk down in a small berth in *Urizen*'s aft section.

The four women were finally left to unpack while Austen and Dorian readied the boat for sailing, and Moriah found that she was exhausted from trying to ignore Austen and from pretending she didn't notice her sisters' speculative stares. Now that she had only Marissa to face, she relaxed her guard a little and began to remove textbooks, notepads and a few personal belongings from her canvas bag.

"Oh, thank God it's safe."

Moriah heard her sister's whisper and sigh of relief and turned to find Marissa clutching her makeup mirror to her chest as if it were a small child. "Better plug it in and check those five adjustments," Moriah cautioned a little acerbically. "You don't want to get caught in the tropics without that daylight setting."

She didn't point out, of course, that Marissa had only to open a window, or porthole as the case may be, to get the same effect. But when she saw the look of sheer panic that came over the other woman's face at the prospect of overdoing her cosmetics because of a bad bulb, Moriah almost reconsidered. Quickly Marissa found a plug and turned the appliance on, spinning the knob furiously to assure herself that all the settings were indeed intact. With that accomplished, she was able to turn her attention to her wardrobe.

While Marissa completed the seemingly colossal task of organizing the single tiny closet their stateroom boasted, Moriah put her few belongings in one drawer beneath the bed and inspected the cabin. It was actually much larger than what she had anticipated. The white ceiling arched just slightly over their heads, and she could easily reach up to skim her fingertips against it. Four portholes and an open hatch offered a generous portion of the warm Caribbean sun, and when night did fall, two small brass wall lamps bolted over the bed would provide all the light they needed. The coverlet atop the mattress was lightweight and the color of a sandy beach, looking very inviting at the moment with an abundance of pale blue and beige throw pillows piled at the head. The solid teak walls, drawers and closet were polished to a golden gleam, cool and smooth to the touch as she ran her fingers lovingly across the louvered doors and brass fixtures. It smelled wonderful, she noted as she closed her eyes and inhaled deeply, reminiscent of lemon oil and the ocean, an essentially masculine scent that reminded her of…Austen.

She opened her eyes quickly and pushed the thought away. She had to get her mind off him and focus on the reason she had come down to the Caribbean in the first place—to work. No, she hastily corrected herself, for *vacation.* Okay, she finally amended, for a working vacation. She glanced over at Marissa, who was looking vexed as she contemplated how she was going to fit a green sequined formal into a closet that was only four feet high. Moriah wondered where her sister was planning on wearing such a thing out in the middle of the ocean, but decided not to ask. Instead she picked up a notebook bulging with loose-leaf remnants of her research and started toward the cabin door. Knowing her sisters as well as she did, it was safe to assume all three of them were struggling with similar wardrobe problems at the moment. Without saying a word, Moriah slipped unobtrusively from the stateroom, knowing she would never be missed, and went in search of a quiet and very secluded corner of the boat.

When Austen went in search of Moriah some hours later to tell her that he and the others would be assembling for happy hour soon, he found her fast asleep on deck, her back against the cabin, her face turned toward the sun as if seeking life itself from the fiery orb. The sea breeze had loosened much of her hair from its severe braid, and the sparkling dark honey curls that had escaped now blew wildly about her face. He noticed with a smile that her eyeglasses lay neglected in her lap alongside a rather large tome bearing the title *Pre-Colombian Cultures in the Fabric of Modern Thought*. She had apparently succumbed to the heat before surrendering to slumber, having pushed her khaki trousers up to her knees and loosening several buttons on her shirt. Below it she wore a white cotton undershirt edged with delicate lace and decorated with a tiny satin bow. It was the kind of undershirt he remembered his kid sister, Molly, sporting when she was about six years old. All in all, the woman before him was a curious mixture of smarts and innocence, of lust and purity, of desire and denial. The realization made Austen's brows draw downward in a frown.

At the moment she reminded him of the Moriah he'd met on St. Thomas, the woman who had hijacked his heart and lassoed his libido within a matter of minutes. She looked carefree and content, completely a part of her surroundings. So who was that woman who had appeared on deck this afternoon? he wondered. That stranger who had seemed so staid and reserved? That person introduced as Mo who had allowed herself to be so easily dismissed by her sisters?

Cautiously, in an effort not to awaken her, Austen stooped down beside her and carefully removed the book from her lap, setting it silently on the deck. Next he removed her glasses from their perch atop her thigh, succumbing to the desire to run his finger softly over the khaki fabric and pausing only briefly when she made a small sound of reluctance in her sleep. But when she sighed and remained oblivious, turning her face more fully toward the sun and exposing the creamy warm skin of her neck and throat in the process, Austen couldn't help but take advantage of the easy access offered. Leaning his forehead softly against hers, he tangled his fingers gently in her curls and pressed his lips against hers in the lightest, most restrained kiss he was able to manage. Evidently it was more restrained than he'd planned, because Moriah didn't budge. His next kiss was more insistent, his lips nibbling at hers in a tender caress that had left other women groaning for more. This time, however, it was Austen who groaned. Especially when Moriah began to kiss him back. She was tentative at first, as if this kiss were her first ever; but as he intensified his ministrations, tasting her mouth more fully, exploring the dark recesses intimately with his tongue, she too began a more thorough expedition into the realm of sensual pleasure.

Slowly it began to dawn on Austen that the reason Moriah was responding so willingly was because she was still half-asleep, so he sought to awaken her to her actions. He let one hand leave the satiny softness of her hair to travel downward and dip into the opening of her shirt, let his fingers strum an erotic serenade against her collarbone and venture lower, between her breasts. Moriah moaned softly and kissed him more deeply, letting her own fingers weave insistently through his dark locks. When Austen could stand it no longer, he stroked his hand gently over the warm fabric of her undershirt, cupping her heavy breast in his palm, thumbing the already-excited peak to new life.

"Moriah," he rasped out against her throat. "Wake up. Look at me. I want you to know it's me, Austen. You aren't dreaming, sweetheart, you're reacting."

For a moment longer she hugged herself against him, continued to run her fingers possessively through his hair and press her mouth curiously against his face and neck. For a moment longer Moriah let herself dream. Then as quickly as she had responded to him, Austen felt her stiffen and try to pull away. She made quite an impressive effort to free herself from his embrace, but he wasn't about to let that happen. Not when he'd just gotten his Moriah back. Instead he gathered her more closely to him, planted his hand firmly at the base of her neck and forced her to stare eye to eye with him.

"Don't even think about it," he told her with an affectionate smile. "You're not going anywhere until we've had a little talk about what *exactly* is going on between us."

Moriah's eyes widened in alarm, and for a moment Austen thought she would never speak again. But she recovered quickly and pushed her fists ineffectually against his chest, then looked up at him with an expression that was adorably affronted and magnificently miffed.

"What's happening is that you have a habit of taking advantage of me while I'm sleeping," she accused him viciously.

"That's true," he admitted readily, so readily that Moriah was once again unable to respond. He capitalized on that fact by rushing on in his defense. "At least *this* time I was taking advantage of you while you slept. Last night I was taking advantage of you because you were drunk. There's a difference, you know. Taking advantage of a sleeping woman is considerably more deplorable than taking advantage of a drunken woman, who really should know better."

Moriah's mouth dropped open in indignation at his suggestion that last night had been her fault. "Are you implying that *I'm* the one who's to blame for that fiasco that occurred last night?" she gasped in horror.

"Well, you were the one who instigated the whole thing," he told her.

"What?" she shrieked.

"Well, you did," he insisted. "Looking so beautiful and desirable, laughing at my jokes, liking all my friends, fitting in so perfectly and making me feel so wonderful. You really should be ashamed of yourself."

"Austen…" Her voice trailed off into a silent plea when she felt herself soften at the way he disguised his compliments. She remembered all the provocative words he'd uttered the night before, the heated ways he'd touched her and the spectacular sensations he'd sent spiraling through her body.

"And then of course there was that little mambo you did against my libido back at your condo," he added lightly.

Moriah couldn't help the small smile that danced about her lips.

Austen felt his heart go haywire. "Yeah, that was a number designed to make thinking men go mad."

"Oh, Austen," she said again, leaning her forehead against his shoulder gently, splaying her hand open over his heart. For some absurd reason he thought she sounded as if she was pleading hopelessly for something that could never be.

"What is it?" he asked her quietly.

His voice stirred the hair at her temple, and Moriah was reminded that she must look frightfully disheveled. She gently disengaged herself from his arms and looked at him forlornly, then shook her head almost imperceptibly before tucking her errant curls back into her braid. Slowly, laboriously, she buttoned up her shirt and pushed the bottom part of her trousers back into place around her ankles, then retrieved her glasses from the deck and donned them with the dexterity of an anthropologist who thinks she knows how she's supposed to look. When finally she picked up the thick copy of *Pre-Colombian Cultures in the Fabric of Modern Thought* and held it up like a shield before her, her voice dropped to an almost soundless pitch. "It can never work, Austen," she whispered. "Never."

She pushed herself up from the deck and began to walk away, unwilling to listen to anything else he might have to say. She wasn't even going to give them a chance, he realized, feeling his earlier irritation return. Dammit, what was with her, anyway?

"Moriah," he called after her. His voice was low, insistent and not a little menacing. He saw her stop, but she did not turn around. "Look at me," he instructed her.

She glanced over her shoulder for a moment, but still she did not turn around. He took five deliberate steps until he was past her, then he turned to face her and hold her eyes steadily. Moriah's vision never strayed, her gaze locked with his, but she remained silent, waiting to hear what he had to say.

Austen took a deep, impatient breath, settled his hands on his hips and told her, "I don't know what's going on between us, but I'm real anxious to find out just how far and wide it's going to travel. Why you seem to think it's already run its course is beyond me because, lady, I think it's barely begun. We've got two long weeks to explore this territory, and I don't plan on doing it alone."

With his roughly uttered intentions stated, Austen seemed to relax somewhat. Moriah studied him with a curious expression, one that was both daunting and inviting. It was a haunting, needful look that made him want to pull her into his arms, but one that also indicated quite clearly that she wanted nothing more to do with him. Angry that a woman he wanted so desperately should be so willing to push him away, Austen forced himself to turn on his heel and leave her. When he remembered that he had originally come looking for her to tell her about drinks on deck, he paused and tossed his well-rehearsed Captain Blye jargon over his shoulder. "We'll be going ashore on St. John for dinner tonight, but happy hour will be starting any minute now. There will be light fare laid out in the galley if you want something to eat earlier, otherwise I hope you'll join us in the cockpit for cocktails."

He should have found satisfaction in the fact that his words came out sounding so cold and impersonal, that the way Moriah's face fell at his statement indicated that she had been hurt by the abrupt manner in which it had been offered. Instead, as he left her behind, Austen couldn't help but feel as if he'd just injured himself far worse than any wound he could inflict upon Moriah.

Moriah decided to give herself a little time before joining her sisters and the others for happy hour. She wanted to return to her cabin first and ascertain that she was back in the proper anthropologist mode. She brushed and replaited her hair, polished her glasses and put on shoes, then inhaling deeply several times, she stood back and gazed at herself in one of Marissa's many mirrors. Seeing that she did indeed appear plain and unremarkable, she was finally convinced that she was back to her old self and ready to face the real world again.

That fact was reinforced some minutes later when she joined the group already partaking of colorful drinks in the cockpit and realized that no one had even noticed her arrival. The sun was hanging low in the sky by now, sinking toward the town of Charlotte Amalie and the island they were fast leaving behind. She could still see St. Thomas quite clearly, and to her right was another small island covered with lush foliage and rimmed by a white ribbon of beach. Ahead of the boat more islands beckoned, all of them looking like green mountaintops jutting up from the ocean's depths, strung together like an emerald necklace. Moriah took a deep breath of the salty sea air and closed her eyes at the feeling of tranquility that settled over her. She had traveled all over the world, seen every kind of natural and man-made wonder there was to see, but nothing, nothing, made her feel more complete and at peace than being near the curiously colored water that was the Caribbean. She didn't know why that was, only that since she had come here, she had quite simply felt a sense of oneness with this world.

When she opened her eyes again, it was to behold the scene of her sisters lounging about the ample cockpit, vying for the sun and Captain Blye's attention. While Dorian claimed the dubious honor of manning the wheel and listening to Christian's more than thorough instructions about piloting a sailboat, Austen had the even more dubious distinction of being flanked by Moriah's two eldest sisters. Morgana wore a flowing caftan of pale green and rose silk, her hair bound up in a scarf of similar design. She cradled a long-stemmed flute of champagne in her left hand and nudged Austen's shoulder playfully with her right, all the while chuckling that low this-man-will-be-putty-in-my-hands-in-no-time laugh of hers. On the good captain's other side, Mathilda sat prettily in a yellow sarong and tank top, batting her eyelashes like a coquette as she asked questions about the boat and feigned indifference to the physical charms of the handsome man beside her.

Boy, she really is an excellent actress, Moriah thought, smart enough certainly to admit that no woman could be indifferent to the charms of Austen Blye. Marissa, Moriah noted, had removed herself from the others to sit against the rail where she could get maximum sun benefit in her simple, no-nonsense, red string bikini. She propped a bottle of beer on her knee, label forward, as if doing a magazine spread for the product, and posed with her face to the wind as if uninterested, unaffected, untroubled and unconcerned. She was actually a better actress than Mathilda, Moriah realized.

All in all, Moriah couldn't help but feel badly for Austen. Although he didn't know it yet, he was about to become embroiled in the oldest Mallory vacation game there was, would in fact become the target as well as the prize for the recreational tradition. Who Gets the Man had always been a favorite pastime for the three elder Mallory sisters, and it was always impossible to predict the winner. The loser, however, was any man they chose as their prey. Moriah only hoped Austen was quick to figure out what they were up to.

She tucked herself discreetly into a corner of the cockpit where she felt she would be safe from the normal vacation perils, but apparently she had been mistaken about arriving unobserved by everyone. Austen must have been watching for her, as he left the ministrations of Morgana and Mathilda without a thought and took up the position immediately to Moriah's right, lodging himself between her hips and the cabin where she was quite certain she had left no room for anyone to fit, let alone this tall, lean, muscular…sinewy… masculine…man. Moriah gulped audibly. My goodness, she thought suddenly. It certainly did get hot fast in the Caribbean, didn't it? And with absolutely no warning at all. Moriah fanned her face with rapidly fluttering hands and tried not to notice the attractive hunk of male flesh beside her.

Evidently, though, Austen had other ideas. He leaned his face close to hers and asked playfully, "Hot, isn't it?" He enunciated the words hotly against her throat.

Moriah glanced over at him quickly and nodded, hoping he didn't detect the quivers of excitement his presence set to dancing in her veins. "Yes," she agreed hastily with a brief smile, trying to still the wild thumping of her heart that always seemed to accompany his arrival. "Yes, it is hot."

"Gonna get hotter," Austen promised her, his voice a quiet caress that only she was meant to hear.

Moriah felt color creep into her cheeks and told herself it was only because of the sun. She must remember to reapply her sunscreen before venturing out on deck again. When Christian approached her and offered her a tall, cool-looking drink adorned with wheels of lemon and lime that floated among the numerous ice cubes, Moriah accepted it gratefully and filled her mouth with the tempting liquid. Her eyes widened with surprise at the fire the concoction started in her throat, then squeezed closed again as the flames leapt up in her stomach. When she began to gasp for air, Austen chuckled good-naturedly and patted her gently on the back.

"Christian's a hell of a bartender," he told her mildly. "Makes some real eye-squinters."

When she'd recovered enough to be able to vocalize again, Moriah wheezed, "Does anyone down here drink anything besides rum?"

"Sure," Austen assured her. "Gin, vodka, bourbon, Scotch, you name it. But rum is definitely the most popular. Not to mention the cheapest and most easily accessible. No matter what island you visit down here, you can be certain that there's a rum distillery on it somewhere. It may be some ancient chunk of machinery way out in the middle of the jungle, but it's there."

"Ever heard of nonalcoholic beverages?" she asked drily.

Austen smiled that disarming smile of his and said, "No, can't say as I have."

Moriah shook her head helplessly at him and stirred the ice cubes with her finger. "Maybe I'll just wait until it dilutes itself a little."

Austen's smile broadened but he said nothing, just sipped his own drink and continued to gaze at her as if she were something worth gazing at. Moriah became inexplicably embarrassed by his obvious interest, especially when she remembered the parting that followed their earlier exchange. She looked away, only to see her three sisters watching her with an enormous amount of interest. That, too, made her uncomfortable, so she leaned farther back against the rail and stared toward the bow of the boat at the destinations that lay beyond them.

"So we'll be having dinner on St. John?" she asked innocuously, keeping her eyes planted firmly on the green islands that rose out of the water before them.

"I know this terrific little restaurant in Cruz Bay," she heard Austen murmur from behind her. "A friend of mine runs it. You'll like it."

"You seem to know everybody down here," she said quietly, still gazing forward, feeling somehow that their conversation now was meant for their ears alone.

His voice dropped to a dangerous pitch as he vowed, "Not nearly as well as I intend to."

Her heart picked up its unsteady beat at the boastful challenge his words offered, and Moriah turned to look at him fully. She was about to ask him what he meant by his pronouncement, even though she was certain that she already knew, but one of her sisters made an indelicate sound behind them meant to interrupt their conversation. Moriah wasn't sure exactly which sister had uttered the sound, as all of their indelicate noises tended to sound alike, but the nasal whine had the desired effect. Both she and Austen turned their attention back to the little gathering in the cockpit and, like it or not, found themselves caught up in the ensuing conversation. Moriah discovered almost immediately that she, for one, did not like it at all.

"So, Captain," Morgana cooed after taking a rather substantial sip of her champagne, "how is it that you met our little Mo before she even came aboard?"

Moriah threw Austen a pleading look, begging him not to divulge the particulars of the humiliating experience that had brought them together. Austen smiled back at her, and for a moment she thought she was safe. Unfortunately he then opened his mouth to speak.

"Your sister here picked me up in a bar on St. Thomas last night," he announced loudly and, Moriah thought, not a little proudly.

Marissa nearly spit out her mouthful of beer, while Mathilda and Morgana only stared at the couple incredulously.

"She did *what?*" Morgana gasped.

"Morgana, I did not do any such—" Moriah began to defend herself but Austen cut her off.

"It was great," he continued. "Moriah knows *all* the best places to go on St. Thomas. She took me to this little bar down on the waterfront, then we discovered this steel-drum band on the beach near her hotel and went dancing until about 4:00 a.m. Boy, can your sister dance!" he added parenthetically. "Quite the little mambo performer, I might add."

"Austen," Moriah pleaded. "Don't do this to me."

"Moriah, what is this crazy man talking about?" Mathilda wanted to know.

"It's a long story," Moriah explained. "And nothing at all like what he's leading you to believe, I assure you."

Austen turned to look at her with feigned affront. "Moriah, how can you say that after all the beautiful things you promised me last night? Do I mean nothing to you? Were you just using me?"

"Austen, stop it," Moriah insisted. "They don't understand that you're just joking. They'll take you seriously." She turned back to her sisters when she said, "It wasn't like that. Some drunks were bothering me in a bar in Charlotte Amalie and Austen stepped in to scare them off, that's all."

Her sisters looked at her for a moment, weighing this information, then looked at one another to see if they would allow it to be accepted. When Morgana nodded slowly, Mathilda and Marissa did likewise, and the earth began to rotate on its axis once again.

"We've warned you about doing things like that, Mo," Marissa told her, sounding like the very voice of experience where being picked up by strangers in bars was concerned. "You're much too young and naive for your own good. Teddy and Diana never should have let you leave Newport to go to that awful school. It only gave you ideas."

Moriah closed her eyes patiently and said, "Harvard, Marissa. I went to Harvard. And some people are of the opinion that college is supposed to give one ideas."

"Well, in this case, your ideas landed you with nothing but trouble, didn't they?" Morgana pointed out.

"Yes," Moriah said obediently.

Mathilda simply cautioned, "Next time be more careful, Mo."

"I will," Moriah replied meekly as an obedient sibling should.

Austen wasn't sure, but he had the distinct impression that Moriah had just been put in her place, though what that place was or why she should allow herself to be put anywhere she didn't want to be was a mystery. Last night she had been a lively, interesting, self-confident woman, vocal and daring and full of fun. Only a short time ago he had stumbled upon her looking beautiful and desirable, and she had responded to him like a woman who knew exactly what she wanted. However, now she was fidgeting like an uncomfortable four-year-old who'd just been scolded for doing something she knew she shouldn't. He wanted to point out to her that she was a grown woman who had the freedom and ability to venture anywhere she wanted anytime she wanted and that she was more than capable of taking care of herself. He'd witnessed that particular fact last night when he'd prevented her from nailing Bart in the loins. Yet at the moment she was acting like an awkward adolescent who had no idea what her place in the world might be. Austen was stumped. When had the change occurred, and what could he do to reverse it?

"So, you ladies get down to the Caribbean often?" he asked with some distraction, hoping to steer the conversation into more agreeable waters.

Moriah was going to offer that it was her first time here, but Morgana waved her hand airily and replied instead.

"Oh, every now and then, but there are so many other places one should see first, I think."

Austen raised his eyebrows in genuine surprise at that. "Really? I can't think of a single area in the world I'd rather see, let alone settle. Where else could you possibly prefer to go?"

"New York," Marissa replied immediately. "Paris, London, Rome. Where all the beautiful, monied people live."

"Those are all wonderful cities," Mathilda agreed. "But you really must appreciate them for their contributions to the arts above all else," she scolded her younger sister.

"No, the wealth is most important," Marissa countered.

Morgana shook her head at both of them. "No, you're both mistaken," she said negligently. "It's the exotic places, the out-of-the-way places that are the most enjoyable. Certainly those are the places where we've had our most memorable adventures."

Moriah closed her eyes and placed her fingertips gently against a forehead that was beginning to throb with a tension headache. She was well versed in what was coming next, another favorite vacation game of her sisters', and as she always did, she tried fruitlessly to prevent it from progressing any further.

"Morgana, do we have to do this every time the four of us go away together?" she asked wearily, not even attempting to sidetrack her sister with small talk.

"Do what every time?" Morgana asked innocently.

"Talk about all of our 'most memorable adventures'?" Moriah felt herself shudder at the memories that were about to be revealed. "You know it generally winds up being a rehash of all the times I've made a fool out of myself."

Morgana waved her off. "Oh, it does not."

"Although there was that one time," Marissa began playfully, "that time in Paris when we taught her how to say in French, 'Hi, sailor, wanna get lucky?' and told her it meant 'Where's the ladies' room?' Remember that?"

Morgana chuckled without reserve. "And we told her to order chocolate cheese whenever she ate out because it was a local delicacy that was relatively unknown to foreigners and everyone would be impressed by her knowledge of the local cuisine."

Mathilda, too, got into the spirit and shared even more instances of Moriah's colossal blunders and errors. All three started to laugh as the stories grew more colorful and embarrassing, and Moriah was helpless to put an end to the onslaught, shrinking farther and farther into her seat with the realization that Austen heard every word uttered. She was certain he already knew that she was a geek after her behavior of the previous evening, but now he was going to see that her geekiness was worldwide and all-encompassing. And the idea of losing favor with Austen, even though she told herself it didn't matter, was the most demoralizing thing of all.

Austen picked up on her discomfort right away and sought to put an end to it. He didn't know why Moriah sat silently by as her sisters made a mockery of her, but he hated to see her looking so damned unhappy.

"Okay, you guys," he began, trying to inject some lightness into his voice, even though he was angry at all the women—at the elder Mallorys for putting their sister so callously on the spot, and at Moriah for doing nothing to stop them. "I think you're embarrassing your sister."

"Oh, Moriah doesn't mind," Morgana spoke for her sister, shrugging off Moriah's embarrassment as if it were no more than a sneeze. "She'd laugh, too, if she had any sense of humor. Unfortunately she's the one member of our family who can't seem to find anything very funny. I think that's why she became a scientist. I don't suppose there's much humor to be found there."

Moriah wanted to tell her sister that there was a great deal to be considered funny in science, especially when she considered the aspects of genetics, but she didn't say a word to counter Morgana's opinion. It would be pointless. How many times had she gone up against her family's viewpoints only to discover that they were so deeply ingrained that to challenge them would be like trying to change the way her relatives looked. And despite the fact that that, too, was a fantasy she also frequently entertained, Moriah was quite simply sick and tired of fighting them.

Austen sat back and waited for Moriah to attack her sister's blatant insult about not having any sense of humor, anticipating with relish the quips and quarrels that would accompany such an outburst. But he waited in vain. Moriah never said a word, silently implying that she agreed with what Morgana said. Austen looked at Moriah for a long time, then looked back at the eldest Mallory, then back at Moriah once more. She seemed to understand what he was getting at, but only shook her head once, twice, three times, then looked over the rail at the quickly passing waves. The Moriah he had met the night before would never have stood for such an affront as the one presented by her sister here. Family or not, intentional or not, Moriah didn't have to put up with the little scene he'd just observed. And why she would do so was a question he intended to have answered. Soon.

Chapter Five

The Islands Restaurant was indeed very casual, Moriah discovered later in the evening, hidden off a side street in Cruz Bay on St. John. Of course that wasn't saying much, as even the main streets looked like side streets as far as she was concerned. As they'd strolled past shops and boutiques housed in buildings that were actually little more than lean-tos, Austen had told her that the tiny town was the most densely populated section of St. John, and that because some two-thirds of the island and its coastal waters were now included in the Virgin Islands National Park, the area would remain lush, beautiful and virgin. Moriah had heard how Laurence Rockefeller purchased the island in 1956 and turned it over to a foundation, insisting it remain unspoiled, but Austen's liberal embellishment of the story and frequent references to all the local gossip from the past two and a half decades made the retelling all the more enjoyable and informative.

The entire sailing party had come ashore at Hawk's Nest Bay, but all had separated for one reason or another. Dorian had hauled a fidgeting Christian off for an obligatory visit with someone named Aunt Agnes, whom, the little boy complained, smelled of too many camellias. The three elder Mallorys had expressed their interest in a quaint little eatery near the beach, but when Moriah had turned automatically to accompany them, Austen had wrapped his fingers gently but insistently around her upper arm and had very quietly reminded her of her earlier agreement to have dinner with him. Moriah had been about to voice the fact that she couldn't remember having made any such commitment, but Austen's fast-talking assurances to the contrary and his swiftly moving feet quickly propelled her away from her family and toward the situation in which she now found herself.

All in all, as she walked alongside Austen and allowed her fingers to be loosely woven with his, Moriah had to admit that she didn't mind a bit. To get to the restaurant owned and operated by Austen's friend, James, they followed the route of two winding roads that first went uphill then came back down. Apparently no one in Cruz Bay had ever thought it necessary to pave some of the narrow, palm-lined streets, a quality Moriah also found very endearing about the town, and dust danced about the couple's feet with every step they took. Although nearly eight o'clock, the sun was not yet ready to set, and stained the sky above them with streaks of orange and red. Moriah's ears pricked up at the sound of the wind whiffling casually through the high palms, and it struck her that even the wind took its time in this part of the world. Again she was filled with a sense of being exactly where she ought to be, and thoughts of her life in Philadelphia were steadily becoming the vague scraps of a dream she could scarcely remember.

When Austen paused in front of a two-story house of wood

bleached gray by the tropical weather, Moriah was curious. She wondered if perhaps the building held some distant memory for him, was maybe the place where he'd lost his virginity or some such nonsense, and she waited for his thoughts to clear so they could be on their way. Then she realized that there was music coming from somewhere above them, from the trees or the evening breeze, and when she looked up to find that dim lights shone from the second floor of the building, she turned her face toward him with a dubious expression.

"You can't be serious" was all she said.

"It's the best restaurant in the U.S.V.I.," he assured her. "In the B.V.I., too, for that matter."

"But it looks like it's about to fall over," she protested. "There's not even a sign. How's anyone supposed to be able to find it?"

Austen winked at her and made a gesture of "okay" with his left hand. "People know, Moriah," he told her with absolute conviction in his voice. "When the food is as good as it is here, and the proprietor as agreeable as James is, people know where to look, and they keep coming back."

Moriah smiled. "You know, for some bizarre reason, this is all beginning to make sense to me. The weirder it gets down here, the more normal it all seems. Does that sound crazy to you?"

Austen smiled back. "Sounds to me like you're catching on just fine."

He lifted her hand to his warm lips, and his amber eyes caught and held hers as he brushed her fingertips lightly over his lower lip. Moriah's breath caught in her throat as she watched the action, and when the wind tumbled a lock of gold-tipped mahogany hair over his forehead, reaching out with her own fingers to push it back amid the rest of the

unruly mass seemed like the most natural thing in the world
to do. Quickly Austen touched the tip of his tongue to the
juncture between her thumb and index finger, and something
inside Moriah squeezed her heart until she thought it would
burst. Then like brief fireworks that dazzled the night sky, the
feeling that had exploded dissolved into sparks, and Austen
once again laced her fingers with his before pulling her
behind him into the darkened building.

The downstairs evidently saw little use as it wasn't even
lighted, nor did any variety of furniture clutter the dusty floor.
Austen led her to a narrow staircase on his right and pro-
ceeded up the stairs with her in tow. As they ascended the
steps, Moriah heard the music grow louder, something
smooth and mellow and sweet, something reminiscent of a
cool Caribbean night. Then she caught the rustlings of quiet
laughter and murmuring, and the impression she had begun
to receive that she and Austen were the last two people on
earth slowly began to diminish.

They passed through a door at the top of the stairs and
Moriah found herself wondering if she had just fallen into a
dream or entered some kind of alternate reality. The room was
big, illuminated with a soft, ethereal golden light and painted
in the most unusual manner she had ever seen. The walls were
canary yellow, the trim bright red and the bar at the other end
where four men chatted and chuckled happily was a vivid
jungle green. Huge, primitive-looking murals of exotic ani-
mals and flowers, the summer sun and sea, adorned every
wall in bursts of blue, explosions of orange and slashes of
purple. Ceiling fans rotated laconically above them, their
gentle *whoosh-whoosh-whoosh* stirring up the warm air and
nudging the curls that had escaped their confinement to dance
about Moriah's face. A single droplet of sweat streamed down
her throat and lingered between her breasts, and she shivered

at the image it evoked of Austen tasting her in the same way the night before.

Austen, oblivious to the avenue her thoughts were taking, strode confidently toward the men at the bar, greeting each of them amiably by name before asking, "Is James around?"

"Yah, mon," one of the men told him. "In de back."

As Austen leaned over the bar and directed a loudly pronounced "James!" toward an open door on the left, Moriah let her gaze wander openly over the small number of patrons who populated the tiny tables dotting the floor. Most appeared to be locals, and all were dressed very casually, more than one of them barefoot. No one seemed to be eating, however, but partook instead of pastel-colored drinks in plastic cups. She was about to address Austen concerning this significant new development, this lack of food and how it might affect their appetites, but before she had the chance to do so, a tall, dark figure who was skinnier than anyone Moriah had ever seen leapt gracefully over the bar and embraced Austen in a fierce bear hug.

"It's good to see you, mon," James greeted his friend warmly. "It's been a long time. Did Dorian come with you?"

Austen nodded. "He's along on the trip, but he's visiting relatives tonight. He said he'd stop by to see you in the morning before we leave."

James nodded briefly and smiled knowingly. "Aunt Agnes," he surmised with a chuckle. Then he turned his inquiring eyes upon Moriah, his smile now accompanied by just the hint of a twinkle in their dark depths. "And who, may I ask, are you?" he wanted to know.

Moriah, too, began to grin as cryptically as the newcomer and opened her mouth to say something flirtatious, but Austen apparently wanted to maintain control of the conversation and hastened to make introductions.

"Moriah, this is James Edison. James, this is Moriah Mallory, a, uh, a close, personal friend of mine."

"Charmed." James's lips pulled back more, exposing perfect, very white teeth as he took her hand briefly in his. Although he turned his attention back to Austen, he looked at them both as he spoke. "So, you here for dinner? Naturally it's always nice to see friends again, but I like it even more when they're payin' customers," he added with a light laugh.

"Yeah, yeah," Austen nodded with a casual wave of his hand. He turned to Moriah and told her, "James is a great friend, but an even greater businessman. It will be his downfall one day."

"I guess you'd be the one to know, mon," his friend told him with a benevolent chuckle. "No one was ever more business oriented or job conscious dan you were the first time we met." Turning to Moriah, James added, "We're talkin' 'bout obsessive behavior with dis man. Austen's job was his *life*. Did you know—"

"The last thing Moriah wants to hear about is my life, James," Austen interrupted abruptly. "And the last thing I want to discuss with a beautiful woman is my former line of work."

James's laugh was a little sad, his eyes a little regretful as he said softly, "Yah, mon, I see what you mean." Then as quickly as the melancholy expression had appeared, it was gone, and James smiled as he went on, "Anyway, you probably want to know what's on de menu for tonight."

"That'll be a good start," Austen agreed, thankful that what could have become an uncomfortable topic had been steadfastly left behind. "What *is* on the menu tonight?"

"Well, to tell you the truth, I'm not sure yet. De fella who does my fishin' for me hasn't come back yet."

Well, that explains the absence of food, Moriah thought drily.

"But," James hastened to add, "I do know we're gonna be

fixin' up some barbecued ribs. Minnie's already got dem on the grill."

"We came for the seafood, James," Austen announced decisively.

James shrugged. "I'll let you know what it's gonna be as soon as Donovan gets back. Take a seat, and I'll send Minnie over with a couple of planter's punches for you."

"Sounds great," Austen said before he guided Moriah toward a table that sat off by itself next to a screenless window opening before a massive palm tree.

James called after them, "I'll drop by your table in a little while to chat."

Austen nodded at his friend as he and Moriah took their seats, and she let her eyes rove once again around the curiously decorated restaurant.

"I can't believe it's after eight o'clock and they still haven't served dinner yet," Moriah spoke her thoughts out loud.

"Most people don't eat dinner until late down here. A lot of restaurants don't even serve meals before seven or eight o'clock. But," he added meaningfully, "you can always come in for drinks."

"I'm sure," Moriah replied tartly.

After a moment, a young woman Moriah assumed must be Minnie approached their table with two tall, yellow, cool-looking drinks. Moriah eyed them speculatively and said slowly, "Planter's punch. Isn't that what you ordered for me at The Green House last night?" She lifted her gaze to meet Austen's, only to find him grinning at her with that wide, knowing, gorgeous smile of his.

"Yes," he confessed.

"It was pink then, wasn't it?" she asked further.

He nodded in the affirmative.

"Why is it yellow now?"

"Moriah, my lovely, curious dreamboat, you have much to discover about life in this little corner of the globe. Lesson number one, and it's a good one—no two planter's punches are alike, but all are delicious."

Moriah leaned back in her chair and studied him with open and acute suspicion. "Will this one have the same effect on me as the one last night did?"

Austen's smile grew predatory. "I'm counting on it."

"I think I'll just stick with a club soda."

"You have absolutely no sense of adventure," Austen complained amiably.

"Are you kidding?" she countered. "I'm stuck on a little boat for two whole weeks not only with an eccentric sea captain with questionable intentions, but with three members of my hyperbolic family, as well! You have no idea what kind of an adventurous soul it takes to face up to such an excursion!"

Austen leaned toward her with his elbows propped casually on the table, his arms crossed before him in a deceptively defensive manner, but his eyes gave away his true feelings as they glittered with the intent to do combat. He took a single slow, deep breath and said, "Which raises an interesting question. One I've been dying to ask ever since you climbed on board *Urizen* this morning."

Moriah unconsciously lifted her drink to her lips in an effort to appear unaffected by Austen's curiosity. She sipped experimentally at the concoction, squinting her eyes at the ratio of liquor to juice, but offered no reply or inquiry to his statement.

The fact that she drank what she had just insisted she didn't want told Austen precisely how uncomfortable she was with the new turn of conversation. So he reacted the way any man in his current situation would react; he pressed his advantage and capitalized on her obvious distress. After what he intended to be a disinterested sip of his own drink, he asked bluntly, "Just what exactly is the deal with you and your sisters?"

Moriah tasted the curious mixture of rum and juice again, this time swallowing with a little less difficulty. "I don't know what you mean," she told him, only able to meet his eyes for an instant before feeling them drop to the scarred tabletop.

"The hell you don't," Austen replied simply, his voice still edged with a dangerous calm. "You know perfectly well what I'm talking about, but I'll be happy to describe it all in gory detail if that's the only way I'll get you to address it."

Moriah had no trouble meeting his gaze when she detected the tone of challenge in his voice that he did nothing to hide. She snapped her head up to face him, jutted her chin defensively and flashed her eyes angrily at the man seated across from her. "There is no *deal* with me and my sisters. We have a few tense moments here and there like millions of other families, but that's to be expected when you grow up in a fiercely competitive household like ours was."

"Moriah, there's nothing wrong with a little competition among siblings," Austen told her. "It's perfectly natural and usually promotes pretty positive results. But I don't see you competing with your sisters. You've surrendered to them completely, and I can't see any indication that you *ever* put up a fight."

Moriah drew in a deep breath and sipped her drink mightily. With no small amount of surprise, she discovered that the rum fortified instead of intoxicated her, and her own voice startled her in her vehement response. "Austen," she began slowly, enunciating each word through gritted teeth, "you're neither my conscience nor my analyst. Therefore this is *none* of your business whatsoever."

She was right of course, he realized. It really shouldn't matter to him one way or the other what kind of relationship she enjoyed with her family. He only knew that for some weird reason, it was extremely important that he help her break out of the smothering, crushing mold in which she'd been trapped for so long. He looked at her for several moments, anger warring with pity in his eyes, wanting to choose his words carefully before he spoke.

As he continued to gaze at her silently, Moriah felt inexplicably as if she were being torn in two. It wasn't any of his business, she repeated to herself. But he was the first person who had ever expressed concern about her as an individual, who had ever seemed to care for her for what she was. For that reason alone, she wanted to offer him an explanation. The only problem was, she wasn't sure that she had one.

Austen stared at her for long minutes before he slowly and wordlessly shook his head. Moriah wasn't sure if he was giving up on his line of questioning or giving up on her, but either way the knowledge was less than consoling. She really did like Austen and wished there was some way she could nurture a future between them, but she told herself that simply wasn't possible. He was a wonderful man, she admitted, more special than any man she'd ever met. But he had his life to live in his world, and she had hers on what seemed at the moment like the other side of the earth. And never the twain should meet, she thought morosely. She had to face the fact that Austen Blye could never be more than a brief vacation fling. And Moriah Mallory, Ph.D., just wasn't the kind of woman to engage in such romantic foolishness. As appealing as one might seem.

Her eyes lowered once again to the droplets of water that streamed down her glass, chasing one with her fingertip to where it joined a perfect circle of moisture on the table. She watched as Austen's strong brown fingers closed over hers, loving the feel of his rough, callused thumb as it stroked over her wrist. From what seemed a great distance away, she heard his quiet voice, and all other sounds in the room receded to the background like so much annoying static.

"Why, Moriah?" he asked her softly. "Why do you give in to them? Why do you let them run roughshod over you? Why do you let them treat you like the family spaniel instead of their younger sister, for God's sake?"

"Austen, you just don't understand," she began. She groped for words that would adequately describe what it had been like growing up in the wake of the elder Mallory sisters, but descriptions eluded her. Finally she drew a weary breath and confessed, "You're right. There's never been any question of competing with my sisters, because the fact of the matter is that I could never even make it into their league." She laughed a little sadly before she told him, "When I was a freshman in high school, I discovered something everyone else called the 'Mallory mystique,' something that had been around long before I ever reached the hallowed halls of the Prescott Academy, something that I'm certain lingers there to this day. You know what that mystique is as soon as you look at Morgana, Mathilda and Marissa together. There's just some presence that surrounds them, something that links them together. Birds sing, violins play, angels dance, the heavens weep."

Austen remembered his initial reaction when he'd seen the three platinum-blond heads at the bow of his boat earlier that day. Yes, he'd certainly detected something about the three women that had hit him squarely in the head, not to mention the libido, but the feeling had been nothing compared to the breath-stealing kick in the stomach he'd experienced upon seeing Moriah the night before. That must have been the Moriah mystique, he reasoned, without question a much more potent natural essence than that tepid potion her sisters manufactured.

"I don't know," Moriah continued with a swift shake of her head. "I just couldn't live up to what they had created, and every day my teachers and classmates reminded me of that fact. 'You're nothing at all like your sisters,'" she mimicked the accusation she had heard so many times as an adolescent. "Although I made a fool of myself on more than one occasion by trying to imitate them, I finally had to accept the fact that it was true, what other people thought. I'm not now, nor was I ever, anything like my sisters. I'm not gorgeous, glittering or glamorous. I'm not spectacular. I'm serious, academic, plain and boring. And when I learned to live with that, my life began to run a lot more smoothly."

Austen felt himself go a little crazy at Moriah's self-analysis. Slowly he turned loose her hand and threaded his fingers through his hair in a gesture of intense frustration, then dropped his fist forcefully onto the table. "Moriah," he began, trying to keep his voice level and calm. "I really believe you ought to rethink this description you offer of yourself, as it's just a tad off base." He searched for his words carefully before continuing. "You aren't…you're not living with what you are—you're letting people force you into a role *they* think is the right one for you. You should rejoice in the fact that you're so unlike your sisters. Yet because others are stumped when they meet you and discover you've managed to break from the mold, *they* feel compelled to cast you into the other extreme, and you've let them get away with it. You've allowed other people to dictate what you should be all these years, and you've actually listened to them when they've told you that you could never be glamorous and witty and romantic, that you'd *better* be academic because that's all you'll ever have going for you."

He was appalled at the tone of voice he heard leaving his lips but was helpless to cease the flow of angry words that escaped him. "Good God," he raged at the woman sitting in confused silence across from him, "can't you see how glamorous, witty, romantic, how *spectacular* you are?"

"Austen," Moriah interjected, pretending to remain unruffled as she attempted to stem the flow of charges.

Yet Austen continued without acknowledging her interruption. "Last night on St. Thomas you were a vivacious, clever woman, full of fun and laughter, making your own decisions. Why were you so different then than you were today on the boat, hmm? Maybe because you were left to your own devices for a change and had no one else to answer to? Maybe because no one reminded you of how you *should* act, because no one was there to put you and keep you in your place?"

"Austen," Moriah tried again to intercede, but he would have none of it.

"Why don't you allow that other Moriah who's trapped inside you to come out the way you know she wants to?" he demanded. "Why?"

When Austen paused long enough for her to understand that he had finally ended his onslaught and expected an answer, Moriah could only sit and stare at him in silence. It had happened again. He was disappointed because she wasn't a real Mallory like her sisters. He wanted her to exude the mystique the way the others did and was turning on her now because she didn't measure up. Moriah sighed in resignation, honestly surprised that the realization caused such a throbbing pain in her chest. She had thought the hurting ended long ago, had thought she was no longer affected by the disillusionment and frustration she saw in the eyes of others when they recognized that she just wasn't like her sisters. Yet the knowledge that Austen was dissatisfied with her the way she was opened a gnawing void in the pit of her soul that quickly filled with cold and anguish.

"I have a 'why' for you, too, Austen," she finally answered him, keeping her voice as cool as the drink she gripped so tightly in her hand. "Why can't you just accept the fact that I'm not the woman you want me to be?"

He gazed at her for long moments before he countered, "Why can't you just accept the fact that you're not the woman *you* want to be?"

Moriah took several long breaths, hoping to calm her pounding heart, before she replied, "That isn't it at all, Austen."

"Isn't it?" he asked as he lifted an eyebrow in obvious and frank speculation.

"Of course not," she insisted. She shook her head for emphasis, but the motion was a good bit more forceful than she meant it to be, and she felt the color rise into her cheeks.

Austen shrugged. "Sorry," he said without a trace of apology, his eyes still shining with accusation. "Guess I'm the one who's off base."

Moriah's back stiffened at his tone of voice before she lifted her drink once again to her lips. "I guess you are," she agreed diffidently, her voice losing the ferocity she'd hoped to carry with her the rest of the evening.

Silence reigned until Minnie came back to refresh their drinks and announce that dinner would be served shortly. Moriah and Austen partook of the shallowest form of small talk while they awaited the arrival of their food, and when James himself placed it before them with his lighthearted banter and an easy sense of humor, the tension at their table eased considerably. The grilled dorado was as delicious as Austen had promised it would be, tartly flavored with curry and dill, pleasantly aromatic from lemon, saffron and peppercorns. The planter's punches that she had requested be kept light on rum, heavy on punch, made her feel mellow and philosophical nonetheless, and as the couple tarried over coffee laced with a local liqueur, Austen discovered to his delighted surprise that Moriah was more than inclined to forget their earlier animosity. Unfortunately, with the topic of herself and her sisters being the taboo that it was, the conversation quickly approached a subject he would rather have seen die a quick death in the dust.

"Tell me more about yourself," Moriah requested dreamily as she placed her oversize yellow pottery coffee mug gently back down on the table. "James mentioned your previous line of work a little while ago. What did you do before you came down to the Caribbean five years ago?"

Austen hoped she couldn't see the slow squirm he felt slithering all through his body. "I, uh, I had a job in Atlanta."

Moriah cupped her chin in her palm and asked, "Doing what? Did you grow up in Atlanta?"

Austen quickly ignored the first question and eagerly grabbed on to the second. "No, I was born and raised on Key West. My father was a fisherman when I was a kid, then chartered his boat out to sportsmen when I was a teenager. I worked for him for a long time."

A soft smile curled Moriah's lips and made her eyes shine like silver in the dim light. "I'll bet you were a hell-raiser when you were a kid. And a teenager."

Austen smiled back and sipped his coffee carefully, hoping the hot brew would calm the rattling his heart took up as he watched the warm look that caused her to appear a little flushed. "That I was," he confirmed. "I can think of more than one skiff, scooter and scandal my friends and I broke." He chuckled at some of the memories crowding into his head. "I remember so many summers when my old man and I would take the boat out and stay for days. It would be miserably hot during the daylight hours, salt and sweat clinging to your skin, sticky and stinging every time the wind picked up. But at night it would be so quiet, so calm, so damned peaceful out there." His voice had dropped to a near whisper as if in deference to the silent nights he was recalling. "Nights at sea," he added decisively, "are just about as close as a mortal man can come to the gates of paradise."

Moriah thought of her relationship with her own father, thought about how the times she had spent with Teddy at sea had been anything but paradisiacal. "How about the rest of your family?" she asked before her thoughts had a chance to become depressing, hungry to learn everything she could about this man before her time with him drew to a close. "Your mother? Brothers and sisters?"

"My mother is a family woman," Austen said simply, as if saying more would be superfluous. "And I have a sister named Molly who's ten years my junior and who is, for the most part, indescribable. However, I'll give it a shot. She's tall, tans easily, would be a professional volleyball player if the money were better, but settles for running a dive shop right now. Tomorrow, who knows? She's too attractive for her own good, has a smart mouth that will get her into big trouble someday and is into and out of more scrapes on any given day than I can count on two hands."

Moriah laughed. "And you love her very much," she guessed.

"And I love her very much," Austen agreed.

Moriah envied Austen this family of his, wished she could speak as fondly of her own siblings as he did his sister. Despite the distance she maintained from them and the complaints in which she frequently indulged, there was no question in Moriah's mind that she cared for her family, even loved them. But for some unfathomable reason, it just wasn't the kind of love she could easily share with them. She couldn't remember hearing the phrase "I love you" spoken by anyone, ever, in the Mallory household. She supposed they all assumed there *was* love there somewhere. At least she hoped they did. But how could one ever really know for sure if it was never voiced?

From the other side of the table, Austen sensed that Moriah's thoughts were becoming troubled. That dreamy, fuzzy expression she had been wearing since they'd been served dessert was fast drawing into a tight, worried frown. He didn't want to go back to their earlier antagonism, so he quickly threw a handful of bills onto the table and pulled Moriah to her feet.

"What?" she mumbled breathlessly, seeming confused by the sudden turn of events. "Where are we going?"

"We have to get back to the boat," Austen told her. "Your sisters are going to be worried about you."

"Actually, they probably won't even notice that I'm miss—"

"Then they'll be there alone with Dorian," Austen interrupted quickly, unwilling to listen to another litany of how much more significant her sisters were than she was herself. "And God knows that idea causes me no end of worry."

"You can't possibly think Dorian would do anything to hurt my sisters," Moriah gasped, clearly outraged that Austen would accuse his friend of such a thing.

Austen smiled at Moriah, bent to press a quick kiss against her lips and brushed back the curls that fell forward over angry gray eyes. "Frankly it was more Dorian's welfare that I was concerned about," he admitted.

Moriah's outrage melted into a warm, mushy feeling when Austen's lips brushed over her own, and she blinked her eyes at the confused emotions crowding into her brain. Her imme-

diate and automatic reaction was to pull Austen against her
and kiss him back, this time with all the insistence she could
muster. For a moment her hands actually reached out to him
involuntarily as if she were planning to carry out her mind's
intentions. However Austen turned away before seeing the
longing that darkened her eyes, and Moriah never had a
chance to fulfill her desires as she found herself being tugged
across the restaurant, past a perplexed James—to whom she
lifted a hand in polite but equally perplexed farewell—and
out into the close, clean Caribbean night.

Chapter Six

Moriah wasn't sure why she awakened when she did. Perhaps it was because of the complete silence that surrounded her. Her apartment on Rittenhouse Square in the heart of downtown Philadelphia normally suffered from any number of night sounds that erupted in the city—car alarms and answering police sirens, Septa buses wheezing and honking until all hours, youthful cries in both celebration and condemnation of life, and traffic that passed ceaselessly by her building through daylight and in darkness.

Here, though, only the darkness was familiar, and even it was not quite so menacing as it seemed in the city. Here the only sounds were those that were almost too quiet to hear—the irregular creaking of *Urizen*'s hull as it rose and fell effortlessly over gentle swells, the occasional smack of sails as they caught the wind, the wind itself as it swept over the open hatch above her. She also heard music—soft music, bewitching music, music that called out to something deep within her soul. It was not the boisterous, joyful music that had permeated the islands, but it summoned visions of stars and the sea just the same. Moriah almost felt as if she were imagining it, as if it were a siren's song carried to her from some fantastic place below the sea's surface. But then she remembered that she was a woman of science not whimsy, and she realized that it was probably coming from a radio somewhere above deck.

Rising carefully so as not to arouse her heavily slumbering sister, Moriah crept toward the open hatch and lifted her face toward the night sky. The moon hung like a bright silver mask above her, and stars dotted the blackness, sparkling like tiny gems. She inhaled deeply, loving the cool, salty scent of the sea that filled her nostrils. As *Urizen* dipped deftly over a soft swell, a cold spray of salt water fell like fairy dust through the open hatch and kissed Moriah's face, and she laughed quietly, closing her eyes before lifting her fingers to her damp cheeks.

Despite numerous efforts to remind herself she couldn't possibly believe in such nonsense, Moriah was nonetheless helpless to prevent the voice inside her whispering that this place was a magic place, unlike anything she had ever known. Austen was right; there was something about the nighttime, something about the sea. And that, Moriah told herself, was precisely the reason she was experiencing the strange stirrings of emotion she'd felt ever since meeting Austen on St. Thomas. The night did funny things to people, made them react irrationally and without thought. There were very real and very good reasons why primitive cultures feared spirits in the darkness, she thought. And so-called civilized man's conviction that such legendary beings were imaginary and ineffectual were not necessarily true. Spirits of the night took many forms, not the least of which for her was a lack of control and a loss of self-knowledge. She told herself again to step lightly and be cautious. Then she ignored those instructions and stepped closer to the open hatch.

Somehow Moriah knew that Austen was up in the cockpit, knew that the music, however mystically inspired it seemed, came in fact from the stereo speakers mounted there. Not bothering to change from the knee-length T-shirt she'd purchased in Charlotte Amalie depicting a scene of sailboats and seashells, she moved soundlessly to the cabin door and left her sister to dream alone. It was completely black in the passageway that led to the companionway, so Moriah had to feel her way blindly through the boat. She headed toward the music that filled the darkness surrounding her, and finally bumped her knee softly against the stairs that led above.

The smell of the ocean was stronger here, she realized as she gripped the handles to pull herself up the steps. And the whisper of the wind and waves was a song whose chorus she had been denied by the walls of her cabin. As she climbed upward, she looked again at the moon and stars, and as her eyes were forced to adjust to the scene that met them, she marveled at how light it actually was outside. The breeze ruffled her hair like a lover's fingers when she cleared the exit, and the cool spray of water stung her skin once more. For the briefest of moments, she forgot that she had come in search of Austen and only gazed around her at the black sea, then lifted her eyes to the creamy stream of stars that crossed the night sky toward the moon.

"It's the Milky Way," she heard a deep, steady voice tell her from the darkness.

Moriah looked at Austen in the corner of the cockpit, his long, muscular legs stretched out before him, his corded arms bent to support his head. He wore navy shorts and a blue-and-white striped sweatshirt. He was barefoot, too. The wind pushed his hair about carelessly, while something else tugged insistently at Moriah's heart.

"I never took the time to really notice it before," she admitted quietly, her voice scarcely above a whisper.

"I would imagine not," he replied. "Not if you coop yourself up the way you seem to do."

Moriah pulled herself from the companionway and stepped into the cockpit, then seated herself in the corner opposite Austen. For long moments neither of them spoke, only looked heavenward and breathed deeply of the salt-scented air. When she felt the silence between them grow heavy, Moriah sought to end it.

"You were right about how peaceful and perfect it is out here at night," she told him softly, referring to the conversation they'd had only hours before. "I can understand why you choose to live your life this way."

Austen lifted a dark eyebrow in surprise at her. "Does that mean you approve of me?" he asked.

"What would my approval have to do with anything?" she wondered aloud.

"Well, personally, *I* would consider your approval the most precious thing in the world," he told her honestly, but his voice carried a puzzling tone. "However *you* seem to value the completely worthless approval of your family more than you do your own."

"Austen," she began, her voice a quiet plea. "Let's not go into this again, okay?"

He drew in a deep breath as if to pursue the topic, then let it go. After a minute he asked her, "Why did you come up here?"

Moriah shrugged a little nervously. "I couldn't sleep. I woke up and heard the music…" Her voice trailed off restlessly and she shrugged again.

"I'm sorry, I didn't realize it was so loud," he apologized.

"I don't think it was the music that woke me up to begin with," she admitted.

Austen looked at her intently. "What was it, Moriah?" he demanded in a low voice. "What's causing *you* to lose sleep?"

She shook her head slowly but said nothing.

Austen didn't push it. Instead he looked up at the sky and told her, "The first thing I bought when I moved down here was a star chart so I could identify all the constellations."

Moriah smiled, picturing a wide-eyed Austen with a cardboard wheel in his hand looking up and down and trying to determine exactly what was what in the night sky. "I took an astronomy course as an undergraduate," she confided. "I really enjoyed it."

His gaze wandered back to lock with hers. "Did you find yourself outside all the time, lying on your back in the middle of a field and staring up at the sky?" he asked her. For some reason she got the feeling he already knew the answer she was about to give him.

"No, but I snuck off to the planetarium every chance I got," she assured him.

"It isn't the same, Moriah," he told her almost urgently. "It isn't the same at all."

Moriah knew he was trying to steer their conversation back down the road that led to her dubious self-discovery, and she quickly ducked down a side route instead. "Why did you come down here to begin with?" she asked him suddenly. "You never really told me what you did in Atlanta or what it was that brought you to the Caribbean in the first place."

A shutter fell over Austen's eyes at Moriah's question, and he quickly looked away. The sail smacked loudly as it caught a stray breeze, and the sound seemed to echo hollowly between them.

"I was a working stiff like a lot of other people," he told her evasively. "I needed an escape from the rat race for a couple of weeks, so I came down here for a visit. A few months later I came back for good."

Moriah wanted to ask him more about himself, wanted to ask him what kind of job he'd held and what had made him decide to leave it, but he easily changed the subject.

"It's so different here than it is in the States," he began, his eyes roving over the ocean toward the almost invisible line that divided the horizon from the sea. "I mean beyond the obvious. Yes, the pace is slower and the weather is more agreeable and the beaches are incredible. But it's more than that. People don't judge you by what you do for a living or the clothes you wear. They don't care where you came from or where you're going. It just doesn't matter what you do or don't have. Everyone is viewed equally down here, and nobody tries to change who you are or what you think." Austen looked at her intently then added critically, "Do you understand how important that is, Moriah?"

He was so serious, she realized with no small amount of awe. He had been so high-spirited and frivolous since she'd met him. She'd never seen him react so solemnly, so emphatically to anything before. Gravity was a characteristic she would never have guessed he claimed. When she saw that he expected an answer from her, she nodded her head slowly but said nothing.

"Do you?" he insisted. "I wonder." But instead of trying to bait her again, he went on. "There's something for everyone down here," he told her. "And there are all kinds of people. Those who are running from trouble and those who have caused it, people who are hiding and people who are seeking, some who want to be left alone and some who want to be a part of everything that's going on."

Moriah smiled at him and pushed a handful of curls back from her face. "And which category do you fall into, Austen?" she asked him.

He thought for a moment and then smiled back. "All of them, I suppose."

Her smile broadened and she chuckled lightly from the back of her throat. "Somehow I believe that's exactly right."

"How about you, Moriah?" he said softly. "Ever think of categorizing yourself?"

Still feeling lighthearted and not a little light-headed, she rejoined, "Do I have to choose from the list you provided?"

"I dare you to try."

She placed her fingers against her cheek and looked at some point past him, reconsidering the categories he'd offered in much the same way he had done. "I suppose," she began thoughtfully, "if I must decide, I would have to say I'm one of those who wants to be left alone."

When her eyes came back to settle on his, she caught her breath at the fire she saw dancing in them. Austen gazed at her for such a long time Moriah wondered if he was ever going to speak again. Finally he opened his mouth to say something, but the words were long in coming.

"Funny," he told her slowly, "but I get the feeling you're one of the ones who are seeking."

Moriah blinked her eyes in surprise. "Why would you think that?"

Austen shook his head. "I have no idea. God knows you try your damnedest to hide it, Moriah, and you've certainly managed to fool those self-absorbed sisters of yours, not to mention having completely duped yourself. But," he added, "you can't fool me."

Her breath came in uneasy bursts as she sputtered, "What do you mean by that?"

In answer to her question, he rose from his seat on the other side of the cockpit and crowded himself against her, dropping one arm casually behind her shoulder, the other pos-

sessively across her abdomen. Before she could stop him, he
leaned down and pressed his mouth against hers, softly,
tenderly, tugging at her lips with his, coaxing, caressing, until
she couldn't help but respond.

But when she kissed Austen back, it wasn't with anywhere
near as much gentleness as he had used with her. From out
of nowhere a passion bubbled up inside her like a hot spring,
blinding her to everything except the sensations coursing
through her body like swirling, fiery magma. Almost of their
own free will, Moriah's hands splayed open across Austen's
chest, and she caught her breath at the feel of strong muscles
rippling below her fingertips. Her damp palms pressed desperately against him as they climbed to curve over his shoulders, then dipped down to squeeze his big biceps. As she
tasted and eagerly explored him, she discovered amazing
things about the male form, and her breathing became more
rapid, her skin more heated, and her heart began to thunder
behind her rib cage as if it were about to break loose. When
she tangled her fingers insistently in his hair and crushed his
lips with her own, the only thing Moriah was thinking was
that she must, somehow, get closer to this man.

Austen had banished all thought and instead was enjoying
the feel of the woman in his arms. When Moriah began to pant
for breath, he took advantage of her open mouth by claiming
it with his tongue. Over and over again he tasted her, groaning
with the need to penetrate other recesses as deeply, settling
for now with more tantalizing pursuits. Slowly the hand at
her waist began to wander toward the creamy flesh of her
thigh that was revealed below the hem of her long T-shirt.
Deftly his fingers sneaked underneath and pressed into the
warm skin below her fanny, lifting her closer until she was
nearly in his lap. Still curious, his hand boldly ventured
farther, dipping quickly under the lacy border of her panties

until he was fully cupping the soft, round firmness of cool, naked skin. As his kisses grew more insistent, he, too, began panting for breath.

Moriah knew she should command Austen to stop his adventurous hand. Yet somehow, for some reason, she just couldn't summon the strength. All she could do was close her eyes and hold on to the strong arms that clamped around her body like a velvet vise, waiting with anticipation to see what would happen next.

When Austen understood that Moriah was not going to protest the liberty he had already taken, his mind began to entertain the challenge of so many more. Holding more firmly on to the silky flesh he'd already claimed, his other hand ventured over the soft pink fabric of her T-shirt until he found the ample mound of one breast. Moriah cried out loud when his fingers closed over her and began a thorough exploration of well-remembered territory, and she dropped her head back in ecstasy when his mouth and tongue replaced the heated touch of his thumb. He tasted and teased her over the barrier of her shirt, as if he didn't even notice it was there. For long, mind-scrambling moments his lips pulled at and suckled her, all the while holding her body and breast determinedly in place for his marauding mouth, until the activity threatened to send them both hurtling down into a dark and dangerous abyss.

"Austen!" Moriah finally cried out, thinking her voice must have sounded much more loudly than the panicked whisper it actually was. "Please. We have to stop this right now."

Austen ceased his ministrations, but placed his flushed cheek against the wet fabric of her shirt, which was already losing heat thanks to the night breeze. He gulped in air as quickly as his lungs could command it, trying to restructure his disordered thoughts and remember where he was. When he looked up and saw Moriah gazing down at him with liquid eyes, and understood that the incredibly erotic fantasy he'd just been experiencing was in fact an erotic reality, he started to become uncomfortable. Not because he hadn't expected and enjoyed, not to mention instigated, their brief interlude himself, but because he wasn't sure what Moriah's reaction to the incident was going to be. Slowly he released her and set her away from him on the cushion, but his hands lingered on her shoulders, softly rubbing her upper arms as if in an effort to warm her. He almost smiled when he realized that, if her feelings mirrored his at the moment, warming was probably the last thing she needed.

"That…uh…" Austen cleared his throat and tried again. "That isn't exactly what I call wanting to be left alone," he managed to say lightly, hoping to take the edge off the uneasy atmosphere that had settled over them.

Moriah was shocked at her behavior and completely at a loss for words. What on earth had come over her to make her succumb to him in such a wanton, hedonistic manner? The breeze blew softly then, mussing her already tousled hair, raising goose bumps on her goose bumps and drawing her attention to a rather large and very peculiar wetness in an extremely curious place on her T-shirt. Her cheeks blazed red when she remembered what had caused it.

"Oh, my God," she muttered in a hoarse whisper.

Here it comes, Austen thought. She's really going to blast me for taking advantage of her this time. But unless she makes a damned strong case for walking in her sleep, there's no way it's going to wash. He knew full well that Moriah had wanted and enjoyed the little escapade as much as he had. Let her rip, he challenged her silently. I dare you to question my intentions this time, Moriah. Because I may have a few questions about yours in exchange.

But contrary to his assumption, Moriah only gazed at him with haunted, fearful eyes. For a brief moment, her brows drew down as if she were in pain, and her lips parted slightly, seeming to emit a silent, pleading cry. Before Austen had a chance to react, she jerked free of his loose hold on her arms, then jumped up from her place beside him and bolted back down the companionway. In her wake she left a star-spattered night sky and a moon masked by wispy gray clouds, a rush of wind that caught and moaned in *Urizen*'s sail, and the feeling of warm fingers tangled carelessly and passionately in his hair. Suddenly Austen realized he was once again alone with the darkness, and he began to wonder if Moriah had ever really joined him at all.

Running his hands quickly through his hair in the hopes of dispelling her lingering caresses, he stretched out again along the length of the cool cushion beneath him. Before, the night surrounding him had seemed welcome and calm. Now, however, Austen felt lonelier and more anxious than he had ever been in his life.

Moriah jabbed viciously with her fork at the pieces of yellow mango that Christian had placed in front of her ten minutes before. Except for the little boy, she was alone in the main cabin, but Austen's laughter reached her ears through the open porthole behind her, mingling with Dorian's as they worked on the boat somewhere up on deck. How dare they all be so carefree and jovial, she thought, when she still felt cranky and irritable after another absolutely hideous night's sleep?

She had avoided Austen and her sisters all day yesterday as *Urizen* slowly sliced through the blue waters between St. John and St. Martin. By imprisoning herself in her cabin, stacking her textbooks around her as if they were a protective wall, Moriah had managed to reestablish the fact that she was indeed an anthropologist with a very important mission. There were ancient cities to explore, for research if not for adventure, and academic worlds to conquer. She would need all her strength for the analyses and studies that would ensue. Her fingers itched to pick up pad and pencil, and already she visualized scribbling her opening words: "In dissecting and analyzing ancient Taino practices, it is imperative that one closely consider the data and conclusions provided here." Yes, that was quite catchy, she thought sarcastically. But that should hook her readers in the scientific community very effectively. She was more than anxious now to get back to her work.

Sometime during the hours following dawn, as Moriah had been tossing and turning, snapping at Marissa's whining complaints about her tortuous sleeping habits, they had put in to St. Martin, and all the other Mallorys had already gone ashore. Knowing her sisters, Moriah thought as she bit viciously into a large piece of mango, they were probably taking in all the shopping for which the island was so famous. They always did manage to miss the best parts of the places they visited, always viewed their trips to exotic and unexplored destinations the way most people looked forward to a trip to the mall. It really was too bad, she added to herself further, relishing the cool, sticky sweetness of the mango as she swallowed it. There were so many things she enjoyed that her sisters were missing out on in life, if only they'd open their eyes long enough to see.

Moriah's next forkful of mango stopped halfway to her lips, dripping with golden juice that fell in tiny splats onto the tabletop. She wasn't quite sure, but it seemed to her for a moment there that she had just been feeling sorry for her sisters. The realization made her fork fall back to the bowl of fruit with a clatter, and her body slumped against the cushion of the settee as if pulled there by an invisible string. Had she actually been doing that? she asked herself. Had she really been pitying her sisters because they didn't claim a quality she herself had always taken for granted? Moriah was stunned. That had never happened before. She was never the one who was to be envied, never the one who did the right thing. She must still be rattled from that little tryst with Austen two nights ago. Yes, of course, that was it. She was still just feeling a little confused. After breakfast and a leisurely jaunt around the island, she'd be feeling herself again in no time.

Before her thoughts had a chance to wander back to her sisters, Moriah gulped down the rest of her coffee and hastily finished her fruit. She ducked into her stateroom long enough to pull her hair back into a hammered-copper clip, and checked to be sure her baggy, dark green trousers and loose-fitting, cream-colored T-shirt hadn't succumbed to the dripping mango. She settled her glasses seriously on the bridge of her nose, then stuffed the things she thought she'd need for the day into an oversize straw Kenya bag—a spiral notebook, a number-two pencil, one felt-tipped pen each of red and black, her summer reading of *Arawak Rituals and Practices: Then and Now* and the latest issue of *Today's Anthropologist.* As an afterthought she tossed in her navy maillot and sunscreen and a paperback copy of *Passion Rides a Spotted Horse,* telling herself it was because there were passages she'd skipped over the first time she'd read it, and she didn't want to find herself put on the spot should Morgana think to ask her a question about the book at some point on the cruise.

She assured herself that she was *not* sneaking away from Austen as she padded silently through the sailboat and slipped discreetly up the companionway. They had tied up at a marina, so Moriah had no trouble getting away from the boat.

Once she found her way along the maze of slips and piers to the main entrance, she also had no trouble signaling a taxi. She had heard Marissa say earlier that Austen had landed them in Marigot on the French side of the island, and she was thankful, as she had learned more than a smattering of French after her humiliation in Paris several years ago, but spoke absolutely no Dutch. When she was seated comfortably in the cab's backseat, she met the driver's eyes in the rearview mirror and requested, *"À la plage, s'il vous plaît."*

The eyes that met hers in response were passive and bored. *"Quelle plage?"* he wanted to know.

What beach? Moriah repeated to herself in English. Of course, you idiot, she chastised herself. It's an island, after all. There's certainly going to be more than one beach here. "Uh…" she stammered, not at all familiar with any of the local recreational areas.

"Look, lady, I don't have all day," the driver told her in perfect but irritated English. "Which beach did you want?"

"I really don't know," she replied sheepishly. "I've never been to St. Martin, and I don't know where anything is."

The driver seemed to soften somewhat at the troubled tone of her voice, then put his car instantly into gear as if he'd already made the decision for her. "I know where there is a very beautiful beach," he told her. "Not many tourists know of it, but it is very popular with the locals."

"Is it far?" Moriah wanted to know, not altogether certain she should openly accept his word.

"Pas du tout," he answered, switching back to his native language.

Not at all, Moriah translated silently, relaxing somewhat at his assurance.

The cabbie was as good as his word, Moriah decided twenty minutes later as she dropped her Kenya bag and spread her towel on the sand of a nearly deserted stretch of pearly white beach. She kicked off her sandals and pulled her T-shirt over her head, revealing the modest expanse of her bathing suit that she'd donned in one of the dressing rooms that lay just beyond the long line of palm trees behind her. Before her the crystal-clear water of the Caribbean rippled as gently as the water in a swimming pool, looking more like fluid glass than ocean depths. The sun hung high above her like a bright lantern, tossing diamonds onto the sea and warming her muscles in the way of a lover's caress. Moriah leaned back on her palms and dug her toes into the soft sand, groaning inwardly with pleasure at her first opportunity to relax and be alone.

She reached into her bag and pushed aside the sunscreen she'd already applied, pulling out the heavy collection of anthropological essays concerning the Arawak Indians. Almost as if mocking her, Morgana's novel tumbled out alongside it, taunting her with its elaborate cover artwork in vivid oranges, yellows, purples and blues, a cover depicting an impossibly luscious and scantily clad redhead caught in the savage embrace of a superbly muscled half-naked man who's only worldly possession seemed to be a thick leather band wound about his huge arm. Moriah forced herself to look away and concentrate instead on the cover of her textbook. It was brown. With off-white lettering of the title and the endorsement of the National Association of Cultural and Social Anthropologists. She glanced once again at the paperback. A reviewer had proclaimed it "Spellbinding! A masterful, sexy romp through the Old West!"

"Oh, what the heck," Moriah muttered as she laid the textbook onto the corner of her beach towel opposite her bag. If nothing else, maybe it would at least keep her towel from blowing sand in her face.

After that, Moriah gradually lost herself in Morgana's

book, became so thoroughly engrossed in the story that she completely forgot it was her sister who had created the world into which she had become a part. She moseyed down dirt streets right alongside the heroine, rode bareback and wild-eyed behind the hero during Indian raids. So caught up did she become with the characters in fact that she started visibly at the appearance of a strange shadow at her side. For a moment she was confused by her surroundings and had forgotten that she was on vacation in the Caribbean. Then she focused on the tanned, masculine feet whose toes were wiggling impatiently in the sand beside her head, knowing who their owner would be before even lifting her face up to inspect him.

"Hi," Austen greeted her amiably when she looked up at him through slitted eyes and raised a hand across her forehead in an effort to blot out the sun's glare.

He wore khaki shorts and a white T-shirt with the sleeves cut off, and he held a half-full bottle of beer in one hand. For a moment she couldn't answer him, as she was stunned by the remarkable resemblance Austen bore to the hero of Morgana's novel. Then she remembered that her sister had described the hero as having hair that fell to his waist like a flowing river of black oil, eyes darker than hell's deepest midnight. It was she herself who had superimposed Austen's mahogany hair and golden eyes over those of the Indian hero. With a stab of panic, she realized that she had also changed the coloring of Morgana's green-eyed, redheaded heroine to match her own.

"What are you reading?" Austen asked as he hunkered down in the sand beside her, seemingly unaffected by the fact that she had yet to even say hello to him.

Moriah quickly tucked Morgana's book behind her back and indicated the larger volume of essays beside her by inclining her head toward it. "It's a new textbook I'm thinking of incorporating into one of my classes in the spring semester," she lied ineffectually.

Austen had been sifting sand casually through the fingers of his free hand as she spoke, but now he dusted them off on his shorts and reached past Moriah to pluck the paperback easily from her grasp. As she grew more and more embarrassed that he had caught her reading something so utterly frivolous and uncharacteristic, he scanned the blurb on the back of the book and then scrutinized its cover.

"I didn't realize you taught sex education," he murmured with a lascivious smile.

Moriah felt her cheeks becoming stained with crimson, and she scrambled for excuses. "I wasn't reading that book," she assured him on a rush of words. "I was just taking a little break from all my studying."

"Uh-huh, sure." Austen's tone of voice indicated that he didn't believe her for a minute. "I've been sitting up the beach from you a little ways for over an hour, and all I've seen you use the big book for is to keep your towel anchored to the sand."

Stung that he should think her so shallow, she overlooked the fact that her thoughts had been identical to his when she'd left the big tome where it lay now. Then his words registered in her brain, and she discovered she had an even better reason for feeling affronted. "You've been sitting over there spying on me all afternoon?" she demanded indignantly.

"I haven't been spying," he replied calmly. "I've been sitting out in clear view of God and everybody, where you could have seen me the minute you looked up. But you were *so* wrapped up in what you were reading that you never even noticed me."

His voice dropped as he uttered his last sentence, making

it sound as if he'd actually had his feelings hurt because she hadn't noticed him right away, and Moriah felt her temper ebb. He tipped back his beer, and she watched in fascination at the way his strong throat worked over the swallow.

"Passion Rides a Spotted Horse," he read the title skeptically. "What the hell kind of a name is that to give a book?"

Moriah made an attempt to snatch the paperback from his hand, but he lifted it out of her reach. "It's a Western," she told him, as if that explained everything.

"So?" he said.

Moriah tried again to reach the book, but Austen kept it at a safe distance as he began to whiffle through the pages. She sighed dramatically and gave up trying to retrieve the silly thing, then explained further, "So the hero is an Indian."

"And?" Austen prodded.

She shrugged. "And he rides a spotted horse."

"And?" Austen made a gyrating motion with his hand as if telling her he needed more to go on.

Moriah felt herself flushing as she quickly mumbled, "And apparently he's very passionate."

Austen's smile broadened when he noted her discomfort. Moriah was embarrassed that she'd been caught red-handed masquerading as a woman instead of an anthropologist. "Apparently?" he asked her. "Is Morgana such a lousy writer that she can't even make passion obvious? She could use a lesson or two from her youngest sister."

Moriah ignored the comment. "Give me back the book, Austen," she requested as politely as she could manage.

He seemed to ignore her comment, too, as he became wrapped up in a particular passage he'd discovered somewhere in the middle of the book. Moriah watched him closely as his eyes scanned over the words, trying to discern the type of scene he was reading by the impassive expression on his face.

Please don't let it be the end of chapter sixteen, she pleaded silently with all the gods, remembering too well the extremely graphic and intensely charged sex scene that she had read over and over again her first time through Morgana's book. If he reads any other section, I can still walk away with some dignity. Just please, please, whatever he's reading, don't let it be the end of chapter sixteen.

"'Plunging Hawk dismounted cautiously and strode with purposeful intent to where Adriana's half-naked, burgeoning body was still lashed to the stake,'" Austen read aloud in an intentionally breathless voice.

Dammit, Moriah cringed inwardly. It was the end of chapter sixteen. She covered her eyes with her hands, wishing that in doing so she could make the entire episode go away.

Austen read further about Plunging Hawk's lengthy exploration and subsequent rapturous defilement of Adriana's ripe, voluptuous body while she was still tied up and helpless, and Moriah became hotter and more turned on with every word that left his mouth. Adriana's rapture, however, was nothing compared to the tempest blowing hot and wild inside Moriah at the mere thought of being so mastered by Austen. By the time he finally closed the book and let it fall into the sand, Moriah's fantasy had thoroughly taken root in her mind. She wanted Austen to reach down and touch her in all the ways and places he'd described Plunging Hawk touching Adriana, wanted him to take her in the sand and again in the sea and later again on the deck of *Urizen*. She was on the verge of revealing her tumultuous desires, but Austen spoke before she had an opportunity.

"You know, your sister makes a lot of references to harvest motifs. I wonder why that is."

Moriah never had a chance to consider or reply to Austen's

statement, as he immediately stripped off his shirt and threw it onto her towel, then shoved his bottle of beer so fiercely into the sand that some sloshed over the top and ran in rivulets toward his feet. Just as Moriah felt her pulse go mad at the sight of his bare chest, he hoisted himself up with an intriguing groan, ran toward the line where the ocean joined the beach, dived as far out into the surf as his muscles would carry him and began slicing through the water toward the horizon. He swam with such strong strokes and traveled so far out to sea that Moriah began to wonder if he had any intention of ever returning to shore again.

Chapter Seven

Austen stayed in the ocean for as long as he could, driving the muscles in his body to every extreme he could conjure, but he discovered to his severe annoyance that the temperature of the water was nowhere near cold enough nor the energy spent in swimming hard near exhausting enough to return his body to the original restless composure he normally felt in Moriah's presence. As he'd read aloud from Morgana Mallory's flaming, feverish fable, the carnal acts in which Plunging Hawk and Adriana mightily partook became all too vivid and tantalizing in his own mind. All he had been able to think about was doing to Moriah everything the hero had done to the heroine, except that he would have done it much more slowly and with significantly more finesse. And instead of focusing on the upper torso, as Plunging Hawk had done with Adriana, Austen would have spent a lot more time with Moriah's—

"Oh, God," he groaned before dunking below the water's surface once again. He had to get a hold of himself.

When he finally thought he could risk a return to shore without revealing to Moriah the large extent to which he had become aroused by a simple paperback novel, Austen began to slowly make his way toward shore. He had followed her for a reason, he reminded himself. He'd been returning to *Urizen* from the marina's office with the intention of asking Moriah to accompany him to a party that evening, when he'd seen her trying to sneak away. He was just in time to glimpse her getting into a cab and had hailed the one immediately behind it, then had tailed her to the beach where they now found themselves. A minute or two later and she would have disappeared entirely, he realized, and the thought of Moriah being someplace where he couldn't find her sent rumblings of a strange emotion through Austen that he couldn't even begin to identify.

He watched her cautiously as he rose from the water and approached her, uncertain how to read the expression on her face. She had disposed of the paperback, presumably having stuffed it back into her beach bag or buried it in the sand, and was now pretending to be totally immersed in the big text-book she'd brought with her. She had put her shirt back on over her bathing suit, Austen noted with a frown, and was once again hiding behind her big glasses. His fingers itched to reach over and snatch them off her face, not because they detracted from her physical appearance—he actually thought they made her look rather adorable—but because she used them as a shield to keep men, particularly one man, at bay.

"Water feels great," he mumbled, unconvincingly he was sure, as he threw himself wetly down beside Moriah onto the towel. Because it was scarcely large enough for one, let alone two, he had to crowd his big body up very close to hers. So much for what little relief he had managed to receive from the ocean, he thought drily, feeling himself tighten and grow warm once again, thanks to the strange mixture of sensual delight that was Moriah Mallory. "Want to join me for a dip?" he asked further. Maybe just another couple of laps was all he needed.

"I, uh, I just put on some sunscreen," Moriah excused herself lamely. "I think I'll wait awhile."

Austen shrugged. "Suit yourself."

For several moments neither said a word, but continued to gaze at each other with expressions that a passerby might compare to the looks of a predator and his prey, although exactly who was playing what role might remain a mystery. Eventually Austen was able to regain some semblance of sanity and remembered to ask his question.

"Are you doing anything this evening?" he inquired experimentally, his voice as melodic and enticing as the water that lapped with a tiresome rhythm so close to where they lay.

The question was so harmless, Moriah thought, so similar to the ones she heard from her students and colleagues that for a moment she wasn't sure she had heard Austen correctly. His carefree smirk and affected swaggering had been completely set aside, and the innuendo that normally accompanied his every comment was ominously absent. Now he looked at her in earnestness and uncertainty. This new side of him, solicitous, even vulnerable, tore down any weak barriers Moriah might have managed to salvage from their earlier battles. He was simply too human to resist.

"I was planning on having dinner with my sisters at a restaurant on Baie Longue that Morgana wanted to try," she told him. "Then I guess I assumed I would go wherever they went after that. Probably out dancing someplace where they could look for ABC guys."

Austen loved the way she was looking at him. Dreamily,

as if she felt exactly the same way he did at the moment. "ABC guys?" he asked automatically, focusing more on the way she was talking than on what she actually said.

Moriah nodded slowly and lifted a shoulder nervously in response. "You know. Armani, Boss, Cardin."

Austen's eyebrows drew downward in confusion. "Your sisters actually go out looking to pick up fashion designers?" he asked.

Moriah's face softened with the curve of her smile. "No, silly," she chastised him affectionately. "They go out looking to pick up men who wear labels like that. I always sort of called them ABC guys."

"Makes them sound pretty simpleminded," Austen said.

"Who? The men or my sisters?"

"Both."

"Well…" Moriah's voice trailed off as if reluctant to contradict his speculation.

Austen bit his lip to keep from smiling. "Anyway, could I maybe change your mind? I have a proposal for you."

"A proposal or a proposition?" Moriah wanted to know.

"Actually it's a proposal I'm hoping will lead to a proposition," he confessed. "But you'll probably be the one who'll wind up doing the specific propositioning."

"You're pretty sure of yourself," she told him, unable to prevent the slight grin that turned her lips upward.

Austen stared at her for long moments with a cryptic expression that darkened his gold eyes. "Not nearly as much as I was before I met you," he said quietly.

Moriah tried to ignore the sudden somersaults her stomach started performing at his roughly uttered admission, and instead took a deep, calming breath before asking, "So what particularly did you have in mind?"

"I have a friend who lives on St. Martin," he told her.

"Gee, what a surprise."

Disregarding her comment, Austen told her, "Nat Malcolm is a real close friend of mine from college. I've known him over fifteen years. His folks owned a little summer house here that they used to use for annual escapes. Now Nat owns 'the cottage,' as his family used to call it, and since he's retired, he lives down here year-round."

"He's only your age and he's already retired?" Moriah asked, not even trying to hide her surprise.

"Nat was a real whiz kid in college, and he carried it with him right to the New York Stock Exchange," Austen explained. "He invested, shall we say, *very* wisely."

Moriah let out a low whistle. "Wow, not bad."

Of course her own upbringing had been rather sumptuous and excessive in many ways, Moriah admitted, but even the wealth of Teddy and Diana Mallory would not have allowed them to retire as early as Austen's friend had, had that been what they wanted to do in the first place. Their assets were of a less liquid nature than Nat Malcolm's apparently were, and then of course there was that matter of raising their four daughters in the style to which they had all become accustomed. At least to which the three eldest had become accustomed, Moriah amended. She herself would have been more than happy to skip the riding lessons and birthday parties for one hundred, in exchange for a show of a little honest affection from either one of her parents. Unfortunately, though, her parents evidently had a different view of what was important for a child's upbringing.

"Anyway," Austen's voice interrupted her thoughts, "I called Nat a little while ago to say hello, and he invited me to this huge, obscene party he's having tonight and told me to bring a date."

Nat had actually said something to the effect that Austen

should bring along whatever little piece of suntanned fluff he found lying on the beach in a neon bikini, knowing full well the type of woman his former college roomie preferred. However, Austen had assured his friend that the woman he was bringing this evening would turn the head of even the great Nat Malcolm, that even Nat, for whom no one was good enough, would approve of this one. Austen also remembered saying some things about how wonderful Moriah was, had in fact gone on for over fifteen minutes rhapsodizing her, but still felt certain that as soon as Nat laid eyes on her, he was going to be thoroughly impressed.

"So, you want to go with me?" he asked. "I promise you'll have a good time. Nat's an interesting guy. Won't wear anything but Hawaiian shirts and listens exclusively to show tunes. He claims rather an impressive roster of friends. I guarantee you *won't* be bored."

Moriah thought it was probably a terrible mistake she was about to make, but she did it anyway. Telling herself it was the perfect opportunity for a fascinating evening of cultural exchange, she told him, "Yes, I'd love to go, Austen." She hoped her voice carried none of the massive doubt she felt settling like cement upon her shoulders.

Moriah had to catch her breath at her first glimpse of Nat Malcolm's "little summer house." Some cottage, she thought. Tucked into the side of a green hill on a peaceful little peninsula overlooking Oyster Pond, awash in pale yellow and orange light from the setting sun, the big white stone structure seemed carved from ivory. As she and Austen strolled hand in hand toward the front door, her eyes roved hungrily over everything in sight, drinking in the limitless sky that was fast succumbing to the colors of the night, feasting on the moon that was a luminous pearl above it all. She listened carefully to the sounds rising like ghosts around her, a smile softening her features as the huge palm trees that stretched over the front entry whispered to her about the tantalizing wonders that lay beyond their guard. When she paused for a moment to take in her surroundings, a warm wind pushed her playfully from behind, tugging at the hem of her pale yellow sundress, scattering her hair softly about her forehead, urging her toward the lively, festive music that rose up somewhere beyond her vision. It was almost as if the island were speaking to her, she thought strangely. Almost as if Mother Nature herself were extending a formal invitation to stay and hang out for a while.

"What is it?" Austen asked her when he noted her stilled steps.

For a moment Moriah only stared at him, confusion jumbling her thoughts. The setting sun lighted fires in his hair, but she felt she would burn her fingers if she reached out to touch them. He wore baggy white trousers and a beige-and-white striped T-shirt, yet somehow Moriah couldn't help but view him as a pirate, a pirate who held her heart captive and might never let it go. What was it about him? she wondered. Why did he make her want to forget her scientific rationale, and how could he possibly be able to send her no-nonsense approach to life zinging out the window every time he was around? She could not forget who she was, she reminded herself. Flights of fancy and stirrings of sensuality were for women like her sisters, not for her. She forced herself to focus on words like *logical*, *resolute* and *staid*, but somehow those words kept moving farther and farther away.

Austen marveled at how lovely Moriah was, how much a part of her surroundings. He wanted to kiss her, to put her back in the rented Jeep and drive her to some secluded beach where he could make slow, sensuous love with her. He wanted to sit naked with her in the sand and watch the sun rise over the sea, then dive into the water and start the cycle all over again, touching her until nighttime claimed their exhausted bodies. He wanted her to stay with him forever. And the idea that she might leave him after their brief time together filled Austen with a fear and anguish like nothing he'd ever known.

"Moriah?" he said quietly. "Is something wrong?"

Finally she shook her head back and forth and lifted a shoulder in an almost helpless shrug. "Nothing," she whispered a little breathlessly. "It's just that I…" Her words trailed off, and her eyes journeyed up to the sky. "I don't know," she said more clearly, though she still felt an odd sensation of displacement. "I just had the strangest feeling…"

Austen was about to press the issue, wanted to do his best to determine what exactly had given her that faraway look, that very brief expression of utter tranquility, what had transformed her for only a moment into a woman who seemed completely at peace. Unfortunately a boisterous group of partygoers who came up from behind them forced them to continue their route toward the house. As their fingers automatically entwined once again, Austen made a mental note to keep an eye on his companion throughout the evening, to watch for the return of that silent, unconscious communication from Moriah that said she was right where she belonged.

The inside of Nat's house was every bit as impressive and overwhelming as the exterior, looking to Moriah like an elaborate Hollywood set. The white tile floors and arching doorways, the ceiling fans and winding staircases, the grand piano and potted palms all reminded her of any number of fabulous '40s films. She waited to see if a white dinner-jacketed Bogart or perfectly permanent-waved Bacall joined the guests, and was almost surprised when they didn't. The music only served to reaffirm the scene when it started up again, a lively Carmen

Miranda number that made Moriah want to flutter her hands and swivel her hips in a raucous rumba.

She found herself becoming easily caught up in the festivities as she wandered from group to group with Austen, smiling when he introduced her to everyone he knew—which essentially was everyone present—and was somewhat astounded that virtually all of her new acquaintances were interested in learning more about her. When she was certain they would all be put off by her dull university work and field study, they were actually very eager to learn more, particularly about her current work in the islands. As she listened to herself talk, Moriah was surprised at the ease with which her words came, was in fact shocked to hear herself laughing and recounting humorous stories with the others. She was actually having fun, she realized with no small amount of awe.

And as the evening progressed, she began to feel somehow as if she were being…reborn. The awkward mannerisms and insecurity that permeated her around her sisters were nowhere to be found tonight. Nor was the dryness and lack of humor that accompanied her when she was teaching and conversing with her colleagues. Oddly, it struck her that a new person was emerging from her former selves, leaving silly little Mo and the too-serious Dr. Mallory behind. Then as quickly as that idea entered her head, Moriah pushed it resolutely aside. That was a ridiculous concept, she thought. She was who she had always been, and nothing would or could ever change that. Just because Austen Blye tried to fill her head with the preposterous, laughable notion that she wanted to be something different, something more, did not mean she believed it to be true. It was *not* true, she assured herself. It wasn't.

And speaking of Austen, she wondered, putting the business of her identity fully to rest as she glanced curiously over one shoulder then the other, where had he disappeared to?

Moriah excused herself from a group that consisted of a Belgian xylophone player, a Venezuelan sailor and a titled but penniless noblewoman from Liechtenstein, and began to search for her escort. She hadn't gone far, however, when she was cornered by a tall man dressed in long khaki shorts and the most obnoxious Hawaiian shirt Moriah had ever seen, one covered with yellow and green fish swimming through pink and purple seaweed. Below an unruly thatch of thinning blond hair, mischievous blue eyes twinkled at her merrily; round wire-rimmed glasses perched precariously on his nose, which like his cheeks and scalp was shining bright red, as if permanently sunburned. In one hand he held what she was certain was the largest rum punch in the world, a massive orange monstrosity decorated with three paper parasols, a thick slice of pineapple speared with maraschino cherries and limes, and boasting a blue plastic swordfish for a swizzle stick. He was a startling study in color, Moriah thought, and she liked him immediately.

He gazed at her for a moment without speaking, then rattled the swordfish around in his drink before pulling it out and pointing it at her. "You must be Austen's mystery woman," he accused her playfully.

Moriah couldn't help but smile at him. "And you have *got* to be Nat," she returned.

He seemed to deflate a little. "Why do Austen's friends always say that when they meet me for the first time? How do you know I'm not some big-time art collector or philanthropist? I could even be a pioneering astrophysicist or hairstylist or something. Why do people always say, 'Oh, hey, you must be Nat,' every time they see me?"

Moriah chuckled at his affected offense. "Austen mentioned that you were something of a, uh, something of an unusual dresser," she confessed.

Nat rolled his eyes theatrically. "Oh, and he's not? This is the Caribbean, honey," he reminded her unnecessarily. "Conventionality equals oddity down here. You want to fit in, you listen to me." He put his arm around her and pulled her close, lowering his voice to a conspiratorial whisper. "Do your own thing," he announced slowly and with grave determination. He released her, then nodded and winked shrewdly, pointing at her once more with the plastic swordfish. "Mark my words," he advised her.

Moriah laughed again and said, "Austen warned me that you were a charmer."

Nat brightened considerably at her statement. "He did? Where is the little son of a fisherman, anyway?"

"I don't know," Moriah told him with a shrug. "I was just going to look for him when you cornered me with what I can only hope was the intention to offer me sound and sage advice."

Nat winked at her broadly. "My intentions always remain secret until I know with absolute certainty what I can and can't get away with." He glanced toward the French doors that led out to the terrace overlooking the ocean and inclined his head in their direction. "Come on," he said lightly. "The best way to find Austen is to go to the nearest view of the water. You can always find him staring pensively out to sea."

But their journey outdoors offered no sight of the man they had gone to seek.

"Okay, let me amend that," Nat offered. "You can usually find him staring pensively out to sea." He leaned against the waist-high stone wall that surrounded the terrace and that rose only to his hip and added, "The second-best way to find Austen is to start talking about him. He always shows up when you get to the best part."

When a waiter strode past with a tray of what looked like

fruit juice, Moriah took one gingerly and sipped it experimentally. It was loaded with rum, but she held on to it anyway, more than anything because she wanted to have something to do with her hands, which suddenly began to feel restless. She turned away from Nat's agonizingly inquisitive gaze and stared a little pensively out to sea herself.

Nat sighed at her uncommunicativeness and hoisted his big body up to sit atop the wall. "All right, all right," he conceded. "I can understand if you're not one of these gabby types. Frankly I was getting pretty tired of all those silly beach bunnies Austen used to bring around, the ones who just talked and talked and talked all the time and never said a single interesting word about anybody or anything. You know the type. They just keep talking and talking without even thinking about what they're saying, as if the act of talking itself is enough to make them sound like they have something to say, something that somebody might be interested in hearing…" Nat's voice trailed off, and he cocked his head to one side thoughtfully. "Anyway, you get the idea," he finished quickly.

Moriah hated herself for the pang of jealousy that shot through her at Nat's mention of meeting other women who had been involved with Austen. It made her wonder again why he was wasting his time with her when he could pick and choose among hundreds of vacationing women every year. She was helpless to voice her thoughts out loud. "Does Austen bring a lot of women here?"

"Women, no," he assured her. "I don't think I'd ever call the creatures he's run around with women."

Moriah felt her spirits sink lower. Girls, then, she thought to herself. Austen probably liked them young and carefree and animated. Girls who could laugh and giggle and be coy, girls who were never serious for a moment. That was the type of woman he wished she could be, she realized sullenly. The type of woman there was no way she could ever become.

Seemingly oblivious to her distress, Nat continued on blithely, "Yeah, it's good to see old Austen has finally settled down with someone special."

Moriah jerked her head up in confusion, then drew her brows down into a frown. She opened her mouth to correct Nat's erroneous assumption about her relationship with Austen, but he rushed on without even taking a breath.

"Frankly I was rather beginning to worry about this tendency of Austen's to run around with nubile, blonde bimbettes and hang out in rough, questionable waterfront bars. He really isn't that kind of man at all, you know," Nat assured Moriah parenthetically. "And he never has been. He just gets a little confused sometimes, mixes up his priorities, that sort of thing. Considering everything he's been through, it's more than understandable, don't you think? And, hey, it does happen to the best of us, doesn't it?"

Moriah was going to say that she agreed with Nat's last statement at least, if with none of the others, simply because she had no idea what he was talking about. But once again her companion never gave her a chance to speak. Instead he continued on with his monologue as if there were no one else present who wanted to contribute to, or even follow, the conversation.

"I'm sure Austen told you that he and I were roomies at Vanderbilt University years ago. Until we were seniors I thought he was a biology major with all those marine science classes he took. And let me tell you, no one, I mean *no one* was as surprised as I was when he announced that he was going to get an MBA on top of his marketing degree and seek a career in the financial field." Nat lifted a hand melodramatically over his heart. "You could have knocked me over with a feather. A *feather* I tell you. Anyway, it didn't last, of course, and it was certainly no surprise to me at all when Austen left that ridiculous vice president's position at the Global Bank in Atlanta. Then again there was that rather upsetting business with Pamela, his fiancée at the time…" Nat paused, taking a deep swallow of his drink. "But that's all in the past now, isn't it?" he concluded happily, as if the words he had just spoken would be of the greatest comfort in the world to Moriah. "No need to dwell on it, right?"

Actually the continuous stream of Nat's announcements caused Moriah's head to spin. Vanderbilt University? she wondered. MBA? The Global Bank? A vice president? None of them were things she would have associated with Austen in even the most remote manner. But more than any of the other startling revelations, Moriah was struck painfully by the words *Pamela, his fiancée at the time*. A fiancée. Austen had once been in love, she realized. Had once loved a woman enough to want to spend the rest of his life with her. And that woman had been someone other than herself. Why the knowledge made her stomach burn, made her heart twist grievously in her chest, Moriah didn't know. She had no right to expect or want Austen to care for her, had no reason to believe that she was the only woman for him. On the contrary, she had persisted in reminding herself that there was nothing between them beyond a superficial physical attraction, insisted that she could never be the kind of woman he needed or desired. Still, at the moment, she felt as if she'd just gone ten rounds with a steamroller, felt as if she might never be able to stand up straight again. This Pamela had no doubt been full of fun and quick to laugh. She had probably been carefree and high-spirited, easygoing and chatty, funny and completely irreverent. She must have loved Austen more than anything in the world. And she had been someone else. She hadn't been Moriah.

What happened to Pamela? Moriah wondered. She didn't realize she had spoken her thought out loud until she saw the expression of surprise that lighted up Nat's round face.

"You don't know?" he asked her, genuinely unaware that she had apparently heard nothing of Austen's past.

Moriah shook her head. "No, of course not. Should I?"

Nat opened his mouth to speak, but for the first time tonight he seemed to have no idea what to say. "I just thought that by now Austen would have filled you in on most of his life's experiences," he finally told her. "I mean, after everything the two of you have shared."

Moriah felt the knot in her stomach clench tighter. "What has he told you about us?" she demanded. "About me?"

"I, er," Nat began. "I'm not at all sure that this is something you should be hearing from me," he finally stammered.

"I've already heard it from you," Moriah pointed out. "I just haven't heard any of the details."

"That's right!" Nat grabbed on to her last statement, apparently realizing that he could use the words later when he would need to assuage Austen's probable fury at the discovery of what his friend had revealed about his past. "That's right, I didn't mention any details. I really think details, specific, concrete details, are something Austen should supply."

Moriah shook her head slowly back and forth, not at all certain how to absorb the information she had been offered in the past several minutes. Nat could easily fill her in on everything she'd been aching to know about Austen since she'd met him, could answer all the questions Austen so deftly sidestepped himself. However, due to his obvious loyalty to his college friend, he was also evidently unwilling to do so. "What did he tell you about me?" she repeated her earlier question instead, her voice a quiet plea.

Nat sighed and looked down into Moriah's face for a long

time before replying. "I know he cares about you very much, Moriah" was all he offered her in response.

Several tense moments passed without words, then suddenly, as if cued for entry, Austen joined them. His grin broadened as he approached, and he said happily, "I should have known I'd find the two of you together." Then he added to Nat, "Nice shirt."

"Thanks," Nat acknowledged. To Moriah he said, "I told you he always shows up just when you get to the best part."

"I see what you mean," Moriah agreed with a slow nod, still reeling from the new view of Austen that Nat had presented and still frustrated that she had been unable to get any more information from him. If she wanted to learn more about the man who stood beside her now, she was going to have to ask him herself. She tried to picture him with a short, conservative haircut, tried to envision his hard, lean body encased in the latest banker's attire. She tried to imagine him with a briefcase. But the only image that came to her mind's eye was of Austen lying shirtless on the beach that afternoon, the salt water sparkling like diamonds as it streamed from his bronzed muscles, the sun streaking his mahogany hair with gold. Austen Blye a banker? Not in a million years.

Austen glanced curiously from Moriah to Nat and back again wondering what he had missed by making himself scarce for so long. The look in Moriah's eyes right now hinted at any number of things, some of them clearly erotic, and his heart picked up speed at the thoughts that exploded in his brain in response.

"Say, Nat," he began slowly, gazing at Moriah instead of at his host. "You wouldn't mind if we blew this joint a little early, would you?" He was finally able to pull his eyes from Moriah and look once again at his friend.

Nat's expression was bland, but his blue eyes danced with

mischief behind the lenses of his glasses. "Why, Austen, whatever for?" he asked with feigned surprise. "You only just got here. And I'm only just beginning to get to know this lovely and intriguing woman you've brought with you."

"That's what I'm afraid of," Austen responded drily.

"Austen," Moriah intercepted, "we don't have to leave. You haven't even had a chance to talk to Nat. I know you two must have a lot of catching up to do."

Austen bit his lip briefly in thought before replying. "Although it's true that I'd sell my sainted grandmother up the river to know what Nat's been telling you this evening, to be perfectly honest, I see more of this guy as it is than I really care to. Mostly the only reason I stay in touch is so I can tell his mother what he's up to."

Nat's eyes widened quickly, and his surprise was genuine. "So you're the one who's been keeping her informed, you rat!" he accused. "I was wondering how she found out about that mambo dancer from Tortuga." Nat shook his finger playfully at Austen. "I've got a serious bone to pick with you, fella."

"Moriah, I think it's time to go," Austen announced decisively.

"But—" Moriah began to decline. However, her escort was insistent.

"No, really, I think this party is about to become bizarre and questionable in nature, and trust me when I tell you that very few have survived a Nat Malcolm party once it gets to that point. "'Bye, Nat," he added before he took her elbow and steered her mindfully toward the exit.

"'Bye, Austen," Nat called after them. "And 'bye, Moriah. It was definitely an honor and a privilege meeting you."

"Likewise," Moriah agreed.

As they found their way back out through the front door, Moriah heard the already lively music take on frenzied tones, and turned her head back in time to catch Nat's voice lifted high with the announcement, "Everybody mambo!" She couldn't help the laughter that bubbled up freely from some recently tapped well inside her, couldn't prevent the urge, even the need, to wrap her arm around Austen's waist and pull him close. As the music behind them grew louder and more festive, Austen spun her toward him in an awkward, animated dance of celebration, and Moriah felt her hands and feet tangle with his until she nearly lost her balance. She fell against him with a breathless giggle, grasping two handfuls of his T-shirt in an effort to keep herself standing. Their dancing ended abruptly then, and Austen gazed down at her with a longing and desire she knew must mirror her own.

"Why do I feel like I've fallen into a dream whenever I'm with you?" she asked him suddenly, unable to remember having chosen to speak her thoughts out loud.

Austen shook his head slowly back and forth, his golden eyes darkening to amber as he looked at her. "I don't know, Moriah," he told her honestly. "But whatever or whoever is causing it, you're not the only one who's been targeted."

For long moments they continued to gaze at each other, then began to wend their way slowly back to the rental Jeep, leaving the music, the dancing and the laughter behind.

Chapter Eight

"Why are we stopping?"

Moriah posed the question to Austen some time later as he slowed the Jeep to a halt and parked it along the side of one of the many hilly, winding roads that crisscrossed St. Martin. After leaving Nat's party, neither had been quite ready to return to the sailboat and the group of people that awaited them there. Instead Austen had given Moriah an informal tour of the island, focusing on the Dutch side because she hadn't yet had a chance to see it. They had enjoyed the late dinner of fresh seafood and a quiet, intimately lighted restaurant in Philipsburg, a tiny eatery tucked into a charming pink building with pale green shutters and a breathtaking view of moonlit Great Bay. Then Austen had taken her to the opposite extreme, had shown her the Casino Royal at Maho Beach, an enormous construction styled after the spectacular, showy casinos in Las Vegas yet nonetheless very Caribbean in flavor.

But now the starry sky hung above them once again. Gone was the artificial glitter and glare of the casino lights, gone the boisterous, manufactured music and the ringing bells of the slot machines that shrilled in alarm as they paid off gamblers with shiny, bright coins. Here there was no need for money, no need to pay for the enjoyment of the pleasures that surrounded them. The sounds that greeted their ears now were the voices of the island—the wind as it stirred the palms, birds chattering and crying at the intrusion of their sanctuary, and somewhere in the distance the continuous, gentle whisper of the ocean as it crept stealthily across the shore. The smell of the earth enveloped them here, a rich, pungent aroma that evoked primitive wants and elemental desires deep within Moriah's soul and dispelled the last of civilization's poisons from her lungs. As her senses worked overtime to take in everything around her, she felt the tension seep slowly from her body to be replaced by a languid, welcoming relief.

"I want to show you something," Austen told her, reminding her of the question she had forgotten she asked.

"What?" she wanted to know.

Austen's eyes caught the moonlight and held it, turning its silver sheen into molten gold. "You'll see," he replied cryptically. "It's something very few people know about. Even people who live on the island might not know of its existence. Nat showed it to me a long time ago. I've never shown anyone else."

He leapt gracefully from the driver's side and circled around the front to her side. All the while his eyes held hers, full of a longing and promise. Try as she might, Moriah could no more have broken contact with his seductive gaze than she could stop her own heart from beating. From somewhere deep inside her head, a loud voice cautioned that something about her was changing and that she had better be careful and watch her step. But instead of coming up with ways to slow her spinning emotions, Moriah could only search for reasons to justify pursuing what she knew she shouldn't want.

"It's this way." Austen's quiet voice parted the darkness that separated them, deeper here than near the shore because the trees were thick and lush and obscured the light of the moon.

As he led her down a path in the jungle, vines and plants tangled gently about Moriah's feet and arms, as if asking her to slow down, to take her time and remain with them awhile. The song of the wind filled her ears with its chorus, and the murmuring surf beckoned to her more insistently. But as the invitation became louder and they drew closer to it, Moriah began to realize that they were taking a course that led away from the ocean instead of toward it. Therefore if what she was hearing wasn't the tireless lapping of the surf, what else could it possibly be?

She had her answer only moments after that when Austen pulled her through an opening in the foliage that seemed to have appeared almost magically before them. They stood on a wide ledge overlooking a small pool, and what Moriah had thought to be the sound of the surf was in fact the result of the continuous tumbling of a sparkling, minuscule waterfall.

"Oh, my," she cried on a soft whisper when she beheld it.

The pool was an almost perfect circle, surrounded by a graceful wreath of tall palms that arched above it, some dripping Spanish moss and bougainvillea all the way to the water's surface. The water itself shone like black onyx in the darkness, the reflection of the moon a glistening diamond that sparkled at its center, its surface fluid and alive where tiny waves rippled forward from the base of the starry cascade that fed the pool from five feet above. Again Moriah was overcome by a feeling that she had just stumbled upon a magic place, that as a mere mortal she shouldn't be allowed such a glimpse at paradise. Yet here she was, she told herself. If she had grown up among the superstitions and beliefs in magic that a member of a primitive Carib tribe would embrace, she would be assuming right now that the gods and the night spirits were offering her a wonderful gift. Therefore, how could she possibly risk offending them by throwing it back in their faces?

She glanced over and smiled at Austen, who had been watching her reaction with more than a little interest. "Do you know," she began slowly, taking an experimental step toward the pool that called out to her with such enticement, "that as much as I've studied and researched the practices and customs of primitive cultures, it's still impossible for me to understand what *exactly* causes tribal members to believe and behave the way they do?"

"Is that a fact?" Austen asked her, uncertain of the route her thoughts were traveling, but nonetheless anxious to find out.

Moriah nodded and took another step forward. "I don't think anyone would disagree that unless one has actually been raised in that type of society, without any knowledge of the progressive lifestyles that lay beyond the village perimeters, it is virtually impossible to fully understand the tribal experience."

"Sounds like a reasonable deduction," Austen agreed.

Moriah took another step toward the pool and could smell the sweet fragrance of the jungle blossoms that grew along one side. "Do you realize," she began again, removing her glasses without comment to tuck them into her pocket, "that you are looking at a scientist who has made it her life's work to study primitive cultures, yet I've never partaken of any kind of primitive behavior myself?"

"Do tell," Austen said with a growing smile.

Moriah shook her head slowly back and forth, sighed deeply with regret and took one more step to the edge of the pool. As she began to loosen the braid from her hair, she told him almost ruefully, "No. Not once."

Austen eyed her with some speculation, then strode toward her with easy, measured steps until he stood at her side. Moriah could feel him studying her profile in the moonlight and wanted more than anything to know what he saw. She turned to gaze at him intently, wishing there was some way she could explain the emotions that were swirling so furiously inside her. But how could she possibly relate them to him when she didn't even begin to understand them herself? Could he tell what she was feeling? she wondered. Did he see that somehow, for some reason, she sensed that she was right where she belonged, right where she wanted to be? Could he detect the fact that all she could think about at the moment was how much she wanted to be something other than the youngest Mallory sister, how she wanted to be more than Professor Mallory, Ph.D.? In spite of all the rational reasons that she should feel otherwise, right now, Moriah realized with a sudden jolt of electricity that shuddered throughout her body, right now all she wanted to be was a woman. And even more alarming than that thought, she wanted Austen to be the man who would help her become one.

With a cryptic smile that was almost sad, she let her gaze wander up toward the sky. "I'm sure this is a very silly question," she said so quietly she wasn't sure he'd be able to hear her. "But have you ever been skinny-dipping before?"

A surprised and very lascivious grin curled Austen's lips as he asked, "What do you think?"

Moriah chuckled nervously. "I think I probably should have known better than to ask."

In response to her assertion, Austen grabbed the back of

his T-shirt in one fist and yanked it over his head. The moon-light tipped the crisp, mahogany hair on his chest with silver, and Moriah's fingers itched to reach out and bury themselves in it. The hard muscles of his abdomen rippled poetically like the ocean's waves, and his bronzed, sculpted arms hardened and expanded as he wadded up his shirt and tossed it care-lessly to the ground.

"Last one in's a rotten papaya," he challenged, letting his hands fall to the buckle of his belt. Almost as if he had re-hearsed it, he pulled the excess length of leather slowly from its loop, then tugged it taut to slip his finger down and free it from the grip of the buckle. Moriah swallowed hard as she watched his long fingers loosen each of the buttons on his trousers one by one, until he revealed more of his hard torso than she had ever seen before. All at once she was able to de-termine the exact course of the springy hair that so anxiously tantalized and preoccupied her, and all at once she began to feel a little faint.

For a moment the world did tilt on its side for Moriah, and she felt herself sway from the momentum of her pulse as her heart heated her blood and sent it surging through her veins. She reached behind her to unzip her sundress, but her fingers were as numb as the rest of her, and she fumbled with the mechanism ineffectually.

"Here, let me," Austen offered when he saw her struggles.

He pulled her body toward him with a gentle tug until it was flush against his, their hearts beating frantically against each other, their breathing mingling with the steamy tropical heat. His long fingers closed over the tongue of her zipper, lingering on the warm flesh of her back as they did so. Very slowly and with utter care, Austen lowered the zipper that ran the length of Moriah's spine, letting his thumb trace over the delicate outline of every vertebra until he knew each of them with an intimate and fiery acquaintance. When the zipper halted just below her waist, Austen pressed his index finger into her heated, sensitized skin and mimicked the movement of closing it once again. Only instead of pulling the fabric of her dress back together, he spread it farther apart until it splayed open across her back, and she could feel the kiss of the island breeze as it caressed and lingered on her skin.

When his rough palms rose higher to cup over her shoulders, Austen pushed the straps of her sundress down over her arms, and only Moriah's movement to cover herself and hold the garment in place prevented it from falling to the ground. Her eyes met his in the darkness with an uncertainty she was afraid to voice, and Austen smiled his encouragement. Gently he twined her fingers with his and lifted her hands away, and like a pale yellow cloud, her dress floated down to encircle her feet.

Austen's breathing became shallow and quick when he beheld her standing nearly naked before him, and his cheeks grew as flushed as she knew her own must be. The fact that he seemed to feel as shaky and nervous as she did made Moriah relax a little, but the thundering of her heart still sounded in her ears like the stampede of a thousand wild beasts.

"You are so beautiful," he told her simply, his voice no longer full of the lightness and easy humor she had come to expect from him. Instead he spoke with reverence and regard.

Moriah didn't know what to say, wasn't sure how she was supposed to respond to a man who made her blood rush like a hot, raging river. No man had ever come close to wreaking the havoc inside her that Austen managed to create by simply being near her, and she had no idea what to do to alleviate the burning sensations that coursed through her every fiber.

"You…you promised me a swim," she stammered softly.

"Did I?" he asked. He could have promised her anything,

he realized, so incoherently were his thoughts coming now. And certainly he would promise her anything more. As long as she swore she would stay with him here forever. He forced himself to turn loose of her hands and respond with as much fortitude as possible, "Then by all means, be my guest. After you."

Despite the tumultuous desires storming down around her, Moriah's modesty was still very much intact, and when Austen released her hands, she was helpless to keep her arms from crossing over her in a protectively insecure gesture.

"But you're still…" she tried to protest, but her words were feeble at best. "I mean, you're not…" She lifted her index finger from her arm and waved it negligently toward his waist.

Austen bit his lip to prevent himself from assuring her that Oh, yes, he was, too, and instead looked down at the trousers he knew she was trying to indicate. He glanced back at Moriah with an expression of mock surprise. "So I am," he agreed, and lifted his hands to his trim waist in preparation for removing his pants.

Moriah snapped her eyes shut like a coward and refused to open them again until she heard the soft splash that assured her Austen was in the pool. Then as quickly and as gracefully as she could, she removed her panties and dived in after him. The water was a cool, soothing balm on her heated skin, and Moriah took pleasure in ducking below the surface again and again. Holding her breath helped slow the pace of her heart and settle her nerves, she discovered, and closing her eyes helped her remember all the reasons why she shouldn't be doing exactly what she was doing.

When she broke the surface of the water after just such a chat with herself, she found Austen standing before her awaiting her reappearance. Due to the difference in their heights, where his chest and taut stomach were clearly revealed above the waterline, Moriah could easily bend her knees and hide whatever she chose. She kept the water level just below her chin and gazed in fascination at the glittering rivulets that streamed down Austen's chest and pooled in some very interesting places. When he began to make his way toward her, Moriah felt her skin grow hot once again and feared the water would soon begin to boil up around them. For every step he took forward, Moriah took a step in retreat, until her back flattened with a jolt against the soft, sandy incline that marked the wall of the pool. Before she could turn and try an alternate escape route, Austen was in front of her, placing his palms smoothly against the incline on either side of her shoulders in a very effective trap.

For long moments she could only gaze at him with a deep and demanding desire, could only try to ignore the yawning void that opened in her heart whenever he came this close. She listened patiently as every part of her body screamed out to her that making love with this man was what she wanted and needed more than anything else in the world. Then Moriah had to force herself to scream back that *that* was the most ridiculous thing she'd ever heard and would her body parts please behave themselves in a manner befitting the adult, rational woman that they composed.

When Austen began to lower his face slowly toward hers, Moriah deftly ducked below one of his muscular arms and easily swam the length of the pool. The water parted into a long V behind her, the moon shimmering at the apex of her wake.

"My, but that's invigorating," she said lamely when he turned to watch her but made no move to join her. "I had no idea that skinny-dipping could provide one with such a sense of freedom and well-being. Perhaps there's more to leading a primitive lifestyle than what the scientific community is aware."

"That's it, Moriah," Austen finally spoke, settling his hands on his trim hips. The water level barely concealed the part of him that so intrigued her, and Moriah's breathing became a little unsteady as she beheld his naked form. "Keep talking like an anthropologist and sooner or later you're bound to remember that's all you were meant to be." He smiled grimly at her, but she knew he intended nothing humorous in his statement. Slowly he began to stride toward her through the water once again, his motions easy, fluid and utterly predatory.

"I can't begin to imagine what you're talking about," she replied on a shallow breath as he began to stalk her again. Once more Moriah swam quickly away to elude him, but found there was little that the small distance separating them in the pool could do to create an effective measure of prevention.

Austen stood where she had left him for a second time, but his eyes followed steadily every movement that she made. The circle of water that had originally seemed of substantial size grew tinier and tinier as Moriah observed him watching her, and finally she decided her only escape lay in the direction of the waterfall. She pulled herself through the water until she stood directly in front of the tumbling cascade, then dipped her face experimentally under the cool, continuous stream of water.

"Oh!" she cried out in delighted surprise. It felt wonderful! Like the cool, luxurious massage of practiced fingers rubbing over her heated skin. She laughed out loud like a child who's just discovered ice cream for the first time, discovered the taste and texture and temperature of something so utterly unlike normal everyday experience.

So caught up in the sensation of the heavy sheaths of water pouring over her, Moriah didn't seem to realize how much of her body she had raised up from the pool in an effort to lift herself as close to the falling water as possible. Austen realized, though. He realized right away. He felt his body go rigid at the sight of Moriah's full, creamy breasts streaming with water and growing round and taut from the cascade's caress. When she lifted her hands to push back her wet hair, her breasts turned into perfect circles, then when her arms stretched out to her sides to catch more of the descending stream, they settled once again against her chest like two heavy globes. His heart hammered hard in his own chest, while his blood boiled and thickened like hot sticky syrup in his veins. Words and thoughts eluded him as moonlight turned her skin to silver, and before he knew what was happening, some invisible string tightened inside him and pulled him helplessly to where Moriah laughed and played.

When she sensed him standing before her, Moriah's light frolic ended, her laughter suddenly died. She had nearly forgotten he was there, she realized, shocked that she could ever forget such a man as he. For long moments she could only gaze at him, losing herself in eyes that blazed with some unknown fire, as if he didn't understand the feelings burning him up any more than she understood her own. She watched in helpless fascination as he, too, leaned his face into the cool rush of water, then pulled her close to join him under the cascade. She felt herself tremble with anticipation as he lowered his face to hers, and the breath dashed from her lungs as he rubbed his rough cheek hotly against hers with a predatory groan. For a long time he only touched her face with his, then Moriah felt his lips move over her temple and her forehead, and down over her nose until only a whisper of the wind separated their mouths. All the while the cascade of water tumbled over and around them, and she was never sure if it was the rumble of the water or the thunder of her heart that sounded so deafeningly in her ears.

"I promised myself I wouldn't let this happen until you

were ready," Austen murmured. "But the only thing that's stopping me now is the fact that you could get pregnant."

Moriah's heart turned over at the way his features softened and grew warm when he added, "And as incredibly appealing, not to mention erotic, as such a concept is to me, I can't help but think that you might feel a little differently."

"No, you're wrong," she heard herself saying before she could stop the words from coming. When the fire in Austen's eyes leapt higher, she quickly clarified, "I mean, I'm just about to…that is, at the moment, there's really no chance that I'll get…"

Austen appeared to weigh her words carefully before asking, "Are you sure?"

Moriah wasn't certain exactly what he wanted her to be sure of, but she did know she wasn't at risk for pregnancy right now. She smiled shakily, but her words were more than certain when she replied, "I am a scientist, after all."

It was evidently exactly what Austen wanted to hear. As quickly as her words were carried away by the rush of water, his lips claimed hers in a kiss that was at once tentative and tempestuous, desirous and demanding. And Moriah could no more resist him than she could prevent the sun from rising and warming the dawn.

At first Austen managed to keep his distance, held his body in check so that only their mouths were touching. With gentle finesse, he nibbled and tugged at her lips, tasted their corners with the tip of his tongue and traced their outline until he knew their shape perfectly. He brushed her mouth over and over again so softly with his that Moriah thought she would die from the sheer pleasure of it all. Gradually his feet moved him forward and brought his body closer to hers until she could feel the hard muscles of his abdomen pressing against the soft skin of her own. The coarse hair of his chest tickled her breasts into taut awareness, and Moriah gasped at feeling them so sensitive for the first time. Then as he drew closer to her still, she could feel the long length of him pressing urgently against her and understood fully his need and desire for her. As water rushed over them in steady streams, and waves swirled gently around them, Moriah felt Austen rub softly against her, and her knees and legs became as warm and liquid as the water in the pool.

When he sensed her about to go under, Austen settled his hands carefully on Moriah's hips to hold her fast in front of him. She moaned quietly at the awareness of such strength and power against her and instinctively pushed herself closer to him. Her action served only to bring their bodies into even more intimate contact and reminded her of exactly how ready he was for her. When his lips took a slow, tantalizing route from her mouth down her neck to her shoulders, licking up the streams of water from her skin as he went, Moriah had to grab hold of his big biceps to keep from losing her balance. When she did, Austen easily plucked her up from the water, using her weightlessness to give him access to the breasts that had so taunted him when she had played under the waterfall. As his mouth closed over one extended peak, Moriah cried out at the exquisite pleasure his tongue provoked. For long moments his lips pursed over her, tasting and teasing her until she wasn't sure where her body ended and Austen's began. Just when she thought her breast would surely burst from the passion welling within, he turned his attention to the other one and raised the same response.

When he finally lowered her back down into the water, they were both gasping for breath and reeling from the burning fires that passion had set throughout their bodies. The water that fell over and surrounded them in the pool was no longer cool enough to temper their hot desires, and neither could summon any more rational explanations or logical excuses to talk themselves out of what they were feeling.

"Moriah," Austen rasped as he pressed his forehead against hers. "I want you. I want to be inside you, making love to you the way no other man ever could."

"Oh, Austen," Moriah moaned, trying to remember all the reasons why she had promised herself this wouldn't happen. "This is crazy," she finally grated out. "We have to stop right now."

"*This* is not crazy," he countered breathlessly. "What's crazy is refusing to acknowledge the feelings we have for each other. What's crazy is lying awake in my bunk every night imagining the things I want to do to you. Fantasizing about what it would feel like to touch you here," he whispered as his palm closed insistently over her sensitized breast. "Trying to imagine the kind of noises you'd make when I did this to you," he added as his other hand slipped slowly down over her hip and settled a long finger between her thighs.

Moriah gasped and cried out on a strangled sob.

"What's crazy is denying ourselves what it is we both want, denying ourselves the one thing our bodies are screaming out for." He situated himself with intent between her legs, then gripped her thighs in his hands and lifted them up around his waist. "Denying to ourselves that what we want, what we need more than anything else, is this," he ground out on a hoarse whisper as he urged his body forward and buried himself fully inside her.

Moriah cried out at the depth of his initial penetration, feeling her senses spin in circles toward some bottomless abyss deep within her soul. As the stream of water cascaded down around them, Austen slowly unsheathed himself from her and then plunged forcefully inside her again. A tautly wound spring began to coil tighter and tighter in Moriah's midsection until she thought it would explode. Austen pushed her under the waterfall then, until they were both behind it, and crowded her back against the sandy incline, gripping her hips insistently to hold her in place for his demanding strokes. Over and over again he claimed her body with his, until she could see nothing but bright streaks of color and spatterings of lights. Higher and higher he carried her, past the moon and stars, beyond all the planets and celestial planes. As they approached a vast, limitless circle of blinding white light, Moriah felt ready to throw herself into its midst. She cried out his name when she did so and wasn't quite startled to hear Austen's voice join hers in celebration of the exquisite culmination their bodies enjoyed.

The trip back to earth was a lengthy one, one in which Moriah experienced clearly every delight and delectation she had rushed by in her initial pursuit of fulfillment. Gradually, though, the darkness of the island enclosed them once again, and the almost-silent sounds of their surroundings lifted into the night. The songs of the birds were less raucous now, and the wind in the trees was a subtle refrain. The waterfall still tumbled casually into the pool before them, and the water settled around them like fluid glass once again. When Moriah remembered who and where she was, she felt Austen still firmly planted deep inside her, felt his breath rushing out at the same speed as her own, felt his heart slowing to a pounding clatter against hers, and she knew they had both just glimpsed the same view of the heavens. As he started to pull away from her, she instinctively tightened her legs around his waist, and for the briefest of moments, tried to prevent his retreat.

"No, don't," she protested, still dazed and uncertain about what had just happened between them. "Don't leave me."

When she heard the note of pleading in her voice and

realized what she had just requested, Moriah was shocked. Immediately her senses returned to her full force, and she was mortified at the situation in which she found herself. Good God! she yelled at herself in horror. What was she doing? What had she *done?*

Austen smiled a shaky smile and took a deep breath, oblivious to the panicked regrets that were speeding through Moriah's feverish brain. "Sweetheart, I'm not going anywhere," he promised her. "I have plans for you yet."

Silence reigned for several long, awkward minutes, then Moriah's quiet words of warning split the darkness.

"Get away from me."

Her voice was an ominous, steely demand, and Austen's heart stopped beating for a moment as he tried to convince himself that what he was hearing wasn't real.

"Moriah, honey," he began uncertainly. "What's the matter? What's wrong?"

Moriah realized suddenly, shamefully, that she was standing naked and wanton behind a waterfall, crowded against an embankment where she had just given herself to a man in the most basic, most primitive way that a woman can give herself to a man. She had done what she had promised herself she wouldn't do with Austen, had participated in the shallow activity of casual sex that she was convinced was so far beneath her. Worse than succumbing to her weakness, though, was the fact that she had capitulated so easily. Worse still was the knowledge that she had taken so much pleasure in the act. And for the life of her, Moriah couldn't begin to explain how an error of such magnitude had come about. Her eyes met Austen's only briefly, then fell to stare into the dark depths of the pool. She didn't want him to see her humiliation at having behaved so spontaneously and without thought, at having allowed her mind to be so easily governed by her body. She didn't want to see the look in his eyes that would doubtless confirm the fact that his reaction to what had just happened between them was one of mere physical relief. Not when her own reaction had been so much more. She didn't want to feel vulnerable the way women always felt after such episodes, didn't want to admit to the weaknesses of desire and need. It was most unsettling, most unscientific behavior.

"Get away," she repeated levelly. "And don't call me 'honey' or 'sweetheart' or any of those other demeaning things men call women to prettify the act of copulation."

"Excuse me?" Austen stammered. It was a weak response, he knew, but it was the only thought that entered his mind at her accusation. Still, he obeyed her, pulled himself slowly from inside her, unable to ignore the catch in her breath and the wounded look that entered her eyes as he did so, then took a single step backward. For a long time Austen could only gape at Moriah and had no idea how to take her withdrawal. In the past he'd received a lot of different reactions from women about his sexual technique, but he couldn't remember a single time when he'd been accused of copulating. Moriah made what they'd just enjoyed together sound like something scientific, clinical and cold. He tugged her back through the waterfall to the center of the pool, hoping the quick rush of water would snap her out of her retreat.

"Copulation?" he finally asked lightly, trying to resurrect some semblance of the closeness and high spirits they had experienced earlier in the evening. "Is that what we just did? Copulate? I always wondered what that would be like. Frankly it was a lot more fun than I thought it would be."

"Stop it, Austen," Moriah told him quietly. "It never should have happened and you know it."

"No, actually, I don't know it," he countered. "What we just experienced together felt like the most natural thing in the world to me. I can't understand why you don't feel that way, too. Usually emotions like these travel in pairs."

Moriah tried to look at him again and failed miserably, instead turning her face up toward the palms that swayed gently against the dark sky above them. "What happened between us just now…" she began, but her words faded along with her convictions. She took a deep breath and tried to begin again. "Our *union*," she said meaningfully, "was simply a result of the sultry night air and our romantic surroundings, a consequence of our natural physical attraction to each other and nothing more. Sexual urges are primitive, instinctive responses," she informed him further. "Feelings, *emotions*, never played any part in what happened here tonight."

Austen bit his lip in an effort to control his growing anger. "Oh, thank you, Ms. Mallory—" he chuckled mirthlessly "—excuse me, I mean *Dr.* Mallory, for clearing all that up for me. I would have sworn that what happened between us tonight was due to this enormous feeling of affection I have for you, an affection I had rather hoped you reciprocated."

"Affection?" she sputtered. "*Affection?* You wouldn't know an honest emotion like affection if it kicked you in the backside." The concept that the best defense was a good offense flashed into Moriah's mind then, and because she didn't understand her current feelings of resentment, she decided they must naturally be Austen's fault. Therefore she attacked accordingly. Taking a menacing step toward him, she placed her hands on her hips in challenge, completely forgetting the fact that they still stood naked beside a waterfall in a veritable tropical paradise. "You can't be serious about anything! Everything's a joke for you, Austen, isn't it? As long as you've got your sailboat and your planter's punch, you can keep the world safely at bay. Well, I've got news for you, Captain Blye. There's more to this life than sensual gratification."

"No, *you're* wrong, Dr. Mallory," he countered viciously, his voice raised in undisguised resentment. "Because *you* think sensual gratification has no place in the human experience at all. Having a good time eludes you, doesn't it? You want to talk about emotions?" he demanded, taking her by the shoulders so forcefully she thought he would start to shake her any minute. "You've spent your entire life surrounded by a family whose members are so shallow and superficial that by their example alone they've managed to kill off any honest display of emotions their youngest child tried to maintain. *I'm* not the one who shies away from my feelings, Moriah, you are. Otherwise you'd have no trouble admitting that you're a passionate, caring woman who has wants and needs like every other human being on earth. Instead you hide behind textbooks and anthropological rhetoric to find excuses for every emotional response that dares brave entrance into your heart."

Moriah listened closely to every word Austen uttered and all the while told herself that none of them were true. "You're wrong," she finally told him softly, feeling the fight go out of her with the release of her pent-up breath. "Oh, Austen, you're so wrong."

Austen looked down into her eyes for a long time, watched as the emotions he swore she didn't claim flashed and warred deep inside their gray depths. "Then prove it," he murmured back to her. "Prove it to me, Moriah. I dare you."

Her brows drew downward almost as if she were experiencing pain, and with no small amount of surprise, Moriah realized that she was. Her stomach knotted fiercely around a cold clump at its center, and her heart actually ached with wanting the man who still held her so insistently. But she forced herself to admit that many of the accusations Austen had just hurled at her had been valid. Emotions weren't things that had come easily for her. Growing up in a family that placed finances first and loving one another last, she'd had to fight and claw to nurture her own feelings all her life. And for precisely that reason letting them go, sharing them with someone else, was a task that was more difficult than anything else she'd ever done.

Wordlessly she pulled herself free of Austen's now-loosened grasp on her arms and swam to the other side of the pool. She glanced quickly over her shoulder at him as she rose up out of the water, hating the look of disappointment that clouded his handsome features. She wished there was something she could say, something she could do that would make everything right between them. She wished she could go back to that first night in Charlotte Amalie and start all over again. But things had happened between them as they had, and no amount of wishing or regretting would ever change what they had said and done. Moriah reached up until she could feel the vines of the jungle floor curl around her fingers and give her a boost out of the pool. Once again she experienced the sensation that the island was asking her to stay. As she struggled to put her dry clothes back onto her damp body, she wondered how she would react if Austen voiced that very same question. With a sinking heart and sagging spirit, she was afraid she already knew the answer.

Chapter Nine

Moriah wasn't sure how she made it through the week that followed. Despite the fact that most of the time she felt as if she were trapped like an animal on the big sailboat, she was nonetheless able to find all the opportunity she needed to hide from Austen. However, every time she succeeded in eluding him for the day, she couldn't help but wonder if perhaps he was making her attempts to avoid him easier by being equally anxious to stay away from her. For the most part she had either kept to her cabin or stashed herself in a convenient nook on deck, always with her textbooks and notepads and always with the intention of totally immersing herself in her work. Yet inevitably her mind wandered back to that night on St. Martin—the night that had been so sultry and alluring, the night that had seemed torn like a flaming page from one of Morgana's torrid books. The night that Moriah, for the very first time in her life, had felt like the woman she wanted to be.

No, she instructed herself as she sat now on deck in the bow of the boat, she would not allow herself to think that. She had been the woman she wanted to be for most of her adult life, she reminded herself, long before she had ever heard of Austen Blye. He had nothing to do with who she was or what she would become. She was happy being herself—serious, sedate and intellectual—and she had absolutely no desire to change.

Oh, sure, a mutinous little voice deep inside of her piped up. Keep on telling yourself that and sooner or later you're bound to start believing it. You just better hope it's not too late when you do.

Moriah slapped closed the thick book on her lap and slammed it onto the deck beside her. She stuck her fingers under her glasses and rubbed her eyes restlessly, then pushed her bangs back from her forehead. The last time she had spoken to Austen had been two days before, when they had put in to Antigua. Before that, they hadn't exchanged words since the stilted ones that had split the air between them on their ride back to *Urizen* after Nat's party and the exquisite session of lovemaking that had followed it. On Antigua she had finally succumbed to her sisters' pointed jabs about not spending any time with them and had accompanied them on a shopping spree in the town of St. Johns. Morgana, Mathilda and Marissa had been deeply disappointed by the lack of pricey boutiques and jewelers, but Moriah had found quite charming the little shops full of locally made crafts and clothes, hand-printed fabrics and artwork. She had purchased several items that she hoped would warm the stark and dreary mood of her office at the university, then had worried that the souvenirs would only enhance the inherent loneliness that she'd always felt there in the first place. And if she placed her newfound treasures in her home, she'd realized more dismally, the effect would only be more disconcerting.

She had run into Austen purely by accident that day, when she had temporarily separated from her sisters to go in search of a particular island liqueur that one of the other professors at the university had requested she pick up for him. Inside a crowded and softly lighted shop whose walls were lined with bottles of liquor the way library shelves would display books, Moriah had glimpsed Austen chatting animatedly with a woman wearing a bikini top and a sarong—a young woman who looked as if she had yet to leave her teens, a beautiful woman with guileless eyes and a magnificent tan. Moriah had seen the two of them together and felt suddenly ill. Then almost as if she had called out to him, Austen's head had snapped up without warning, and he had caught her looking at him with who knows what kind of expression on her face. She'd hoped it was indifference, but had thought it more accurate that he'd seen desire and melancholy, because that's precisely what she had been feeling at the time. She had quickly looked away and made her purchase, hoping to escape into the passing stream of tourists before he approached her, and hadn't been surprised to hear him call out her name as she'd made a hasty retreat.

"Moriah, wait," he had requested breathlessly as he'd come up behind her, wrapping his fingers gently around her upper arm to slow her progress and turn her around to face him.

She had pivoted quickly to gaze at him, but had been unable to speak, uncertain what she should say.

"I really think we need to talk," he had told her. "About the other night. About what happened on St. Martin."

His eyes had been as tired and haunted-looking as her own had been when she'd looked in the mirror that morning, and she'd almost felt as sorry for him as she did for herself. Then she'd remembered the blonde in the sarong, remembered the way he had been smiling at her and touching her shoulder, and Moriah had become defensive.

"What's there to talk about?" she had demanded. "You've obviously found someone else with whom to pass the time. Why would you have anything to say to me?"

She had hated the sound of her voice as she'd said the words, had wished she'd sounded like something other than a jilted lover. She recalled that Austen had looked confused for some moments before he had finally spoken.

"You mean Candy?" He had inclined his head toward the shop they had just left and had started to chuckle like a man with a private joke on the rest of the world.

Candy, Moriah now repeated to herself with derision. What an apt name for the girl. She had wanted to hurl accusations at Austen, had wanted to tell him to go straight to hell. But then she had remembered that it was she who had decided that there was no future between the two of them, had reminded herself that what he said and did was of no interest or consequence to her. She had forced herself to remember that she couldn't care less. Then she had wanted to slap herself for being such a fool.

"Candy's the daughter of a good friend of mine," Austen had offered negligently. "She works there. I just stopped in to say hello and ask about her old man."

Moriah had felt relief wash over her then, had wanted to believe him more than anything in the world. Instead she had responded to him in a quick, unsteady rush. "I was supposed to meet my sisters fifteen minutes ago. I'm late. I have to run."

"Moriah, we need to talk," Austen had repeated insistently.

"Austen, I don't think we have anything to talk about," she had replied, turning her back on him once again. She had begun to briskly walk away, but the words he had called after her had slowed her steps to almost a halt.

"I see you've spent the day collecting souvenirs, Moriah. You might be sorry about that when you get home."

The fact that his warning had been so similar to her own earlier fears had stung Moriah deeply. But instead of turning around to face up to him, she had hastened her steps once more in an effort to flee as far from him as possible.

And she had been running ever since, she realized now as she sat on deck in her navy bathing suit and shorts, letting the heat of the midday sun warm the chill that had somehow settled into her bones despite the eighty-five-degree temperature. They were on their way to Martinique now, but everywhere Moriah looked she was surrounded by water. She had discovered that sitting in the bow of the boat with her back leaning against the forward mast was her favorite place to be on the fifty-one-foot ketch. Here she had a clear view of what lay before them and on all sides; here she did not have to see or care about what had gone before. The ocean was deep blue and gentle today, the sky cloudless and perfect, the air crisp, salty and clean. She could see for miles that it was smooth sailing ahead. She only wished she could say that was true of her life, as well.

Unfortunately she was still haunted by the specter of Austen Blye standing dripping wet and naked behind a waterfall with passion-darkened eyes. She wondered if there would ever be a time in her life when she would be completely free of him.

The following evening found the entire sailing party seated at dinner together for the first time since that fateful happy hour the first day they had set sail on *Urizen* nine evenings before. Austen had announced upon arriving in Martinique that morning that he knew unquestionably the best place for seafood on the island, and now the seven of them sat in eager anticipation of the delicacies they had ordered. Actually six of them sat in eager anticipation. Moriah sat in glum reluctance. If she was eagerly anticipating anything, it was a swift and final departure from the group that now surrounded her.

The restaurant was a small one, referred to by Austen as one of the many "feet in the water" restaurants in the tiny fishing village of Tartane on the Caravelle Peninsula. Although the building claimed a roof, there were no formal windows or doors, and Moriah felt as though she were dining outside, despite the candlelit room. Austen had recommended ordering the *oursin* or *boudin,* his personal favorites on the menu, but when Moriah had discovered that meant a choice of either sea urchin or creole blood sausage, she opted to go with the langouste instead, a clawless Caribbean lobster, with some *accras,* or vegetable fritters, on the side. She had, however, been helpless to prevent Austen from ordering a round of "le 'ti punch" for everyone, and having learned the hard way that punch in any form in the Caribbean packed more than a wallop, she sipped it experimentally. She had to admit that the curious mixture of rum, sugar, syrup and lime over crushed ice was quite refreshing.

Somehow she had managed to become seated directly across from Austen, and every time she glanced up from her menu or her plate or her lap, where her thumbs twiddled nervously, she was unable to see anything but his handsome face and the bland expression that made her feel as if he were looking straight through her. He was flanked on his left by Mathilda, more dressed up than usual, and by a dreamy-eyed, chattier-than-usual Marissa on his right. To Mathilda's left at the large round table was Dorian; beside him was Morgana, who sat at Moriah's right. Christian claimed Moriah's attention from her left, where he laughed continuously at his own childish stories of life at sea. Moriah tried to be as enthusiastic about his anecdotes as she had from the beginning, but unfortunately all of her attention was commanded by the scene being played out for her across the table.

"Do you know, Captain Blye," Marissa said sweetly as she draped her arm casually over the back of Austen's chair, "that I have been to Martinique once before on a photo shoot and didn't even realize that this was the same island until Morgana pointed it out to me?"

Somehow that didn't surprise Austen at all, but he politely replied, "No. Isn't that the strangest thing? I hate it when that happens."

"It happens to you, too?" Marissa asked brightly, plainly delighted to discover that she wasn't the only one who suffered from such a malady.

"All the time," Austen assured her good-naturedly. "Doesn't it, Dorian?"

Dorian nodded ruefully in agreement. "He's always gettin' Martinique mixed up with Dominica," the other man told their guests with a broad smile.

"Well, they are right next to each other, after all," Austen pointed out.

"Seems like that kind of confusion would be a tad inconvenient for someone who makes his livelihood taking paying customers from one island to another," Moriah mentioned tartly.

Austen glanced over at her then, loving the note of anger in her voice when she spoke to him. She cared, after all, he thought whimsically. Maybe there was hope for Moriah yet. "Nah," he told her. "I always remember at the last minute. Dorian reminds me."

Moriah raised her eyebrows at him skeptically but said nothing, turning her attention to the busy bar. Austen considered her attempt at indifference to be a very good sign.

"Anyway," Marissa went on, "it just goes to show you that these islands all start to look alike after a while."

"They only look alike to those whose vision is rather limited to begin with," Morgana muttered.

"Oh, you're one to talk about vision, Morgana." Mathilda was quick to jump to her younger sister's defense, not because she was anxious to stand up for Marissa but because she relished an opportunity to argue with Morgana. "Especially tunnel vision. When are you going to write a book that features something a little different? Like a solid plot or three-dimensional characters?"

Great, Austen thought. Here we go again. The war of the Mallorys wages violently onward. Ever since they'd left St. Thomas the three elder sisters had indulged in a continuous flow of backbiting and power-playing as some perverted form of familial and social intercourse to pass the time. He had noted long ago that Moriah remained conspicuously silent whenever the group of women congregated, letting her sisters go on with their bickering without ever challenging any of them—even during those times when they targeted her with what they honestly seemed to believe was innocent teasing, but which in fact left Moriah clearly feeling hurt and insulted. Maybe tonight would be different, he thought suddenly. Maybe tonight they'd go too far, and their youngest sister would break free from the mousy, insecure facade she hid behind whenever her siblings were around. Maybe tonight she'd face up to her desires, he added, thinking that if he was going to fantasize, he might as well do it thoroughly. And maybe tonight she would admit that she cared for him as much as he did for her.

"Marissa," he interrupted the sisters' heated conversation quickly, hoping to defuse the potentially explosive discussion that might ensue otherwise. "That really is a lovely outfit you have on. What did you say that was called?"

Marissa positively beamed at the singular attention she was receiving from Austen, and her triumphant smile made Moriah's stomach clench. "It's a Bundy," she announced smugly at the revealing two-piece miniskirt and halter set. "The Australian designer, T. Q. Bundy, designed it specifically for me. He fell in love with me at first sight when he met me in New York, and he did an entire line inspired by the cool, detached attitude I assume when I do runway work."

"I see," Austen replied with a nod, hoping he sounded properly impressed. "It's quite becoming."

"Thank you," Marissa acknowledged, sounding very satisfied.

Not one to play favorites, Austen turned then to Mathilda and said, "It finally hit me this afternoon why it is you look so familiar. You've done commercials, haven't you?"

Mathilda looked stunned. "Why, yes," she told him. "But that was years ago. They aren't shown on television anymore. And I'm thankful for that, I might add."

"But why?" Austen asked, hoping he sounded surprised. "That one where you played Lady Macbeth to a cornflake was a classic. And maybe they don't show them in the States anymore, but I've seen that cornflake one down here a dozen times in the past few months."

Mathilda's face went white. "Where's a phone?" she demanded with a gasp. "I have to call my agent immediately."

"And by the way, Morgana," he added as Mathilda pushed her chair quickly and with a violent scrape away from the table, "I read part of *Passion Rides a Spotted Horse* not too long ago. Moriah loaned me her copy. It was incredible. Really, just incredible. I don't think I've ever been quite that, uh, moved by a book in my entire life."

Morgana smiled with utter confidence, clearly indicating she heard such praise all the time. "I'm glad you like it, Austen," she told him. "Men so seldom seem to take my books in the spirit in which they are intended. It's good to know you aren't one of the shortsighted."

"Oh, no way," he assured her. "I definitely took it in the spirit in which it was intended. Didn't I, Moriah?"

Moriah, who had been trying her best not to hear the praise Austen heaped so freely on her sisters, started visibly then, her eyes wide and full of panic when they came to settle on him. "What?" she stammered quickly. "I…I'm sorry. I wasn't paying attention."

"Austen was just telling me how much he likes *Passion*," Morgana said, using the shortened form of her title the way she normally did with her books.

Moriah blinked in confusion, wondering why Austen would have revealed something of such a personal nature to her sister. "He what?" she asked vaguely.

"He said you had shared it with him and that he found it quite enjoyable," Morgana repeated.

Moriah's face paled at Morgana's statement. Her eyes flew to Austen's face, and her heart hammered hard in her throat at the curl of his silly smile and the laughter in his eyes. How could he have told her sister about what had happened? she wondered in stark horror. And how could he find it so funny that he had? "Oh, Austen, how could you?" she murmured miserably.

Austen's face fell at her question. "How could I what?" he asked her, obviously very confused.

"How could you have told them about what happened between us?" she insisted.

"Moriah, I didn't tell them anything," Austen assured her. "I just told Morgana how much I like the book you shared with me on the beach on St. Martin," he added meaningfully.

When Moriah realized the colossally embarrassing mistake she had made, what color was left in her cheeks quickly drained, only to be replaced by a vivid scarlet flush. "Oh," she said very quietly.

"Oh, ho," Marissa rejoined with a victorious smile. "So what's been going on between our little Mo and the charter-boat captain?" the model wanted to know.

"Nothing," Moriah pledged hastily.

"That's not the impression I get at all," Morgana said with genuine interest, eyeing her youngest sister with intent speculation.

Mathilda chose that moment to rejoin the group with the unhappily muttered explanation that her agent was currently unavailable, and gazed with curiosity at the group of diners. "What's up?" she asked Morgana, whose eyes fairly glowed with the light of discovery.

Morgana sat forward and tented her fingertips on the table, and Moriah would have sworn she licked her lips eagerly before she said, "It seems that our little Mo has been promoting a dalliance with the dashing Captain Blye."

"No!" Mathilda chuckled with delight. "Oh, this *is* going to make for some interesting conversation."

"Please don't start up, you guys," Moriah pleaded with her sisters. She would never hear the end of it if she didn't put a stop to their teasing right now. She could already hear future vacation exchanges between the elder Mallorys about that little trip to the Caribbean when Mo fell madly in love with the charter-boat captain who scarcely knew that she was alive except to wish that she was someone else. "There's nothing to discuss," she told them.

Marissa's smile broadened as she turned to Austen. "Is that true, Captain?" she asked him sweetly.

Austen had never felt more trapped in his life. He told himself that Moriah had gotten herself into this by jumping to the conclusion that he would be shallow and callous

enough to discuss their lovemaking with her sisters. But
he hated to see the way they baited and taunted her, and
he hated even more the fact that she would let them get
away with it. He told himself to let her fight her own battles. But he knew that she would not. He thought for a moment to himself. Not, that is, unless she had the proper
ammunition. Or, more correctly in this case, the proper
provocation.

"Actually," he began, trying to choose his words carefully,
"I think you're all misunderstanding Moriah's reaction to
what Morgana just said."

Oh, thank you, Austen, Moriah thought, mentally releas-
ing a deep sigh of relief. I knew I could count on you.

"While it's true that Moriah has tried to keep her feelings
a secret, I do believe she's nurturing rather a large crush on
me. But," he hastened to add, "I can assure each and every
one of you that I've done nothing to promote any kind of 'dalliance,' as you call it, between the two of us."

"What?" Moriah gasped in stunned horror.

But Austen continued on blithely as if he'd never heard her.
"I think you'll all agree that she's just too innocent and vulnerable to understand complicated emotions like love."

Moriah's jaw dropped down in amazed and righteous
anger. How dare he? she thought indignantly. How *dare* he?
He was talking about her as if she weren't even there, was
dismissing her as easily as her sisters always did. Well, if he
thought he could get away with that, he had another think
coming. She opened her mouth to blast the smug little grin
right off of Austen Blye's charming face, noting absently
that he was looking as if he actually welcomed such an outburst, when Morgana interjected.

"Of course that's true," her eldest sister said with a decisive
nod. "It's always been that way. She's always been so stu-

dious, so wrapped up in her lessons, that she's never had the opportunity to experience most of life's basic education."

No, that wasn't true, Moriah wanted to say. She'd never had the opportunity because no one in her family had ever allowed her the chance. *They* had all been the ones who insisted her studies were the only thing she'd be capable of pursuing successfully, and they were the ones who had prevented her from reaching out to touch life.

"Teddy and Diana never should have let her out of their sight," Mathilda agreed. "She just hasn't been the same since she went away to Harvard. She didn't get a fully rounded education because she was so focused on anthropology. She's always been so bogged down with her tribal cultures and has so many confused and primitive ideas about how the world should work. She doesn't give a thought to the way things really are."

You're so wrong, Mathilda, Moriah wanted to scream. I know exactly how things really are, but that doesn't mean they have to remain that way. I'm not the one who's confused at this table. Everyone else with the last name of Mallory is.

"And she really doesn't have a clue about the rules of the fashion industry," Marissa added, the only thing that had ever really bothered her about her youngest sister. "I've tried my best with her, but she's just impossible."

All right, that does it, Moriah decided silently. This has gone far enough. There is absolutely nothing wrong with my wardrobe, and it's perfect for the lifestyle I lead.

She looked at each one of her sisters carefully, repeating to herself her objections to every statement they had made. She opened her mouth to voice her protests out loud, very loud, but something deep inside her kept the words from coming out. Why bother? she thought sullenly. Suddenly Moriah was very tired. Tired of listening, tired of arguing, tired of the Mallory battles that waged continuously on and on. What difference would it make to fight them? she asked herself. As she took in her three sisters' countenances, the vague looks, the expressions of utter confidence in their self-righteousness, she knew it would be fruitless to challenge their accusations. They would believe what they wanted to believe, and nothing she said would ever change that. As she always did when confronted by her sisters' invalid charges of incompetency and lack of emotion, Moriah folded miserably. She chose not to ponder the fact that she had always in her adult life reacted in such a cowardly way, chose not to accept that by being silent after so many such sessions, she was as guilty of allowing their misinformed, disheartening analysis of her character as they were of offering it.

On the other side of the table, Austen had watched Moriah's growing indignation with respect and anticipation. He loved the black looks of exasperation and disbelief that crossed her face, loved the glitter of combat that made her eyes flash with fire. She was beautiful when she was angry. She wasn't going to let them get away with it this time, he thought. She was going to tell her sisters exactly where to get off, was going to assert her power as an intelligent, well-rounded individual to instruct them all to go straight to hell. He waited for the words that would free her from the mold she had allowed her family to enclose her in all her life. And waited. And waited. And waited.

But no contradiction came. No assertion of her character, no defense of her feelings and emotions, no condemnation of her sisters' thoughtless behavior. Moriah just sat dumbly in her place, silently indicating to everyone present that she agreed with every patronizing, demoralizing word her sisters said about her. And that's when Austen got angry. Angry with Moriah's total lack of response, and angry with himself because maybe he'd been wrong about her, after all. Maybe her emotions didn't run as deeply as he'd thought. Maybe she was just as shallow and superficial as her sisters. Maybe she was as dry, humorless and unfeeling as she claimed to be. Then he remembered the first hot night on St. Thomas, recalled their steamy session on St. Martin. Moriah Mallory shallow and emotionless? Not a chance.

Then why was it so impossible for her to stand up for herself? Why was she so willing to be stuffed into the shell of a woman she didn't really want to be? Why couldn't she allow herself to be the Moriah he'd met in Charlotte Amalie, the Moriah with whom he'd made love under a rushing waterfall, the Moriah he was so absolutely certain that she wanted to be? Why couldn't she be the woman he loved?

Austen had never been confronted by such a question. Because, quite simply, he had never before been in love. And the idea that he had fallen in love with a woman he had seen only a few times, a woman who insisted she was not who he thought her to be, was more than frustrating. It was enough to drive a man insane. She *was* the Moriah he'd met on St. Thomas, wasn't she? That *was* the real woman who lay beneath the facade, wasn't it? Or was it? Maybe he *had* fallen in love with who he wanted her to be. Maybe she *wasn't* what he thought she was. Was it possible that he could be so mistaken? Could it be that Moriah Mallory was in fact no more than the quiet, unassuming little sister who sat so dispiritedly among her family as they chatted on blindly about her?

Austen was getting a headache. He lifted his fingers to his forehead and pressed hard, but relief was not to be had. When their dinner was served, he found that the food he normally loved held no appeal for him tonight. All he wanted, he discovered, was a golden-haired woman with dangerous curves and no inhibitions to come back to him and laugh as freely and as confidently as she had the first time he'd seen her. Instead he ordered another drink, hoping it might alleviate at least some of the frustration that gripped him so acutely when he looked at and wondered about the woman seated across the table.

The following morning found Moriah lying alone on the white-sand beach at Les Salines near Ste. Anne on the Caribbean side of the island. She'd been told by one of the locals to avoid the northern stretches of Atlantic coastline as the surf was far too dangerous for swimming, and had been pointed in this direction instead. Although most of the women around her were sunbathing topless and apparently harbored no concern whatsoever, Moriah couldn't even entertain the thought of seeing herself so exposed in public. In a way she felt uncomfortable because she was so obviously and thoroughly covered, but to be so uninhibited was an alien concept to her. Of course, she reminded herself, she would have thought that making love under the moon and a waterfall in the middle of the jungle would be something of an alien concept to her, too, but that hadn't prevented it from happening, had it?

Moriah pushed the frustrating thought away and instead tried to concentrate on relaxing. She had purposely left all reading material and notes aboard *Urizen,* determined to spend at least one day without a care in the world. Of course, that was going to be very difficult when thoughts of Austen Blye kept thrusting themselves so forcefully into her brain, but Moriah had convinced herself that she *would* enjoy herself on this vacation if it was the last thing she ever did. And that was that.

When she felt the sun blocked from her view, she had a swift reminder of the afternoon on St. Martin when Austen had joined her on the beach, and she was relieved when she opened her eyes to see Christian standing over her instead.

"Well, hello there, Mr. Christian," she greeted him by the name that always made him giggle. Today it had the same effect. "Where did you come from?"

"Dorian's been helpin' me dig a big hole in de sand," the little boy told her.

"Why would you want to do that?" Moriah asked him. "Wouldn't you rather build a castle instead?"

"Nah," Christian told her with a swift shake of his damp head. "De ocean, she always tear de castles down. But if you dig a hole big and wide enough, you can catch her for a little while."

Moriah laughed. "Only for a little while?"

Christian sighed ruefully. "She always get away somehow. Dorian say de ocean is very aloo…aloos…"

"Elusive," Dorian helped out his younger brother as he joined them. "Just like all women," he added with a smile. "Hello, Moriah, how are you?"

Moriah smiled back. "I'm fine, thanks. And I do believe you just made a sexist remark, but I'm not sure."

Dorian shook his head resolutely. "I hold women in de highest regard," he assured her.

Moriah raised herself up on her elbows and squinted at the glare of the sun. "I think you've been hanging around Austen too long."

Dorian laughed. "You might have a point dere."

Half expecting the other man to show up at the mention of his name, Moriah was somewhat surprised to find that Austen wasn't with his friend. "Where is he?" she asked before she could stop the question from forming on her lips.

"At Shinty's," Dorian told her. "Visitin' friends."

"Shinty's?" Moriah asked.

"It's a bar down on de waterfront."

"Oh." Moriah couldn't keep her voice from sounding small and insecure, because small and insecure was exactly how she felt at the moment. She remembered Nat's words about Austen's habit of frequenting such bars with "nubile, blonde bimbettes." Digging her fist violently into the sand beside her towel, Moriah came up with a handful of the sun-warmed granules and watched as they sifted slowly through her fingers and back to earth.

"Have you known Austen a long time?" she asked Dorian, no longer trying to deny her constant curiosity about the man who had monopolized her thoughts, dreams and fantasies since the day she had first met him.

"'Bout five years or so," Dorian told her, watching with obvious loving care as his little brother scurried toward a spot on the beach just beyond reach of the waves to start another excavation. "I met him on St. Thomas a few months before he came down here for good." He laughed sadly and shook his dark head in rueful memory. "Boy, what a night dat was," he remembered aloud. "Austen was blind drunk. I had to pull him up outta de gutter where he'd fallen. Somebody had lifted his wallet, and he had no identification. He told me he was a banker, but I didn't believe him."

"I still can't believe that about him," Moriah admitted.

"It's hard to imagine," Dorian agreed. "I brought him back to my boat and got him sobered up. But he kept on mumblin' 'bout some woman named Pamela, kept talkin' 'bout how much he hated his job at de bank. He was pretty bad."

"What did he say about Pamela?" Moriah asked slowly, hoping she sounded indifferent, knowing instead that she was probably as transparent as glass.

Dorian turned to look at her, clearly sympathetic to her reasons for asking, and shook his head. "Nothin' I could understand," he told her. "And when he was sober again, I didn't think to go askin'. I did tell him, though, dat if he was so unhappy in his job, den maybe it was time to work elsewhere, where he might be happier. After all," he added, looking Moriah straight in the eye, making her feel as if they were no longer talking about Austen, "one life is all we get, you know? We better make sure we take de right road down, otherwise, we gonna wander until de wrong one ends in darkness."

When he glanced back to where his brother had wandered out into the surf, Dorian jumped up and shouted, "Christian!" with a laugh, running to pull a squealing, delighted Christian back up to the shore. Moriah watched the two brothers tussle affectionately for a long time, thinking about what the elder one had just told her. So Austen had gone on a bender after something had destroyed his relationship with Pamela, she thought. Obviously he had loved her very much to have been so utterly shattered by their separation. The knowledge made Moriah's heart hurt. She told herself that it didn't matter, that it was better she knew that Austen had once loved a woman with such complete devotion. It offered her yet another excuse to assure herself it would be wrong to become involved with him. He probably still carried a raging torch for the other woman, could probably never give fully of himself again.

Even as she presented herself with that logic, Moriah knew it was seriously flawed. There was no foundation on which to base her assumptions, no solid evidence to support them. Still she clung to the idea that Austen couldn't love her the way she wanted and needed to be loved. Because her earlier conviction that she wasn't his type was beginning to crumble fast. More and more she felt herself changing, becoming the kind of woman Austen told her she wanted to be. She'd been having stirrings of unfamiliar emotions ever since she'd met him on St. Thomas. She didn't understand the new feelings, didn't want to even admit to having them. She only knew that slowly but surely they were making their presence known, and for some reason, she wasn't all that disturbed by them. It struck her that somehow an entirely new person was emerging from the ashes of awkward little Mo and the staid Professor Mallory, as if the two had meshed and would ultimately result in a stronger, more determined woman. How this could happen when both had been such spineless saps to begin with was a mystery, but Moriah suspected that a strong helping of Austen Blye had acted as a catalyst.

But there was still a lot of the old Moriah left in her, still a good portion of the uncertain, awkward woman she had been all of her life. The metamorphosis, she realized uneasily, was nowhere near complete. Because all of these new feelings were still quite alien and unfamiliar. And as much as it galled Moriah to admit it, they scared her. They scared her a lot.

Chapter Ten

That afternoon Moriah returned to the sailboat long enough to change from her bathing suit into a conservative white cotton shirt, a navy knee-length straight skirt and flat blue espadrilles. She replaited her hair and donned her glasses, then went in search of a cab to take her to the Musée Départmental de la Martinique. She was not only very interested in viewing the exhibits of early island cultures the museum had to offer, but had the added intention of keeping an appointment she had scheduled before leaving Philadelphia, meeting with a fellow anthropology professor from Paris who was doing research on the island. Dr. Maurice Parmentier was very well-known within the scientific community for his studies of the ancient Arawaks, and Moriah was very much looking forward to meeting him, having been a fan of his books and essays since she was a student at Harvard.

As she stood anxiously by the curb to hail an approaching taxi, she noted larger, darker fingers lifting high above her own, and followed the length of corded, bronzed arm attached to them until she came eye to eye with Austen.

"Hi," he greeted her with his most disarming smile. "Where ya goin'?"

Seconds ticked by as she gazed at him, still unsure of her feelings about the whole situation surrounding them, but loving the way he looked in his loose khaki trousers and breezy white cotton shirt. The sun was very bright that day, as it had been every day, and Moriah felt herself wanting to reach over and trace the lines that fanned out from his eyes as he squinted down at her in the blinding glare. He was so handsome, she thought. She'd never met anyone who smiled nearly all the time. It knocked her off guard and made her heart skip and dance in irregular rhythms.

"Hi," she returned his salutation automatically. "I'm going to the museum. I have an appointment with a professor there."

"Another anthropologist?" Austen asked her.

"Yes."

"Can I come, too?"

She lifted her brows at him in surprise, wondering why on earth he would want to. "I really don't think you'd enjoy it," she told him. "It's going to be pretty dry stuff for someone like you."

His smile fell at her statement. "Someone like me?" he asked her. "You mean someone immature and uneducated who can't be serious for a minute?"

Moriah sighed quietly, wishing she could take back the words she had so thoughtlessly hurled at him on St. Martin. "No, I don't mean that at all," she told him softly. "I just mean that since you're not an anthropologist yourself and apparently don't take any interest in what I do for a living, you probably won't find much to keep your attention, that's all."

"Who says I don't take an interest in what you do for a living?" he wanted to know, and if she hadn't known better she would have thought he sounded almost hurt.

She lifted one shoulder in a careless shrug. "You keep insisting it isn't what I want to do," she pointed out. "And you just don't seem to think it's a very important pursuit."

Austen shook his head at her slowly, biting his lip as if he were guarding his words carefully. "You've misunderstood me, Moriah," he said. "I want you to be and do whatever you want. I just want you to be sure that what you are is a result of your desires and no one else's. And I'm not quite convinced that's the case."

His assertion was offered with such quiet sincerity that Moriah found it impossible to be angry with what he said. There was also the fact that she could no longer completely disagree with his analysis of her character. She wasn't sure of her motivations lately, either. She was more confused about herself and her life now than she'd ever been before, but more than anything else, she was confounded by the feelings Austen Blye aroused in her. She knew she should tell him she had no desire for his company today, but if she was honest with herself, she knew that simply wasn't true. Despite her confusion and everything that went along with it, she had to admit that she still preferred being with Austen to being alone.

"All right, if you really want to come, you can," she acquiesced. Then she cautioned him firmly. "But I don't want to find myself involved in any conversations about not doing and being what I want to do and be."

"I promise," he vowed, lifting his hand once again to summon a cab. He added silently to himself, *I just want you to be happy, Moriah. I want you to be yourself.*

* * *

Professor Maurice Parmentier looked as much like an anthropologist as Moriah did not. He was a small man, well past his sixties, with thinning white hair that fell carelessly past his collar, thick-framed glasses, rumpled, outdated clothes and crepe-soled shoes. During the trio's exchange of introductions, he smiled at Moriah and shook her hand vigorously up and down, telling her how much he had genuinely enjoyed her book on the primitive tribes of Peru and Venezuela.

"You never told me you'd written a book," Austen said softly from behind her as Professor Parmentier led them toward the exhibits on the Arawak tribe.

"You never asked," she replied absently over her shoulder.

"And I read your series of articles on the Taino Indians in *Today's Anthropologist*, Dr. Mallory," Professor Parmentier told her further when he overheard Austen's remark. "I was quite impressed with your treatment of the Spanish enslavement of the tribes on Puerto Rico in the 1500s. You should make that the premise of your next book."

"It's interesting you should say that, Professor Parmentier," Moriah told him. "Because that's precisely what I have in mind for my *third* book. My second focuses on the migration routes the Arawaks may have taken from one island to another and where their origins actually lay."

"That's wonderful," he applauded her. "That's a topic that has needed further inspection for some time. I look forward to your new book's publication."

"I'll send you an advance copy," she offered.

"Merci beaucoup," he thanked her with a dazzling smile that charmed Moriah all the way to her toes. "I would very much appreciate it." He placed his hand protectively in the small of her back and extended his hand forward. "Come. The exhibit we discussed on the phone last month is this way."

Austen watched through slitted eyes as Moriah followed the French scientist toward an entry to their right. He listened closely throughout the rest of the afternoon as the two professors exchanged heavy anthropological rhetoric, noting with something akin to resentment the animation that overcame Moriah when she talked with such precision and specificity about her studies. She was utterly absorbed in her conversation with Professor Parmentier that grew more and more incomprehensible to Austen with every new exhibit, and she hung on every word the older man uttered. With a start of surprise, Austen realized he was jealous, not only of the attention Moriah was paying to the other man, but also of the subject matter about which he was completely ignorant. She really did love her job, he recognized with awe. She really did take an interest in what she did for a living, and she was clearly well-informed and well respected within the academic community. She really was extremely intelligent and very intellectual. It shouldn't be such a surprise to him, he told himself. And it shouldn't hurt to discover it.

But it did hurt. Because now Austen really began to wonder if he *had* been wrong about Moriah, after all. His doubts had started forming over dinner the previous evening, when he had begun to doubt that she would ever break free of the domination she had allowed her family to have over her for years. And now to see her with her colleague, spouting words and quoting theories he couldn't begin to understand, as if she used them over breakfast every morning, only served to air his crumbling convictions. Maybe the Moriah he'd met on St. Thomas *was* a fluke, he thought. Perhaps the only reason she had been the way she was that night was because, as she had said, she'd had too much to drink. After all, she had been drinking that night at Nat's party before they'd made love, he remembered, because she'd been holding a rum punch when he found her talking to his friend. Of course, drinking is as common as breathing in the Caribbean, he reminded himself, but still…

He looked at Moriah once again as she stood at Professor Parmentier's side inspecting examples of early Arawak tools. Her spine was as straight as an arrow, her clothing plain, conservative and very much befitting a cultural anthropologist. She spoke crisply and confidently about an ancient tribe that was long ago crushed by the invasion of civilization, and it was as if it were the only thing of importance in the modern world. Her eyes were bright, her skin flushed, all with the excitement of intellectual intercourse, and the man who commanded her attention at the moment was aged, balding, stoop-shouldered and small. Austen began to wonder what she had ever seen in a simple charter-boat captain to begin with.

As they left the museum, Moriah was full of plans for her research when she returned to Philadelphia. As Fort-de-France disappeared behind the back of their taxi and they headed toward where the boat was anchored at Tartane, she chatted happily and with excitement about her return.

"I can't wait to get back home and get to work on my new book," she told Austen as she gazed out the window at the passing scenery, loving the way the green mountains rose up to greet the blue sky. "I have so much to do. Talking with Maurice really got me inspired. I have so much to do!"

"Maurice?" Austen asked petulantly. "Isn't that a little informal for such a distinguished scholar? The guy's old enough to be your grandfather," he pointed out.

Moriah turned her head to look at Austen in confusion. "He asked me to call him Maurice," she said blankly.

"Yeah, I'll just bet he did."

His derisive tone of voice raised Moriah's hackles. "Just what are you trying to insinuate?" she demanded.

After feeling slighted and ignored all afternoon, Austen couldn't have controlled his angry emotions now if he'd wanted to. "Oh, come on, Moriah, I saw the way the guy was looking at you," he told her.

"What?" she cried in disbelief. "As you just pointed out, the man is a scholar and old enough to be my grandfather. How could he possibly have been looking at me as anything other than a colleague?"

"Oh, right," Austen sneered. "If that's the way he looks at a colleague, I'd hate to see his reaction to one of the women who hang out down by the waterfront. Of course, you were doing nothing to discourage him," he added spitefully.

"Oh, so now you're calling me a prostitute?" she challenged in a deceptively controlled voice.

"Of course not—"

"Now you listen to me, Austen Blye," she quickly cut him off. "Just because it's impossible for you to look at a woman as anything but a sexy toy doesn't mean there aren't men, real men, out there who can view a woman as an intelligent human being who might have something substantial, even intellectual, to offer."

"Moriah, that wasn't what I—"

"I have *had* it," she went on relentlessly, "with your suave innuendos, your continuous sexual implications and your juvenile approach to any kind of attraction we might happen to have for each other. I don't want to hear another word!"

"But—"

"Not one word. I've told you what kind of woman I am all along, but you've insisted on seeing me as the kind of woman I am not. If you can't look beyond the basic, physical similarities I just happen to have in common with other women and see that I'm not like the ones with whom you're so used to associating, then you're the one who has a problem, not me. I'm not who you think I am, Austen," she said slowly, enunciating each word as if she were talking to a simpleton. "Deal with it."

Austen didn't say another word after that. She had spelled out for him precisely what had been nudging his suspicions in the back of his mind since last night. She *was* Professor Mallory, Ph.D., and she *was* little Mo Mallory, youngest sibling of the spectacular Mallory sisters. She wasn't the laughing, high-spirited Moriah he had met in a bar in Charlotte Amalie. Apparently that woman only existed at the bottom of a glass of planter's punch. Several planter's punches, he amended. With some nautical nogs thrown on top. The realization quieted him, made him feel dismal and bereft. He had fallen in love with a woman who didn't exist, a woman who would haunt him until his dying breath and a woman who wouldn't, couldn't, ever love him back.

Unfortunately Moriah wasn't nearly as easily swayed by her assertion as Austen had apparently been. She had offered it with all the conviction she could muster, hoping to convince herself as much as she did him. She assured herself that all it would take was a little chat with herself to reestablish all her earlier confidence in the path she'd chosen for her life. However, she still wasn't certain if she'd actually chosen the path or been pushed in that direction by her family's treatment of her all those years. If she were honest with herself, she knew she couldn't blame them exclusively, as convenient and appealing as that course might be. If her life wasn't exactly what she wanted it to be, it was because she had allowed it to reach such a point. And for that reason, if for no other, Moriah *had* to believe she had been doing what she wanted to do all along, *had* to believe that her life was precisely on the road she had always wanted it to take.

As the two of them sat in stilted silence for the rest of the drive back to the boat, Moriah was able to convince herself that her forcefully delivered words were true. As a result, she—and Austen, who'd obviously come to the same conclusions—was in no mood to join the others for dinner that evening and wandered off to be alone. *Urizen* would set sail at midnight that night for a final destination south that Austen had promised them all they would love. At the moment, Moriah thought, the only thing that seemed attractive to her was the prospect of ending this farce and returning to her normal ways of life. The fact that she might never be able to enjoy it in quite the same way again was something she was afraid to consider.

When Moriah heard *Urizen*'s anchor dropping two days later, she was sitting in her cabin with a pencil clenched between her teeth, organizing the notes she had taken during her visit with Maurice Parmentier. Even with the portholes and hatch open to allow in the breeze, the heat of the early afternoon had gotten to her in the tiny room, and she had changed into her navy bathing suit and shorts once again. She heard Austen cry out the words, "Land ho!" as he had done whenever they'd arrived at their destination, and she rolled her eyes heavenward at the unnecessary announcement. During the entire cruise, they had seldom been completely out of sight of the numerous islands dotting the string that comprised the West Indies, and the fact alone that they had dropped anchor, and that the rattle of the chain had slowed when no more than a dozen feet of line had fallen, indicated to Moriah and anyone else who might be listening that they were indeed quite close to land.

She raised her head to the sound of footsteps racing along the deck, then the excited laughter and remarks from her

sisters as they passed by the open portholes, extolling the
wonders and beauty of the sight that met their eyes. Telling
herself she was only curious to know what could possibly
have them behaving like children without reservation or in-
hibition, Moriah pulled the pencil from her teeth and stuck
it in her hair below her braid. She tucked her notes neatly and
methodically into their color-coded folders and stacked them
alphabetically on the floor beside the bed. When she could
find no other excuse to stall, she left the cabin that had become such a sanctuary for her and joined the others up on the
deck.

When she rose from the companionway, Moriah saw the
sight she had seen so many times before, the endless stretch
of the Caribbean as it traveled out to meet the horizon. However, when she turned toward the bow of the boat where her
sisters were standing with Austen, Dorian and Christian, she
was drawn to the scene before them like a daffodil turns to
the morning sun.

The beach that stretched across the island before them
like a bright white ribbon was one of the most beautiful sights
Moriah had ever beheld. It was perfect—pearly, spotless
sand, a gentle swell of surf, waters of crystal and emerald and
sapphire, and utterly, completely deserted. At the middle of
it all stood what she supposed was a hotel, though no sign
proclaimed it as such. It was a two-story structure made of
wood long ago bleached gray by the sun and salt. Several sets
of French doors were thrown open in welcome on the upstairs
level, while the first floor boasted a wraparound porch beneath a wide veranda. Behind the building, stately palms
reached high for the sky, while before it smaller versions of
the trees grew just above the second story. Stairs led down to
the beach, but no one was there to appreciate the setting.
There were no other boats anchored offshore as there had

been everywhere else they had traveled, and Moriah got the not quite unsettling feeling that the small group aboard *Urizen* might be the only people left on earth.

"Where are we?" she asked no one in particular.

Austen came up behind her silently, and she started visibly when she heard his deep voice only inches from her ear. "I told you you'd love it," he said softly.

She turned to meet his gaze then, entranced by the mysterious intensity with which he looked at her, and whispered, "I've never seen anything more beautiful."

He stared at her for a moment longer before murmuring, "I have."

Moriah felt her heart take flight at his words and ordered herself to stop acting like a teenager with her first crush. She closed her eyes briefly then opened them again, but Austen was still looking at her the way he used to, with the sparkle he'd always had in his eyes before. Before she had convinced him she wasn't the woman of his dreams. "Where…where are we?" she repeated.

"Yes, Austen, where are we?" she heard Marissa demand insistently, and Moriah was forced to recall that her sisters were along with her on this trip.

"This island doesn't have a name," he told them, letting his attention wander reluctantly from Moriah to return to the other women who encircled him. "But Dorian and I make it a stop on all of our charters. It's a nice place to spend the last couple of days unwinding. And I have a very good friend who lives here," he added.

"Oh, you do not," Moriah stated adamantly in disbelief. "You can't possibly have a good friend on every single island in the Caribbean."

Austen smiled at her smugly. "I hate to break this to you, Moriah, but I do have a good friend who lives on this island.

Actually she used to live on this island," he amended. "But she's visiting again for a few months this summer—"

"She?" Moriah was helpless to stop the petulant sounding interruption from leaving her mouth.

"—with her husband and daughter," Austen finished with a grin.

"Oh." Moriah looked quickly away from his self-satisfied expression and back toward the beach.

"When can we go ashore?" Morgana wanted to know.

"Anytime you want," Austen told her. "You can either swim or we can take the dinghy."

"A swim sounds lovely," Mathilda said. "Who'll join me?"

"I'll go with you, Mathilda," Christian piped up immediately.

"Oh, I might as well swim in, too," Morgana agreed.

"I always swim from the boat to shore," Austen added. "It's a terrific workout."

"I…I think I'll wait for the dinghy," Moriah mumbled.

"Me, too," Marissa nodded.

Dorian looked over at the two women and shook his head almost imperceptibly, clearly disappointed by their absence of adventuresome spirit. "I'll get it ready," he told them.

By the time Moriah and Marissa made it to shore with Dorian, the others had already been in the hotel and helped themselves to beer and rum from the bar. Austen urged the newcomers to do likewise, assured them that they shouldn't feel uncomfortable about taking charge in such a way, explaining that this was the way things were done on this particular island. They would simply keep track of their own tabs and pay the bill before their departure. No problem.

When Moriah looked to Dorian for confirmation, the other man nodded his agreement. "It's cool," he told her. "We know de owner."

Yet still no one appeared to claim the hotel—no owner, no manager, no custodian. Moriah began to feel as if the place were almost unreal, as if it were a type of Brigadoon that simply appeared out of a timeless dimension for one day at a time for their exclusive enjoyment. It was a wonderful place, she had to admit as she explored the spacious building. The whitewashed walls were adorned with some of the most breathtaking watercolor paintings she had ever seen, scenes of the beach, the ocean and the hotel done by someone who obviously knew this island very well. And in a small room off the lobby, there was a most amazing library for an island so tiny. She quickly scanned the hundreds of titles that rose floor to ceiling, before her eyes settled on a book she had not read since she was a teenager. *Jane Eyre* had always been one of her favorites, she remembered. It had been ever so long since she had retreated into the kind of escape such a novel could provide.

Hugging the book to her heart in an unconscious gesture, Moriah began to head back out to the beach. When she approached the spot on the sand where the others had spread towels and started happy hour, she realized there were more people present than there had been when she left. Quite a few more. As she drew closer, she heard Austen making introductions.

"General and Mrs. Ruben Morales," he said of the eldest couple who were tethering two horses to one of the palm trees near the hotel. The man was very tall and had made up for his loss of gray hair by growing a thick, bushy mustache. His wife, who identified herself as Teresa, was petite and quick to smile, with salt-and-pepper curls and eyes that glittered with mischief.

"Diego and Gabriela Santos," Austen introduced the second couple, close in age to the Moraleses, but both heavier set, he with wavy white hair and she with a bright orange chignon.

"The writer?" Morgana asked with great interest.

"Yes, I'm afraid so," Diego told her with a modest smile.

"It is *so* nice to meet you," Morgana said, and Moriah couldn't remember a time when she'd ever seen her sister genuinely impressed by another human being. "We have a lot to talk about."

The last couple that joined the small group had lagged well behind the others, strolling hand in hand in the surf as they kept a close eye on the laughing little girl who splashed before them. This couple was much younger than the others, and Moriah had to honestly admit that she had never seen a more attractive family. The woman, wearing a flowered sarong the colors of a sunset, was deeply tanned with hair that fell to her shoulders in straight shafts of bronze, copper and gold, and eyes that were a curious light brown that caught the sun and warmed it. The man was big and well built, wearing ivory shorts and a loose-fitting green T-shirt, his dark hair barely sprinkled with bits of silver, his eyes bluer than the ocean behind him. And the little girl, she noted, was an extraordinarily beautiful child. She guessed her age to be close to two, her coloring that of her father, but her face a mirror image of her mother. She ran along in front of her parents, chasing the tiny silver minnows that hugged the shoreline, her laughter echoing like music when the fish let her get almost close enough to catch them before quickly swimming away.

"And these are the Durans," Austen said as the family finally joined the others. "Silas and Hester," he indicated the adults, then when the little girl shrieked with delight and ran up to hug his leg, Austen laughed and added, "and this little starfish is Madelaine."

"Hi, Austen," the child said, throwing her head straight back to squint up at him.

"Hiya, kid," Austen replied with a huge smile, lifting Madelaine high above his head as she giggled with happy excitement.

Austen introduced the members of the sailing party to the new arrivals, and because Moriah was hanging back, he identified her last. When he did, she couldn't help but detect the hesitation with which he voiced her name, nor the note of confused disappointment that laced his tone when he did so. She was sure the others had missed it, but the knowledge that he was reluctant to acknowledge her presence stung.

For the rest of the afternoon, the group lounged on the beach, and Moriah watched as Austen and Hester spoke with animation about everything that had happened since they had last seen each other. She couldn't help the pang of jealousy that shot through her when she noted the ease with which he conversed with the other woman, nor could she help but notice the obvious affection he held for her. She wondered where they had met and what kind of relationship they had enjoyed in the past. Was Hester a former lover of Austen's? Moriah wondered. She was undoubtedly a well-educated woman and close to Moriah in age, a far cry from the nubile bimbettes of Austen's rumored past. But she was blonde and very beautiful. Then Moriah turned her attention to Hester's husband, Silas, who sat in the sand beside her, helping Madelaine build a lopsided castle. He obviously harbored no concern about his wife's relationship with the other man, and Moriah could sense he wasn't the type who would tolerate the presence of old boyfriends. Of course, any man who looked like Silas probably didn't have to worry about his wife straying, either. He was definitely handsome, Moriah thought as her eyes wandered back to study Austen, but he wasn't nearly as attractive as the man who had commanded her attention for the past two weeks.

Her eyes fell back to the book in her lap that she had been trying to read for the past hour. Yet her mind wandered freely over everything but the developing love between Jane and Mr. Rochester, and inevitably her thoughts circled back to the events of the previous two weeks. There were only three days left on her Caribbean idyll, she realized. They would spend today and tomorrow here on this island, then set sail for St. Vincent at midnight. The night after that would be spent in a Kingstown hotel, and Sunday she would return home. Back to her Rittenhouse Square apartment where the night sounds would no longer include the songs of the sea and the islands, back to her office at the university where her only reminders of these two weeks in paradise would be the books that told her of ancient times and people here. She would never see Austen Blye again, she realized morosely. Never again. The words echoed in her head and in her heart as if both were no more than empty chambers. Moriah had to admit that such a concept was only half-true. Her head would never be empty again, would always be filled with memories of a handsome sea captain. Her heart, however, would not be so lucky. It would probably remain empty forever.

Chapter Eleven

That evening, because of the arrival of the sailing party, an impromptu celebration was thrown at the hotel, hosted by the island's tiny population. They were joined by another man who had been absent that afternoon and who was introduced simply as Desmond, the manager of the hotel. The guests had each been assigned a room upstairs, and Moriah took great pleasure at the prospect of having such a spacious room all to herself. The close quarters of the boat had made it virtually impossible to find much private time, and sleeping with Marissa, who snored like a chain saw gone mad, had caused Moriah more than one sleepless night. Now as she sat in the hotel lobby on a rattan sofa covered with a pink-and-green jungle pattern, watching as the others chatted freely and danced to the mellow reggae music that radiated seemingly from nowhere, Moriah began to relax. Austen had disappeared with Dorian, Desmond and Silas to walk up the beach and smoke Diego's Cuban cigars, and the tension that always seemed to fill her body when he was around slowly seeped away to be replaced by a languid sense of relief. She closed her eyes momentarily, only to feel the couch sag beside her as someone else joined her on the seat.

"Hi," Hester greeted her as Moriah opened her eyes once again.

The other woman was still wearing her sarong, looking quite stunning, Moriah thought dismally. She wished she had worn something a little more exotic than her own baggy khakis and cream T-shirt.

Hester extended her hand and offered her a cool-looking, pale amber drink that was dripping wet with condensation in the tropical heat. "Would you like a rum and tonic? No offense, but you look like you could use one."

Moriah shook her head slowly back and forth, not wanting the other woman to think her rude, but in no way desiring what she was sure would be a strong drink like all the others she had tasted in the Caribbean. "I don't think so," she declined almost reluctantly. "Thanks, though."

Seeming to read her mind, Hester smiled and said, "Don't worry. I don't make them nearly as heavy on rum as you normally find them down here."

Moriah couldn't help but smile back and took the drink that Hester offered, sipping it experimentally. It was very refreshing, not nearly as overwhelming as what she had become accustomed to receiving. "It's good," she told the other woman as she traced the tip of her tongue over the excess on her lips. "Thank you. I suppose I could use one." Actually, she amended silently, I could probably use several. Enough to drink myself into oblivion, wake up feeling lousy and assure myself that the past two weeks have been nothing but an alcohol-induced hallucination. However, she kept her wishes to herself.

"Are you enjoying your stay down here?" Hester asked her. The question was innocent enough, but Moriah thought she detected an underlying intensity to the woman's curiosity.

"Yes, I am," Moriah replied. "Everyplace we've visited has been gorgeous, and the people have been so wonderfully nice. I've also discovered that I love sailing." The revelation came as a surprise to Moriah even as she uttered it. She had always hated sailing when she was growing up in Newport, so why her sudden enchantment with the sport? Maybe her enchantment with the boat's activity was a direct result of her enchantment with the boat's captain.

Hester wrinkled her nose in comic disgust. "Well, I'll agree with the first part of your statement, anyway. Frankly, I'm not much of one for sailing."

"Why not?" Moriah asked, honestly not sure how anyone could be put off by what she had come to view as the ultimate opportunity to find peace, solitude and escape.

Hester waved her hand toward nothing in particular and said, "Oh, I just don't have any aptitude for it at all. If you ask Austen, he'll tell you the same thing."

Moriah's back straightened involuntarily at the other woman's mention of Austen's name. She didn't understand why she suddenly felt so possessive, but the feeling rose in her unbidden nonetheless. For some reason, the idea that Austen had gone sailing with someone besides herself didn't set well with Moriah at all. She knew it was ridiculous to expect a charter captain of five years to have had no female charters, but nevertheless, the flesh-and-blood example of such an excursion sitting before her made Moriah feel defensive. "You, uh, you've been sailing with Austen, too?" she asked, hoping she sounded nonchalant.

If Hester's expression was any indication, Moriah had

sounded anything but nonchalant. "Don't worry," the other woman told her. "It wasn't what you think at all."

"Who says I thought anything?" Moriah charged, realizing her true feelings must be nowhere near secret now. She wondered if everyone she'd met in the past two weeks knew about the deep longing she felt for Austen Blye.

"I used to work for Austen and Dorian," Hester explained, taking no offense at Moriah's tone of voice.

"Oh," Moriah remarked quietly.

"It was years ago, right after they started the business. I had come to the Caribbean in a panic to get away from a lousy life I was leading in New York, and to make myself useful I told myself I needed to find a job."

"I see." Moriah had expected that to be the end of their discussion about Austen, but Hester continued the story without provocation or reservation.

"I was visiting on St. Thomas one day and saw an ad on a bulletin board that Austen had put up looking for someone to crew on a new charter service. Despite the fact that I had absolutely no sailing experience, I applied and he hired me. It was their maiden voyage, and I figured, Hey, how hard can it be?" Hester laughed derisively at her own ignorance. "Boy, was I in for a rude awakening."

Moriah laughed, too. Having watched Austen and Dorian closely throughout the trip, she knew there was an enormous amount of information and practical training she would have to absorb if she ever wanted to help sail *Urizen*. Then she reminded herself that there would never be any need at all as she would never go sailing on Austen's boat again.

Hester continued her story as Moriah took another sip of her drink. "We put in here one night, and Austen suggested quite discreetly that Diego really needed someone to manage this hotel, and wouldn't that be just the perfect job for me seeing as how I wasn't really working out as a crew member? Knowing that if I didn't accept, he and Dorian would probably keelhaul me for being such a disable-bodied seaperson, and having established an immediate rapport with Diego and Gabriela, I decided to stay. But I still saw a lot of Austen, because he puts in here with his charters so frequently. He and I became very close over the years."

I'll bet, Moriah thought.

Seeming to read her mind once again, Hester grinned and said, "But not the way you think."

"I wasn't thinking anything," Moriah told her.

"Mmm-hmm," Hester muttered with a knowing look. "Don't try to fool me, Moriah. I'm in love with a man myself."

Moriah's eyes widened in alarm at the other woman's statement. "In love?" she sputtered. "What on earth gave you that idea?"

"I've seen the way you and Austen look at each other. And I heard the way his voice dropped when he introduced you this afternoon. I know him too well," she added almost sadly. "He and I shared a lot of the same experiences in our lives before we moved down here. It only made us that much more sympathetic to each other."

Moriah couldn't disguise her curiosity. "What kind of experiences?" she asked.

Hester looked at her for a long time before she replied, studying Moriah's face as if searching for answers there. "No, of course he wouldn't tell you any of it," she finally said with a shake of her head. "He only told *me* about his past because it mirrored my own so frightfully well. It's a shame he has such trouble communicating with other people about his life before he came to the Caribbean," she added absently.

"Especially with those who care about him so much. A lack of communication in a relationship can lead to nothing but disaster. You can trust me on that."

"Tell me about him," Moriah requested almost on a plea. It might be her only chance to discover exactly what made Austen the man he was. And even though she knew the knowledge would probably only make leaving him behind that much harder, she wanted more than anything to find out all she could about him.

"Well," Hester began, "he used to be a banker in Atlanta."

"That I heard," Moriah told the other woman. "Even though I find it impossible to believe."

"You and me both. But it was never Austen's choice to become one," Hester informed her.

"What do you mean?"

Hester shrugged. "His father, who struggled for years to make a decent living for his family as a fisherman, decided when Austen was a boy that his son would go to college and never have to do the kind of backbreaking labor he was forced to do himself in order to make a living. He told Austen he wanted him to major in business and go after a career in the financial field, and Austen, not wanting to disappoint his father, did exactly that."

"But if he didn't want to do it…" Moriah began, her words trailing off when she felt as if she already knew the answer.

"He told himself he did want to," Hester said. "Austen spent years trying to convince himself that he was doing precisely what he had always wanted to do. For ten long years he perpetuated the charade that he honestly believed he was living the life he chose."

Moriah absorbed Hester's words reluctantly, thinking Austen's behavior sounded vaguely familiar.

"He even let his family talk him into getting engaged to a woman he worked with, because they felt she would complement his lifestyle so perfectly."

"Pamela," Moriah guessed.

Hester raised her golden brows in surprise. "You know?"

"Only the name," Moriah said quietly. "And the fact that he really went to pieces because she left him."

Hester's surprise was doubled at Moriah's assertion. "Who told you that?"

Moriah looked at the other woman blankly. "Dorian said he found Austen facedown in the gutter drunk one night, and that Austen kept mumbling about some woman named Pamela. I assumed it was because he was so hurt by their separation."

Hester shook her head in vehement denial. "I don't doubt that Austen was blind drunk when Dorian met him for the first time, but it wasn't because of Pamela, it was because of his whole life."

"What do you mean?"

Hester took a deep breath, obviously trying to choose her words carefully as she continued. "He never loved Pamela," she told Moriah assuredly. "And Pamela never loved him. They both just got caught up in the games their families were playing. Austen's father wanted to see him living the good life as a wealthy banker with a beautiful, well-bred wife and children. Pamela's parents were from very old money and were trying to keep her away from this poor art student she had dated all through college. They saw Austen as the man to keep her respectable. And because he and Pamela were both the type of people who wanted to please their families more than themselves, they let themselves be guided toward a life together that neither of them planned or wanted."

Again Moriah listened closely to what the other woman

said, again feeling Hester's words were describing her own life as much as Austen's. "So what finally drove them apart?" she asked.

"Pamela never stopped seeing the artist," Hester told her. "She got pregnant by him, and that was enough to make her realize what she wanted for her own future. She left Austen as gently as she could, and she went after what she wanted."

"But how can you say Austen didn't love her if he reacted the way he did to their separation?"

"Austen didn't fall apart because Pamela left him," Hester told her. "He fell apart because Pamela's departure only served to illustrate his own weakness at letting himself be forced into a life he *hadn't* wanted for ten years. Her leaving finally compelled him to face up to the fact that he'd spent ten years of his life doing what other people had arranged for him. Ten years living a lie. That's why he drank himself silly that night. Because he couldn't tolerate the idea that he'd been so blind to his own unhappiness."

Moriah took a deep swallow of her drink, surprised to find that she had finished it during Hester's story. Thoughts crowded into her head at the other woman's explanation of Austen's behavior, thoughts that Moriah really didn't want to acknowledge. At least she understood now his hang-up about the importance of doing one's own thing, of being exactly whatever one wanted to be. And she had an explanation for why he never wanted to discuss his past. But those weren't the thoughts that were bothering her. She couldn't help but feel that so much of what Hester described in his life reflected her own actions and feelings over the years, couldn't help but think that maybe Austen wasn't the only one who was guilty of living a lie. Yet she couldn't, wouldn't, allow herself to think of that. She pushed the upsetting realization angrily away and told herself that the behavior Hester had illustrated wasn't like her at all. Moriah was happy with the life she led, the life she had *chosen*, she added insistently. She was.

Unbidden then, Dorian's words of their day at the beach on Antigua came back to haunt Moriah, as well. One life is all we get, he had told her. And we're the only ones who have control over where it goes. We better make sure we take the right road, otherwise the wrong one will end up in darkness. No, she denied vehemently, she *was* on the right road, the road that she wanted. Wasn't she? Or was she?

"I think I need to go out and get some fresh air," Moriah announced suddenly.

If Hester was surprised by Moriah's wish to escape, she didn't let it show. Instead she nodded as if in understanding and said, "I need to go look for Silas anyway."

As if cued for entry by her statement, Hester's husband appeared to seat himself on her other side on the sofa. "Did I hear someone mention my name?" he asked. "I brought refills," he added, pressing two freshly filled glasses into the women's hands. "Just tonic for you, though," he said meaningfully to his wife.

"Moriah and I were just chatting about the men in our lives," Hester told him, taking the drink he offered, a bright, cryptic smile her only comment for his second statement.

Moriah thought she should probably say something to deny that Austen was the man in her life, but then had to admit that she wished it was true. And since she would undoubtedly never hear him called such again, she said nothing.

"Austen's out wandering on the beach somewhere," Silas told them. "I don't think I've ever seen him in such a crummy mood before. He's completely uncommunicative. I don't understand it."

Hester glanced over at Moriah expressively and asked, "Do you want me to join you outside?"

Moriah shook her head. "No, that's okay. I'm just going to take a walk up the beach a little ways."

"Besides, I don't think it's a good idea for you to be out in the night air in your condition," Silas added, taking his wife's hand in his and lifting it to his lips with undisguised devotion.

Moriah almost felt like an intruder as she watched him gaze at Hester with such unabashed longing, and she couldn't help but feel a little envious of the deep love they so obviously felt for each other. Then the import of his statement struck her squarely in the brain. "Your condition?" she asked with a smile.

Hester ducked her head a little shyly and flushed most becomingly. "Well, we're not positive yet, but we're pretty sure we're going to have another baby."

Silas shook his head with determination and puffed out his chest proudly. "No, we *are* going to have another baby," he vowed definitely. "All the signs are there, and I just happen to know for a fact that it's true."

Hester chuckled at her husband. "There's just something about this island," she told him with a knowing smile.

"Yeah, we'll have to start coming back every summer," he agreed.

Moriah smiled and excused herself from the couple then, feeling their undeniable desire to be alone. She wandered out onto the veranda and descended the stairs that led to the beach. Bright stars liberally dotted the night sky, and she could easily see the white line of surf as it twisted down the ivory sand beach. Less than a hundred feet to her right, Moriah saw a dark shape standing at the water's edge, staring out to sea, and she knew it must be Austen. So she chose a path to her left and began her slow, meandering journey in the opposite direction.

When she felt she'd put enough distance between herself and Austen and the happy sight of Hester and Silas Duran that had made her feel so empty and melancholy at the hotel, Moriah stopped suddenly and dropped to a sitting position in the sand. She realized absently that she had brought her drink down to the beach with her, and she sipped it casually as she lost herself in thought. In a little over twenty-four hours they would be leaving this island. They would arrive on St. Vincent late Saturday morning, and she would catch a flight home early on Sunday. She would never see Austen Blye again. Was that what she wanted? she asked herself. Was that *really* what she wanted?

Moriah reflected with a start that she had never asked herself that question before. What did she really want? For herself, for her life, for her future? She had chosen her career because she had always taken an honest interest in primitive South American cultures, and at the time, teaching had been the only way to make a living with such a fascination for the subject matter. But she was doing well with her writing, she reminded herself. And as much as she liked her job at the university, writing and research were actually the things at which she excelled and the things she most enjoyed. Once she completed her new book, she would be able to eke out a modest living as a writer and researcher. And really, when she got right down it it, she had to admit that such a career was what she had secretly envisioned for herself all along.

The admission left Moriah feeling a little light-headed. Had she just made a conscious, individually inspired choice about her future? A single small chuckle escaped her lips, and she placed the fingers of one hand uncertainly over her mouth to keep in the laughter she felt threatening. My, but it felt good, this decision making, this laying out of plans. Why hadn't she done this years ago? she wondered. Well, there was no sense stopping now. If her intention was to give up her position at the university in order to pursue a full-time research and writing career, why then was it necessary to keep living in Philadelphia? She'd never actually cared for the city that much, had kept her life and activity restricted to the university and her apartment. There was an awful lot of traffic, she thought, already dreading her next entry onto the Schuyl-kill Expressway, and getting to the Jersey shore was next to impossible in the summer. Of course the shore itself would hold even less appeal, now that she had visited such pristine and secluded beaches as the one upon which she now sat. And face it, she told herself, aside from The Chart House, there were no restaurants in Philly where she could get seafood done the way she liked it. So really, what was the point in keeping her apartment there?

She could move down to the Caribbean, she thought suddenly. After all, it made sense for a person whose current research revolved around primitive Caribbean cultures to live in the Caribbean, didn't it? It would be ex-pensive, but no more so than living on Rittenhouse Square. Why hadn't she realized that before? She wasn't one for living the high life anyway. And she had enough of her advance left over from the sale of her second book to keep her going until the royalties from the first one became more substantial as it was picked up for instructional use. She could live in the Virgin Islands, she told herself. Supple-ment her income with essays in trade and educational journals… It would be so easy, so perfect. Why hadn't she thought of it before?

Could she really do it? she asked herself, feeling giddy with the prospect of making such changes. Moriah took a deep, fortifying breath and another sip of her drink, hoping the rum would slow her racing pulse.

"Moriah."

Austen's voice came at her out of nowhere, and Moriah turned quickly to see him standing over her, an inscrutable expression darkening his handsome features. When she didn't reply, he took a few slow steps forward and sat down in the sand beside her. He pulled his knees up before him and stared unseeingly out at the black water that stretched to the hazy dark line of the horizon. Propping his forearms on top of his knees, he let something he was holding pass from one hand to the other as if he had forgotten about it. For long moments neither of them said a word. Then when she couldn't bear the silence any longer, Moriah finally broke it.

"What have you got there?" she asked softly, pointing to the object he was fingering so gently in his hand.

He looked over at her with a startled expression, as if he was surprised to find her sitting beside him, then let his eyes wander back to his hands. "It's a shell," he told her, holding up the small, perfect, pink scallop for her inspection. He gestured toward the direction from which he had joined her and said, "I found it lying on the beach a little ways from the hotel. It reminded me of you. You don't find whole, beautiful shells down here very often. Most of them are broken and discolored, rough and full of flaws. When you do see one this perfect and lovely, it strikes you right away, and you know better than to leave it where it is, to let it go for someone else to find." He gazed at the scallop for a moment longer, then turned back to Moriah. "Here," he told her, extending his hand to her, "you take it back to Philadelphia with you."

Moriah's fingers closed over the ones holding the shell with such gentle care, her eyes searching his for some indication of his feelings. "But you just said you shouldn't let it go," she reminded him on a shallow breath. She removed her hand from his and shook her head. "It belongs down here with you," she told him.

He studied her features for a long time, and nodded very slowly as if not quite convinced. Then he rose to leave.

"Austen, don't go." Moriah's voice halted his steps. "Stay here and talk to me." She wasn't sure why she wanted him to, she realized. Maybe because she wanted to tell him about the new plans she had been making for the future, or maybe just because she wanted him to be close by. Whatever her reasons for doing so, Moriah only knew that she didn't want him to leave her. Not until she was fully able to consider everything that had happened between them and everything that was yet to take place.

He seemed to hesitate briefly, then sighed almost as if in resignation and took his seat beside her once again. "What do you want to talk about?" he asked.

Moriah lifted a shoulder halfheartedly, honestly unsure of the course she wanted their conversation to take. She was afraid to describe her plans for the future to him, afraid that she might still change her mind and go back to what was familiar and predictable instead of trying something new. There remained in Moriah a fear of striking out on her own. Despite her new conviction that the life she had been leading before coming to the Caribbean was not necessarily the life she had originally and currently planned to pursue, there was still one little part of her that couldn't quite pledge its allegiance. One little part that continued to nurture the cowardly, spineless Mo and the dry, humorless Dr. Mallory. Her life may not be exactly what she wanted, she realized, but it was all she had ever known, all she had ever been used to. Was she really the sort of person who could just throw all that away?

"I don't know," she finally told Austen, answering both

of their questions at once. "I was just sitting here thinking about things, and a little conversation seems like a welcome distraction."

Austen lifted his eyebrows at that. "What exactly were you thinking about that would cause you to need some distraction?"

Moriah's gaze fell to where she was digging her toes nervously into the sand, and she decided she might as well come out with it. "I, uh, I was just thinking about my future."

All at once, Austen seemed very interested, and he eagerly encouraged her to go on. "What about your future?"

Moriah shrugged again. "I'm not sure," she admitted. "I was just thinking that maybe… I mean I might perhaps give up teaching and focus more on a career in writing."

"Really?" Austen was afraid to believe what she was saying was true. "What else?"

Moriah looked up at him quickly, but was unable to tolerate the intensity of his gaze. "I…I might leave Philadelphia," she added.

"To go where?" he asked a little breathlessly.

Moriah took a hearty swallow of her drink for fortification, and Austen noted the gesture with a frown. "I might…I might move down here," she told him on a quick rush of words, then added hastily, "maybe."

Austen had always prided himself on being very fluent in body language, and what he saw of Moriah's now made him stop to rethink his momentary lapse of optimism at her announcements. She stammered her intentions out uncertainly and couldn't look him in the eye as she spoke, instead focusing her attention on feet that furrowed restlessly through the sand. The tall glass clenched tightly in her trembling hands was nearly empty, so obviously she'd consumed some amount of alcohol. He thought of the other times that she'd been drinking, when her actions and words had been so carefree and uninhibited, only to be regretted and denied once her senses returned to claim her. His shoulders sagged in defeat, and he shook his head slowly back and forth in resignation.

Moriah Mallory was talking through her hat, he realized. She had panicked at the prospect of her vacation's end and had been swept away by the sultry tropical night once again. She had let her thoughts go wandering, and they had gotten carried away. She had no more intention of following through on her plans to move down here than he had of leaving. The knowledge that she would try to build up his hopes only to tear them down again cut into Austen deeply and made him angrier than he'd felt in a very long time. He naturally sought to retaliate, to injure her in the same way a wounded animal would strike back at its aggressor.

"Moriah, look at yourself!" he demanded harshly. "Look at how difficult it is for you to talk about making changes! You couldn't strike out on a new life now if you had to. You've let your family pin you down in a choke hold for too long, and you're too cowardly to try and fight back." His voice had risen in volume as he'd listed her shortcomings, and now he stood suddenly, clutching tightly in his hand the small scallop she hadn't taken from him. "I was a fool to think you were different, Moriah! Do you hear me? A fool!" With a savage lunge that drove the air from his lungs in a painful groan, Austen hurled the shell out into the ocean as far as he could.

"Austen, don't!" Moriah screamed out at the action.

But it was too late. The nighttime had already swallowed up the gift it had so graciously offered him, and now he would never see it again. He looked down at the place where Moriah had been sitting, only to see that she had struggled to her knees and reached out her arms to where he'd cast the shell away. He was stunned to see that she was crying. Fat tears tumbled down her cheeks, catching what little moonlight fell from the thin crest of silver above them.

"Don't," she repeated miserably, and he felt his heart twist as if a great fist squeezed it in anger. Her voice fell to a whisper as she added belatedly, "Please, don't throw it away."

But Moriah realized it was too late. Nothing would bring it back to them. Austen couldn't trust that she would turn her life into what she really wanted it to be, and as a coldness crept into her soul and settled there, she realized she really couldn't blame him. As he turned his back on her and left her alone in the darkness, Moriah's eyes traveled upward to stare at the moon. It had been nearly full the night they'd left St. John, she remembered, and now the thin sliver of light just barely hung on to the black sky consuming it. Tomorrow night when they left the island for St. Vincent, the moon would probably be gone. Just like everything else, she realized. Just like everything else.

Chapter Twelve

As the first pink and yellow fingers of dawn reached over the hills outside Kingstown, St. Vincent, on Sunday morning, Moriah lay awake and restless in her hotel room, anticipating and dreading the wake-up call she had left at the desk the night before. She hadn't had more than an hour's sleep, she was sure. The hotel was very comfortable and attractive, but it was located in the center of town, so all night long as she had stared into the blackness of her room, Moriah heard nothing but silence, punctuated now and again by reveling tourists and noisy taxis in the street below. She found, not much to her surprise, that she missed the continuous, subtle rocking motion of *Urizen,* missed the sound of the water as it splashed halfheartedly against the bow of the boat. She missed the way the wind caught and hummed in the sails, and more than anything she missed the sound of Austen's rumbling voice and easy laughter as it drifted into her cabin through the portholes and open hatch.

Moriah sighed deeply and turned to lie on her side, noting that the darkness in her room was slowly fading to gray. She thought about the last day they had spent on the tiny island, the day she had not seen Austen, who most certainly was avoiding her. She had wandered desperately up and down the beach all morning and afternoon, telling herself it was because she craved the opportunity to absorb as much of the view as she could take back to Philadelphia with her, but searching, she knew, for the shell Austen had tossed into the sea the night before. She hadn't been able to find it.

That evening at midnight they had left the little island. Moriah had stayed ashore as long as she could, using the excuse that she wanted to get Hester's address before she left, realizing that she was actually frightened to get on board because she knew it would be the last time she ever did so. She had hoped Austen would talk to her, would at least look at her as she climbed up from the dinghy to the cockpit, but he had only ignored her. The only time he'd touched her had been when she had nearly fallen backward climbing over the last rung of the ladder, and then he had grabbed her with such a ferocity and yanked her on board with such a jerk that she had been afraid he would loosen her arm from its socket. When she had glanced back to look at him, he had been staring down into the dark waters of the sea, breathing heavily as if the exertion had cost him every bit of strength he possessed. She had thought for a moment he'd glanced up at her with an expression of utter fear and desolation, but it had happened so quickly she knew now it must have been a trick of the moonlight. Then she remembered there had been no moon that night. It must have been a trick of the stars.

They had arrived in Kingstown early enough yesterday to enjoy the last opportunity to shop at the market in town. Moriah had found enchanting the motley booths offering everything from plaintains to teapots to straw elephants. The people of the island, who laughed and haggled with her so freely, seemed to be earthy, honest and real. She remembered at one point looking over her shoulder to see her sisters following coolly behind her—Morgana in her white silks, Mathilda in her beige shirtwaist, Marissa in her black jumpsuit—and comparing them to the pastels of the buildings and bright clothes of the people who surrounded her everywhere she looked. They had no more been a part of their environment than a trio of polar bears would have been. Then Moriah had looked down at herself, at her baggy T-shirt, shorts and sandals, at the light tan she had nurtured during the past two weeks, and the straw bag that held all the treasures she had collected on the islands—pieces of broken seashells and coral, a pale blue starfish, an envelope she had filled with sand from St. Martin, papayas, mangos and a bottle of local rum. She had no idea why she had accumulated some of these things, she realized. Whimsy must certainly have overcome her normally staid rationale at several points. Whatever the reason, she knew the islands would remain a part of her forever.

Moriah tossed fitfully to lie on her stomach amid the tangle of sheets in the king-size bed. She wondered where Austen had been when she had left *Urizen* for the last time. Dorian had been the one to see that the four sisters made it off safely and had been driven to their hotel in town. Christian had been there to say goodbye as well, but Captain Austen Blye had been ominously absent. Dorian had said it was because there had been some very urgent business with a friend of Austen's that the other man had needed to address immediately upon arriving on St. Vincent, but Moriah had found that very difficult to believe. Not only could she think of very few things Austen might consider urgent, but she seemed to recall that two weeks ago he had made a date to meet her at the botanical gardens. Oh, well, she told herself. None of that was her concern now.

She contemplated what awaited her on her return to Philadelphia. The first order of business was to organize her notes for the upcoming fall semester. She really wished she wasn't teaching so many classes this year, she thought. It was going to cut significantly into her writing time, and frankly, she was getting tired of repeating the same material again and again. She had been trying to convince Dr. Fulkerson, the department head, to introduce some new subject matter into the curriculum, but he was close to retirement and very set in his ways, and he didn't want to be bothered with schedule changes. He had told Moriah more than once that the material offered by the anthropology department was sufficient to satisfy the students' needs, and a broader view of South American and Caribbean cultures wasn't necessary. Yet despite his unwillingness to expand the program, Moriah had continued diligently with her extracurricular research. It was what had ultimately led to the publication of her first book and the current undertaking of her second.

She felt herself wishing that she was staying down here, then immediately silenced such desires. There was nothing here for her, she reminded herself. And anyway, money would have been tight for the first several months if she had given up her job at the university. Her next royalty check wouldn't come for at least another three months, and the pay for writing articles for the trades was spotty at best. She had been fooling herself to think she could give up teaching to pursue a life down here. There was no way she'd be able to make it alone. And there was no one down here who wanted her with him.

Resigned to the fact that she simply was not going to go back to sleep before her wake-up call came, Moriah rose from bed and went to her phone to cancel it. She sat at the desk for some moments with her chin propped in one hand, the fingers of her other tapping impatiently and unnoticed on the scratched surface. After some moments she rose thoughtfully and began to pace the length of her room before suddenly stopping in the center. The first time she had awakened in a Caribbean hotel room it had been to a massive hangover and the memory of nearly making love to Austen the night before. This morning she felt hungover and lost in memories again. Hungover from partaking excessively of a handsome sea captain for two weeks, haunted by memories of one particular night where she had felt free and unburdened and loved.

Loved, she repeated to herself. Oh, if only that were true. If only she were indeed loved by Austen Blye. But any feelings he had for her were for the woman he thought she had been on St. Thomas, a woman who simply did not exist. If he truly cared for her, he would have seen beyond the woman he wanted her to be and would have loved the woman she was, who loved him so deeply in return. Moriah sighed and felt her depression grow. What a cruel joke fate had played. To offer her a man to love who could only love her back if she were someone else.

As tears threatened to gather in her eyes, Moriah wiped them away and hurried to take a shower. She would not think about it, she decided. She would be leaving the Caribbean within a matter of hours and would return to all that was familiar and predictable in her life. That was what she wanted, after all, wasn't it? To go back to the way things had been? Before Austen Blye had come along and made her question everything she had ever known and felt, made the life she was living seem like a lie. Well, she would show him, she told herself with determination as the hot spray of water stung her body all over. She would go back to her job and way of life in Philadelphia, and she would enjoy it and excel. She had always been competent, she remembered rather desolately, assuring herself that there was certainly nothing wrong with such a trait. She was the woman she had always been—Professor Moriah Mallory, cultural anthropologist and research writer, and youngest child of the celebrated Mallorys of Newport, Rhode Island. Likewise, her place in the world was where it had always been—in academic and scholarly settings. And for now anyway, Moriah believed that to be true.

When the cab arrived that was to ferry the four Mallory sisters to the airport, the driver, a slight man who probably weighed no more than Moriah did, alighted from the front seat and eyed the pile of luggage with reservation.

"All dese bags belong to you four ladies?" he asked cautiously, apparently hoping they would deny it and point only to the small handbags each had slung over her shoulder.

"Of course it all belongs to us," Morgana told the driver.

"Although it does seem to have tripled since we arrived," Moriah mentioned absently, gazing at the bags with speculation.

"Well, most of the new ones are yours, Mo," Mathilda pointed out.

"Yes, because I only needed to buy one for the things I bought on St. Thomas," Marissa added.

Moriah recognized with no small amount of surprise that what her sisters had said was true. She had more luggage than any of them now, a fact that was completely outrageous to consider. She really had done a lot of shopping while she was down here. It startled her to realize it. "Yes, well, most of it is for the visual enhancement of my university lectures," she explained.

"Oh, right, that green-and-blue sarong you bought at the market yesterday ought to add quite a new dimension to your discussion of cannibals," Morgana commented drily.

Moriah lifted her chin defensively. "That's to wear in my apartment when the city heat becomes unbearable, as it inevitably does every summer."

"You could turn on your air conditioner," her eldest sister offered.

Mathilda joined in the fun by remarking, "Oh, I don't know, Morgana. Mo could probably convince her students that her sarong was actually authentic native wear. It's all those papayas and mangos she bought that I'm wondering about."

"Papayas and mangos are excellent sources of vitamins A and C," Moriah sniffed indignantly.

"So are carrots and grapefruit," her middle sister told her. "You just better hope customs doesn't give you any trouble."

"Just wear your sarong and they'll never notice," Marissa suggested, chuckling at what Moriah was sure she thought was a comic picture of her youngest sister dressed in such exotic attire.

Here it comes, she thought then, as she bent to pick up the largest of her bags that remained on the sidewalk in an effort to help the driver who was huffing and puffing after lifting only half of their luggage into the back of the awning-covered open-air taxi. The traditional conclusion to the typical Mallory vacation—making sport of everything Moriah had done, to elicit a good laugh. This year's festivities ought to be especially fun for the others, she realized dismally. She had committed numerous and colorful crimes with which to embarrass herself. There was of particular significance that little item where she had fallen in love with a handsome sea captain who couldn't possibly ever want her for the woman she was. It would be a long time before that one was put to rest.

"At any rate," Marissa went on as the last of their luggage was placed in the back of the taxi, "I'm wondering how those bottles of rum are going to add to Mo's lessons. Isn't there a law in Pennsylvania that prohibits the distribution of alcohol to minors?"

"My students are all seniors or graduate students," Moriah reminded them. "Besides, the rum is for me." I'm probably going to need it in excessive quantities by the time this day is over, she added silently. "I thought a little taste of the islands now and then might warm me up come this winter."

Marissa's lips curled into a knowing grin as the four women ascended the cab and took their seats toward the front. "Yes, well, I'll bet you wish you were taking back a taste of something besides rum to warm your upcoming cold nights," she said suggestively.

"Yes, like that nice Captain Blye," Mathilda added with a teasing smile. "That nice, strong, muscular, sexy—"

"Virile, hard, bronzed, sculpted…" Morgana added with a leer.

"Handsome, uh…" Marissa stammered, her own supply of adjectives much more limited than her sisters'.

Moriah, however, could come up with more than enough adjectives for Austin Blye. Haunting, tormenting, unforgettable… She could go on forever.

"You know, you never did tell us exactly how you found him in the first place," Morgana said suddenly. "Aside from having met him in a bar where you shouldn't have been sitting alone in the first place."

Moriah closed her eyes for a moment, wishing she was anywhere but here. Alone. She knew Morgana's words were more than idle curiosity. They were a command to tell her sisters everything that had transpired the night she met Austen Blye. Now that they had spent two weeks in his company and knew as well as she did that he was no ordinary man, they were insistent on discovering why he would ever have had anything to do with such an ordinary woman as Mo Mallory. "No, I don't suppose I did ever tell you," she said simply, trying to indicate that it was a subject she didn't care to discuss, knowing, however, that such a protest was the last thing that would put her sisters off.

"Well?" Morgana asked pointedly.

Moriah looked into the faces of her three sisters, so similar and so vague. They were all equally curious to know about that night. As the taxi pulled away from the hotel and out into the traffic of Kingstown, Moriah felt her anger at them beginning to accelerate, as well. It's none of your damned business, she wanted to snap at them. But instead of voicing the words she wanted to say, she heard herself reluctantly recounting exactly what they wanted to hear.

"There were some divers bothering me, and Austen came to my aid by pretending to be my boyfriend."

"Oh, that must have been some stretch for him," Mathilda said with a chuckle. "The part of 'lover to an anthropologist' is probably the one role I would never be able to play convincingly."

"He wasn't acting," Moriah replied coolly in her own defense. "He was himself the entire night, and he really enjoyed my company."

Her sisters' expressions indicated they did not believe Moriah for a minute, but she continued anyway, trying to keep her anger in check. "He stayed with me until the divers left, then he invited me to meet some friends of his at another bar." Not quite reluctantly, and with a definite touch of pride, she added, "There was a band, and we danced some."

"You? Dancing?" Marissa was incredulous. "I thought Austen had been kidding about that part."

"It's true," Moriah insisted indignantly. Then before she

could stop herself, she challenged, "Why is that so difficult for all of you to believe?"

"Oh, Mo, be serious," Morgana said, then laughed at her own joke. "Of course, serious is all you ever are. Which is precisely my point. You simply don't have it in you to have fun. The only place I can envision you dancing is at some kind of weird tribal celebration that would result in the furthering of your knowledge of the primitive cultural experience."

Moriah opened her mouth to retaliate, but Mathilda interrupted her as if knowing her youngest sister would have nothing to offer in the way of a comeback.

"So what else happened, Mo? Did the dashing Captain Blye try to take advantage of you when he took you back to your hotel?"

Mathilda's tone of voice clearly stated she knew that to be a laughable impossibility, and the snicker of her sisters indicated they agreed. But Moriah couldn't prevent the uncomfortable and obvious squirm that worked its way slowly through her entire body. Nor could she prevent her sisters from seeing it.

"He didn't!" Morgana gasped.

"He couldn't!" Mathilda insisted.

"He wouldn't!" Marissa agreed.

Moriah's lips turned up in the first genuine grin she'd felt on her face in a long time, loving the horrified expressions that made her sisters appear so comical, loving more the fact that she was about to horrify them even further. "Actually," she said very slowly, "*I* would, *I* could and…*I* did."

"You *what?*" the three of them shrieked in unison.

Moriah shrugged lightly, as if her announcement were the most commonly spoken statement in the world. "I seduced Austen Blye." There. It was out. She had finally admitted it. She didn't see why she had to tell them that the seduction hadn't exactly run its course because she had passed out. She was quite certain that had she remained conscious that night on St. Thomas, she and Austen would have wrestled and sweated amid the sheets until dawn. The confession felt wonderful, she realized in a rush. For the first time in her life, her sisters were hanging on her every word, awaiting with eager anticipation whatever she was about to reveal. Feeling inordinately powerful and smug, Moriah opened her purse to pull out an emery board and went studiously to work on her nails.

Morgana was the first to reply with a single, quick release of air, followed by Mathilda and Marissa who promptly pulled up their jaws from where they had dropped them down in gapes of disbelief.

"That…that's quite amusing, Mo," Morgana said with an unsteady laugh. "You've made a little joke. Well, well, well. Maybe you're not so humorless as we all once thought."

"It wasn't a joke," Moriah assured them. "We made love on St. Martin, too."

"I beg your pardon?" Morgana said.

"Yes, under a waterfall no less," Moriah added with victorious glee. "If you'd like, Morgana, I can go into lengthy and graphic detail so you can take notes for your next book. Naturally, though, I'll want an acknowledgment."

Moriah couldn't remember a time in her life when her sisters had actually been left speechless. She wanted to laugh out loud at the feelings that were bubbling through her like warm Jell-O. She had finally stood up to her sisters, something she had been so certain she would never be able to do. That could only mean one thing, she realized suddenly. Moriah Mallory had a mind and a will of her own, after all. It had taken her thirty long years to realize it, and now that the knowledge was wedged soundly and squarely in the front of her brain, Moriah also realized that she had thirty years of allowing herself to be suppressed, repressed and oppressed to make up for.

"Just for the record," she began evenly as she looked up from the last of her fingernails, "I am *not* serious, humorless, dry, awkward, staid, logical, rational, obedient, naive, conservative or any of those other unsightly labels with which you have all so conveniently tagged me for years. I am, let's see…" She tried to remember all the things Austen had said of her over the past two weeks. "I am witty, glamorous, romantic, vivacious, clever and desirable, full of fun and laughter." She smiled a secret smile she knew none of the others would understand. "I am a curious, lovely dreamboat. I am, in a word, spectacular. A passionate, caring woman who has wants and needs like every other human being on earth, and I'm not going to let the one good thing that's ever happened to me get away without a fight. Driver!" she shouted to the man she was sure had been eavesdropping on every word she had uttered. "Turn this heap around!"

"Mo, what are you doing?" Morgana asked mildly.

"Mo, you have got to be kidding," Mathilda agreed.

"Mo, knock it off," Marissa instructed.

But the driver had apparently detected something in her voice that her sisters did not, an unquestionable indication that she did not want to be trifled with. He quickly and deftly pulled his cab to the side of the busy downtown street and stopped. The realization that someone would jump so obediently to her commands gave Moriah all the strength and encouragement she needed to go on. She was finally going to tell her sisters where to get off. Literally.

"Number one," she said, lifting her index finger confidently into the air, "this taxi is being rerouted *away* from the airport." Before her sisters could interrupt, she lifted a second finger and added, "Number two, anybody who doesn't want to stay in the Caribbean for the rest of her life had better get off here and find another cab." Lifting a third finger to join the other two, she took a deep breath and said, "Number three, don't ever call me Mo again. My name is Moriah. Use it."

Dead silence was the only reply she received for long moments. Then without a word, Morgana, Mathilda and Marissa rose from their seats and exited the taxi. Moriah and the driver watched soundlessly as the three women plucked their bags one by one from the back of the cab and piled them onto the curb. As Mathilda lifted a hand to signal another red-and-white awning-covered truck that was approaching, Morgana turned back to look at Moriah.

"We'll discuss this when you get back to the States, Mo…riah," she said slowly.

Moriah smiled in smug satisfaction and promised her sister, "I've done all the talking I'm going to do. Now comes the time for action." Without another word for any of her sisters, Moriah twisted back in her seat in the cab and gave the driver instructions on how to get back to the marina where *Urizen* was berthed. The cabbie quickly put his rig into gear, and with a lunge and a lurch, Moriah went to meet her destiny head-on.

When she returned to the sailboat, her first impression was that it was completely deserted, and her heart sank at the prospect of waiting all afternoon for Austen's return. Then she heard Dorian down belowdeck whistling what had become a familiar tune, and she smiled.

"Dorian," she called out to him as she climbed into the cockpit. "It's me, Moriah."

Dorian's dark head quickly appeared in the companionway, a huge white grin splitting his dark face. "Moriah, you came back," he greeted her, clearly delighted by her return. "Did you forget something?" he asked playfully.

Moriah shook her head. "No, I remembered something. I remembered that I fell in love with someone I didn't ever want to leave behind."

Dorian nodded in understanding. "Dat happened to me once on St. Lucia. I finally had to bring de girl back to St. Thomas with me."

"Maggie?" Moriah guessed.

"I suppose I'm gonna have to marry her," he admitted. "De last two weeks have been very educational. I've seen what happens when people try to deny what dey feel for each other. No offense, Moriah, but it doesn't look too healthy."

"It feels even worse," she assured him. She hesitated a moment before asking, "Where is he?"

Dorian ran a hand thoughtfully over his cheek before telling her, "He went into town to dis little bar down on de waterfront."

Moriah's expression fell a little. Her plane hadn't even left the ground yet, and he was already out auditioning new talent. "He went out to pick up women?" she asked Dorian miserably.

"No, no!" he was quick to assure her with a definite shake of his hands. "He went down dere to drown his sorrows on cheap rum, not easy women. De way he gets when he's dis depressed, I don't think even de easy women would have him."

I would, Moriah thought to herself. I'll take him any way I can get him. It had come to her so clearly on the ride back to the boat. She had been telling herself all along that Austen couldn't see the woman she was because he was looking for someone else that he wanted her to be. But the fact was that Austen had been the only person who *could* see the woman she was, the only one who could look past the image she had been trying to project all along in an effort to deny her true self. Why hadn't she listened to him sooner? she wondered. More important than that, why hadn't she listened to herself?

After Dorian told her where she would be able to locate Manny's Tavern, Moriah asked him if it would be all right to make use of her former cabin one more time. Once there, Moriah took a long look at herself in the mirror and frowned. But it was only a moment before a slow grin began to curl her lips in mischief. As plan upon plan began to hatch in her head, Moriah began to disrobe. Her glasses came first, to be neatly tucked into their case and stowed back in her purse. Then she loosened the braid from her hair and brushed it until the dark honey tresses shimmered and tumbled in curls around her shoulders. She opened one of her new bags and withdrew the short denim skirt and scooped-neck black T-shirt she had worn her first night on St. Thomas. Then she affixed large, hammered-silver earrings she had purchased in Antigua and slid the four matching bracelets over her left wrist. As her frumpy anthropologist clothes pooled in a messy heap about her ankles, Moriah contemplated her new tan that covered all of her except her white abdomen that had been obscured by her maillot. First thing in the morning she was going to buy a bikini, she decided. A red one. Grandma Maxine's calves notwithstanding, she had a remarkably good body. Why had she never realized that before?

When she finished dressing, Moriah remembered that there were a few telephone calls she needed to make, and after completing them, she climbed back up the companionway to be greeted by Dorian's long, low wolf whistle.

"Goin' fishin'?" he asked her with a smile.

"Nope," Moriah told him. "I'm going on an all-out manhunt."

Dorian laughed. "I hope you bag a big one."

"Count on it," she replied.

Manny's Tavern was everything Moriah would expect of a seedy waterfront dive and then some. There were the requisite disreputable-looking characters slouching over drinks at the bar; the lighting was muted and yellow, the music some garbled and wretched copy of a Louis Prima recording. "All of Me," Moriah thought it sounded like, but she wasn't absolutely sure. As her eyes adjusted to the difference between the bright sunshine outside and the musty, dim interior of the establishment, she quickly scanned its occupants for one that might be familiar. She finally saw Austen seated with his back to her on a stool at the very end of the bar, crowded against the wall as if he'd tried to stuff himself thoroughly into the corner. Like everyone else, he slumped over his beer with his head in his hands, but he was nonetheless easy to identify because of the ripple of muscles that strained against his blue T-shirt and corded down the bare legs visible below his shorts. Moriah sighed. He really was quite magnificent.

Ignoring the lascivious leers and comments that were offered her halfheartedly as she crossed the room, Moriah sidled up beside Austen at the bar. He didn't seem to notice her, instead focusing on the empty beer bottle that stood sentry on the other side of his glass, so she slipped an arm possessively across his shoulders and leaned in very close.

"Hi, sailor," she murmured as throatily and suggestively as she could. "Wanna get lucky?"

Austen shook his head back and forth slowly and said, "No thanks, honey, I—"

And that's when he looked up to find Moriah, his Moriah, the Moriah he had met and fallen in love with on St. Thomas. She was staring back at him with sparkling gray eyes and a huge smile, looking as if she were ready to tumble him to the floor and have her way with him this instant.

"Hi," she said. "Did you miss me?"

Austen closed his eyes for a moment and then opened them again. It did no good. She was still here. He'd had only two beers so far, he reminded himself. He never started hallucinating this early.

"Moriah?" he heard himself ask stupidly.

She gave herself a quick once-over, then met his eyes again. "Well, it certainly isn't the staid and academic Professor Mallory, is it?" she asked him lightly. "And I told my sisters never to call me Mo again, so it can't be her, either." She shrugged. "Guess that only leaves one woman it could possibly be."

"Moriah," Austen said with a satisfied smile.

"Moriah," she confirmed with a nod.

"I'm so glad you're back," he told her, throwing his arms around her to pull her into his lap. "I did miss you."

"Austen!" she protested, pushing at his shoulder in a half-hearted effort to climb back down from his lap.

"It's okay. Manny is a friend of mine, and this sort of thing happens in his tavern all the time."

Moriah stopped her reluctant struggles. "Why doesn't that surprise me at all?" She gazed at him a moment longer, then let her own arms prowl across his back to hug him close. "Oh, Austen, I love you," she mumbled into his neck.

Austen could hardly believe his ears. Holding her tightly in his lap with one hand, he cupped her chin in his other and turned her head to face him. "Say that again," he ordered.

Moriah smiled and placed her palm softly against his cheek. "I love you," she repeated. "I love you, Austen. I love you."

"Moriah, what are you saying?" he asked before he realized what a silly question it was. "I mean, what are you going to do?"

It was all the urging Moriah needed. Grabbing two fistfuls

of Austen's shirt, she leaned forward and took his mouth in a searing kiss. He responded immediately, of course, clamping his lips over hers until their teeth rattled together, silently promising he had no intention of ever letting her go. When she pushed away from him to gasp for breath, he let her have one before pulling her back to him. He let one hand wander from her waist up to her rib cage until her breast was snuggled comfortably just above the curve of his thumb and index finger. When she moaned her approval, Austen's tongue ventured casually into her mouth, exploring there for quite some time before exiting again to trace slowly around the lips that so intrigued him.

"What are you going to do, Moriah?" he repeated his question roughly and with unsteady breaths.

Moriah's breathing was none too steady either as she gazed at Austen's passion-darkened eyes and flushed cheeks. She felt his heart pick up speed the way her own did when she inclined her head toward the exit and offered quietly, "I, uh, I noticed a little hotel not too far up the street when I was coming in."

Austen smiled his approval, and she could tell it was costing him plenty when he said, "Later. First I want to know what you're going to do right now. About the future. About your family. About your job. About…us."

"My future is down here in the Caribbean," she told him without hesitation. "As for my family, well, my sisters probably found a taxi to take them to the airport all right. That was a pretty busy street corner where I made them get off."

"You actually told your sisters where to get off?" he asked with a delighted chuckle.

"In more ways than one. As for my job, I've already called in my resignation to the university, and I'll mail a formal letter tomorrow. So much for getting tenure. Oh, well." She shrugged as if completely unconcerned. "I've accepted another job, anyway. One that I was offered some time ago, but that I never really seriously considered taking until today."

"What job is that?" Austen wanted to know.

Moriah grinned and pulled him closer. "You happen to be holding on your lap the newest writer for *Today's Anthropologist.*"

"Today's Anthropologist?" he said as he nibbled a particularly tempting section of her neck.

"It's the magazine for the hip and savvy anthropologist inside the cultural scene," she informed him loftily, shivering at the sensations his tongue aroused on her collarbone. "I'm going to be covering the Caribbean beat."

"Do tell."

"There's only one problem though," she added, meeting his eyes as he rose to stare at her with languid desire.

Austen couldn't imagine a single problem in the world right now. It was a perfect place for the very first time. "What's that?" he asked her, hoping his smile wasn't too goofy or annoying.

"My new career means I'm going to have to do a lot of interisland traveling, and frankly, that can get pretty expensive. Not to mention the fact that the pay for a writer of this type isn't all that great and comes sporadically at best. Even when my royalties kick in from my books, I may have to moonlight at a second job."

"Gee, that's tough," Austen said, knowing he didn't sound a bit regretful. "Maybe you'd be interested in crewing on a charter boat?"

Moriah's feigned disappointment cleared. "You know someone who's hiring?" she asked.

Austen nodded. "My partner is talking mutiny. Dorian's going to bail out on me. Says he's getting married. Wants to find a job where he doesn't have to travel so much."

"Gee, that is tough," Moriah agreed. "You're pretty lucky I came along when I did."

"That's for sure. And I'm even luckier that you came back." He hugged her close once again. "I love you, Moriah. I don't know what I would have done if you hadn't come back, if you'd left me here alone."

"It will never happen," she assured him as she tangled her fingers in his hair and kissed his temple.

"Wait, there's something else," he told her, shifting her to the side only far enough to reach into his pocket. He smiled happily as he held up a perfect pink scallop shell.

Moriah drew a startled breath as she plucked the shell from his fingers. "Oh, Austen," she sighed. "You got it back."

He held her to his heart and nipped softly at her ear. "Yeah," he said on a warm rush of air. "I got it back. Promise me I'll have it forever."

"You'll have it forever," she vowed.

His hold on her relaxed somewhat, but he still refused to let her go. "Answer me one more thing," he requested.

"Anything."

He hesitated for a moment before saying, "When we get married, are you going to invite your family?"

He felt her quiet laughter stir his hair. "Only if they promise not to stay."

Austen let out a long sigh of relief and kissed her gently on the mouth. "Good," he whispered comfortably. "Now, where was that hotel you mentioned earlier?"

* * * * *

Fall in Love with...

MEN
in UNIFORM

YES! Please send me the exciting *Men in Uniform* collection. This collection will begin with 3 FREE BOOKS and 2 FREE GIFTS in my very first shipment—and more valuable free gifts will follow! My books will arrive in 8 monthly shipments until I have the entire 51-book *Men in Uniform* collection. I will receive 2 free books in each shipment and I will pay just $4.49 U.S./$5.39 CDN for each of the other 4 books in each shipment, plus $2.99 for shipping and handling.* If I decide to keep the entire collection, I'll only have paid for 32 books because 19 books are free. I understand that accepting the 3 free books and gifts places me under no obligation to buy anything. I can always return a shipment and cancel at any time. My free books and gifts are mine to keep no matter what I decide.

263 HDK 2653   463 HDK 2653

Name _____ (PLEASE PRINT)

Address _____ Apt. #

City _____ State/Prov. _____ Zip/Postal Code

Signature (if under 18, a parent or guardian must sign)

Mail to the **Harlequin Reader Service**:
IN U.S.A.: P.O. Box 1867, Buffalo, NY 14240-1867
IN CANADA: P.O. Box 609, Fort Erie, Ontario L2A 5X3

* Terms and prices subject to change without notice. Prices do not include applicable taxes. Sales tax applicable in N.Y. Canadian residents will be charged applicable taxes. This offer is limited to one order per household. All orders subject to approval. Credit or debit balances in a customer's account(s) may be offset by any other outstanding balance owed by or to the customer. Please allow 4–6 weeks for delivery. Offer available while quantities last. Offer not available to Quebec residents.

Your privacy: Harlequin is committed to protecting your privacy. Our Privacy Policy is available online at www.eHarlequin.com or upon request from the Reader Service. From time to time we may make our lists of customers available to reputable third parties who have a product or service of interest to you. If you would prefer we not share your name and address, please check here. ☐

MUBPA10

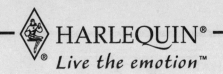

HARLEQUIN®
Live the emotion™

The series you love are now available in

LARGER PRINT!

The books are complete and unabridged—
printed in a larger type size to make it
easier on your eyes.

HARLEQUIN® *Romance*

From the Heart, For the Heart

HARLEQUIN®
INTRIGUE

Breathtaking Romantic Suspense

HARLEQUIN® *Presents*

Seduction and Passion Guaranteed!

HARLEQUIN® *Super Romance*

Exciting, Emotional, Unexpected

Try LARGER PRINT today!
Visit: www.eHarlequin.com
Call: 1-800-873-8635

LPDIR09

HARLEQUIN® *Romance*®

The rush of falling in love

Cosmopolitan
international settings

Believable, feel-good stories
about today's women

The compelling thrill
of romantic excitement

It could happen to you!

EXPERIENCE
HARLEQUIN ROMANCE!

Available wherever Harlequin books are sold.

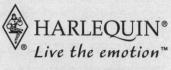

HARLEQUIN®
Live the emotion™

www.eHarlequin.com

HROMDIR09

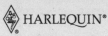
HARLEQUIN®

American ★ Romance®

**Invites *you* to experience
lively, heartwarming
all-American romances**

Every month, we bring you four strong,
sexy men, and four women who know what
they want—and go all out to get it.

From small towns to big cities, experience
a sense of adventure, romance and family
spirit—the all-American way!

American ★ Romance®

Love, Home & Happiness

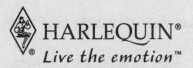
HARLEQUIN®
Live the emotion™

www.eHarlequin.com   HARDIR09

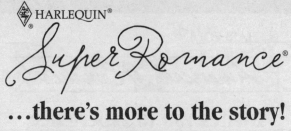

...there's more to the story!

Superromance.
A *big* satisfying read about unforgettable characters. Each month we offer *six* very different stories that range from family drama to adventure and mystery, from highly emotional stories to romantic comedies—and much more! Stories about people you'll believe in and care about. Stories too compelling to put down....

Our authors are among today's *best* romance writers. You'll find familiar names and talented newcomers. Many of them are award winners— and you'll see why!

If you want the biggest and best in romance fiction, you'll get it from Superromance!

Exciting, Emotional, Unexpected...

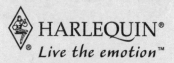

Live the emotion™

www.eHarlequin.com   HSDIR06

HARLEQUIN®
INTRIGUE®

BREATHTAKING ROMANTIC SUSPENSE

Shared dangers and passions lead to electrifying
romance and heart-stopping suspense!

Every month, you'll meet six new heroes
who are guaranteed to make your spine tingle
and your pulse pound. With them you'll enter
into the exciting world of Harlequin Intrigue—
where your life is on the line
and so is your heart!

THAT'S INTRIGUE—
ROMANTIC SUSPENSE
AT ITS BEST!

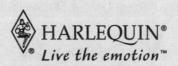

HARLEQUIN®
Live the emotion™

www.eHarlequin.com   INTDIR06

passionate powerful provocative love stories

Silhouette Desire® delivers strong heroes, spirited heroines and compelling love stories.

Silhouette Desire features your favorite authors, including

Ann Major, Diana Palmer, Maureen Child and Brenda Jackson.

Passionate, powerful and provocative romances *guaranteed!*

For superlative authors, sensual stories and sexy heroes, choose Silhouette Desire.

passionate powerful provocative love stories

Visit Silhouette Books at www.eHarlequin.com   SDDIR08